WORTH THE HEAT

ETERNITY SERIES

JENNIFER J WILLIAMS

Cover design by KB Barrett Designs

Cover Photography by Lindee Robinson Photography

Cover models: Daniel & Kayle

Editing by Brenda Bastien

This book is dedicated to the real Rick and Amelia.
Fuck you.
Have the day you deserve, assholes.

A NOTE FROM JEN

Hi friends! In case you're new to my world, mental health is very important to me. Because I recognize that not every reader responds to things in the same way, I always provide a list of triggers that may be upsetting to some readers. While the majority of this book is the typical fluffy and cozy romance you expect from a JJW book, this is my most suspenseful romance to date.

It is important to know that this book does *NOT* include the MMC, Sebastian, involved in any of the following triggers.

Within Worth the Heat, there are mentions of:

- Suicide
- Attempted SA
- Assault
- Anxiety/Mental Health/Mentions of Therapy
- Kidnapping
- Destruction of Property
- Drug Use/Drug Paraphernalia
- Suspense as a result of stalking/bullying

As always, take care of yourself!
Jen

Play List

Listen to the playlist on Spotify.

Heat Waves Glass Animals
HOT TO GO! Chappell Roan
As It Was Harry Styles
Sweetest Pie Megan Thee Stallion
Sugar Maroon 5
Lavender Haze Taylor Swift
All About That Bass Meghan Traitor
bad idea right? Olivia Rodrigo
Who's Afraid of Little Old Me? Taylor Swift
Dirty Thoughts Chloe Adams
Slow Hands Niall Horan
Vigilante Shit Taylor Swift
I Feel It Coming The Weeknd, Daft Punk
Lover Taylor Swift

Chapter 1

"Belly, I'm a little concerned for your mental health," my sister, Arianna, frets from behind me as I maniacally throw glitter all around me. I'm covered in it, but I don't care. Arianna has called me Belly since she was a baby. It's our 'thing,' and definitely not a diss at my size or weight.

"I'm fine. This is fine. Everything is fiiiiiine," I say, stuffing a handful of party sequins under the couch cushions. A very fine glitter covers the table and flooring, and I even stuck some handfuls *under* the fitted sheet on the bed. My subsequent giggle is high-pitched and frenzied. It's possible everything is not fine.

My mental health is, for the most part, fine. My overall sanity is taking a hit, as is my self-confidence, but what else is new? I've been rocking the dumpster fire life for at least a decade, and that certainly didn't change with the demise of my most recent relationship.

I found my boyfriend in bed with my best friend. God, such a cliché!

When I introduced Rick to Amelia, I was thrilled when they seemed to get along great. They had this brother-sister camaraderie that made me so happy. I had visions of double dates, whenever Amelia would finally settle down. Couples vacations. All the things.

Amelia has been my ride-or-die since the fifth grade when she tripped a snot-nosed brat who was bullying me under the slide at our elementary school. I'd always been a little plumper than my peers, and boys really honed in on that the closer we got to middle school. Amelia, on the other hand, was beautiful from the moment I saw her. Gorgeous blond hair in natural waves down her back, and crystal clear blue eyes that always sparkled. As we got older, she became an absolute knockout. I, on the other hand, stayed plump.

Last week, when I decided to leave my bakery early for a change, I planned to surprise Rick by being naked in his bed when he got home from work. He lives on the outskirts of Denver, working as a financial analyst at a large bank downtown. I didn't notice his car in the apartment parking lot, nor did I notice Amelia's. I sure as hell wish I had.

I didn't have a key to the apartment, but I'd looked over Rick's shoulder once and had seen the code for the keypad. The apartment complex he lived in was all hoity-toity, with every bell and whistle a young professional could want. I found it all to be a little over-the-top, but never told Rick because I didn't live there. I figured we could cross that bridge if and when we came to it. We hadn't been together long, and I wasn't entirely sure if he was the one I wanted to be with forever anyway.

So I snuck into my boyfriend's apartment, and I even giggled merrily as I set my bag down on the couch.

And that's when I heard the moaning.

In hindsight, I should have walked right back out. Clearly, hearing moaning meant Rick had someone in his bedroom with him. I knew that. But it seemed like my feet took me to the doorway against my better judgment. The door was slightly ajar, and peeking in, I could definitely see Rick's profile as a woman rode him.

"You gonna come for me, baby?" he grunted. I stood, transfixed, watching his face. Bile slowly climbed up my esophagus, and I remember wondering if I would throw up right on the floor. Then the woman answered him as she threw her head back in bliss, and I forgot how to breathe.

"Yes! Yes, I'm coming!" Amelia moaned.

My best friend, my ride-or-die, was fucking my boyfriend. For a moment, I thought that it made sense. Honestly, Rick was probably out of my league with his all-American good looks. Tousled brown hair and hazel eyes weren't anything to write home about, but when he smiled, it was like angels sang in my head. When he directed that smile toward me, I was putty in his hands.

"Shit!" Rick shouted, and he pushed Amelia off him. She shrieked as she fell off of the bed, but our eyes met for a brief moment before she was out of sight. "Izzy, it's not what it looks like ..."

God. The number of times I've asked him not to call me Izzy has to be in the thousands, and we'd only been dating for six months.

Rick jumped off the bed and approached me, not even trying to cover himself. I dragged my eyes down his torso to see one glaring issue: a lack of condom. He fucked my best friend raw, but always — *always* — used one with me.

"Oh, God, Belle, I'm so sorry," Amelia said after she wrapped herself up in a blanket. I stared at her, unable to speak. She was sorry? Like, oops, somehow she fell and landed on my boyfriend's dick?

I turned around, walked out, and blocked both of their phone numbers.

Which brings us to today.

I could seriously be arrested for this, but I don't care. I've let men walk all over me for so long, and I'm done with it. With them. I'm in my early thirties, and I'm over how men treat me.

Maybe it's just me. Maybe women with blond hair, bubbly personalities, and skinny butts are treated better. Not me.

"Belle, we really need to go. He's going to know you did this!" Arianna hisses. Taking a quick glance at my younger sister, I see sheer panic on her face. The woman I just described fits Arianna to a tee, except for the blond hair. Arianna could flirt outrageously, even at a young age, whereas I never felt comfortable with the opposite sex. I'd rather be baking or reading.

"I just have a few more things to do," I tell her with a cackle. Whipping a gallon-size bag full of cooked shrimp out of my tote, I shove it in front of her. "You wanna help?"

Arianna sighs. "I mean, I guess? I'm already an accessory, might as well add me as a full accomplice at this rate."

"Great!" I yank a smaller bag out and hand it to her. "Go shove one in every air vent you can get to."

"Isabella!" she shouts, horrified. "What is this?"

"Seven-day old shrimp."

Her mouth drops open in shock.

"What?" I ask innocently.

"I'm scared to ask what else you have planned," Arianna whispers.

I shrug. "Nothing too bad. Well, I guess it's all subjective. I debated on switching out his contact solution with vinegar, but figured that would actually cause physical harm, and it probably would involve a longer time in jail. So everything I'm doing will just aggravate him. Laxatives in his protein powder, and food coloring in his laundry detergent. Gonna superglue his shoes to the floor. Honestly, he leaves them in disarray all over the place. He has that one coming to him. If I can, I'm also supergluing all of his silverware together too, and replacing his cologne with toilet water. Oh, and I raided Ben's leftover Legos that he never plays with, and grabbed all the super tiny ones that are hard to find on carpet." Ben is our nephew, the son of

Alex, our oldest brother. He's smarter than everyone in our family.

"I am incredibly concerned with your imagination."

"I can't take full credit. I found this grandma on TikTok who did a whole series of videos about what to do if your man cheats. I just never thought I'd be using them myself."

"And you're sure he doesn't have cameras in here?" Arianna asks, looking around warily.

"Nope. He doesn't trust the cloud, and spent an hour one night ranting and raving about how 'the government is always listening.' He doesn't even trust having a doorbell camera."

"Well, let's get going with all of these criminal activities. Stone's meeting me with the girls for a family trip to the Denver Zoo." Arianna's smile is blinding. I'm low-key jealous, but also so incredibly happy for her. Arianna was dealt a crappy hand throughout childhood. A rare disease called Hemolytic Uremic Syndrome caused her kidneys to fail, and she underwent a kidney transplant at the age of eight. She outgrew that kidney in her early twenties, and had another transplant. She'd been in love with Stone, our brother Alex's best friend, for as long as I can remember, and it was really special to witness her getting her happily ever after with him. Now my baby sister is married with two daughters, and I'm still the same train wreck I've always been.

I mean, almost all of my siblings are married with children, and here I am, destroying my ex-boyfriend's apartment for sport.

"Are you absolutely sure he won't try to get you arrested for this? I love you, Belly, but you're not cut out for jail time," Arianna says with an exaggerated shudder.

"I'd do better in jail than you would."

She winks at me. "I never said I'd be better. I'd make someone my bitch pretty fast, though."

I giggle. "Sure, Ari. You're tiny. Someone would totally overpower you."

"Nope. When it's the choice of making someone my bitch or eating the taco, I'm gonna find every ounce of power in my body to win."

"Eating the taco — Jesus, Arianna." I look over at her to find her smiling innocently at me. "Just go deposit the shrimp so we can leave."

Her face screws up in distaste. "I'm putting it off so I don't have to touch them. Do you have any collateral if he figures out it's you?"

"He's going to know it's me."

"Isabella!" she shouts, horrified.

"I caught him in bed with my best friend. He can easily deduce that I'm the most likely suspect," I point out. "But I have collateral."

"Really?" she calls out from the bedroom. "What?"

"You know how Rick works for a bank?"

Her head pops out of the bedroom. "Please tell me he's stealing pennies, or something completely asinine."

"Worse," I tell her gleefully. "He bragged to me about how he approves fake loans to improve his own sales targets. Then doubled-down to tell me he's got a file on his computer where he keeps all the information."

Ari's mouth drops open. "Seriously? That sounds incredibly illegal."

"It is."

"Belle, you can't just sit on this info. You need to report him." Arianna walks toward me, her eyes wide. "This isn't just collateral. This is fraud."

I smile wickedly. "The bank already knows. I emailed the manager and suggested an audit of the loan department."

She gasps. "Can't they track the IP address?"

"I thought about that. So I drove to a public library, created a new email account from one of the computers there, and sent the email. I researched it, and found that many email providers require a period of time before an account is deleted, except for mail dot com. Those can be deleted immediately."

"You thought this through."

I sigh, a sound full of aggravation and anger. "I'm just so pissed off, Ari. I'm sick of men taking advantage of me. I'm tired of men making me feel like I have to settle just because *they* think I'm fat. Frankly, I love my body. I'm not gonna settle just because a man thinks otherwise. And I also don't understand why an introverted woman who has her own business is apparently a bad thing to ninety percent of the male population. Everyone in this family is happy, but everyone also thinks I'm not. Well, I guess Leo isn't all that happy, but he's never really been super happy, so that's nothing new. It's not that I'm unhappy, but I see all of you finding your partners, and I can't help but wonder why I haven't.

"Belly," Arianna says quietly, her head tilted to the side, her eyes full of sympathy.

Walking to the sink in Rick's kitchen, I wash the remaining glitter off my hands. "I want to find someone who accepts me as I am. Who sees me as a diamond in the rough. Who won't say one thing and do another, especially not when they want to do my friends. I want what you and Gia have. The men who could see our chaotic family, with our demanding brothers and involved parents, and not run away screaming."

"I know," Arianna whispers, "I want that for you, too. The right man is going to come along, and he'll be the lucky one who gets to experience how wholeheartedly you love."

"I won't hold my breath," I mutter as I remove a small piece of folded paper from my pocket.

"What is that?" Ari asks.

"A note."

"And it says what?"

"That he should probably get tested, because I know Amelia has herpes."

"Seriously?" she gasps.

I shrug. "Who knows. But it'll stress him out for a few weeks, until he finally mans-up and gets the tests. He probably has an STD too. Looking back, I don't think she was the only one he was screwing behind my back."

"Should you get tested?" Arianna wonders.

"Already did. But we always used condoms. The one silver lining to all of this, I guess."

"Won't the note really give it away that you destroyed his apartment?"

My eyes meet hers. "I really don't give a fuck."

As I march toward the door, Arianna's loud cackle reverberates against the stark white apartment walls. "Kinda loving this zero fucks given attitude, Belly."

Yeah, I kinda am too.

FOR AS LONG AS I CAN REMEMBER, I'VE WANTED TO BE A PASTRY CHEF. Nothing made me happier as a child than helping my mom and *Nonna* bake. I'd learn the changes they made to recipes, how to alter a recipe for high altitude baking, and listen to them gossip about everything in our small tourist town. Being the second youngest in our group of seven kids, I was used to falling through the cracks. When you have a brother with NHL aspirations, and a very sick sister, it's rough. Add in the rest of the crew, and I struggled to find my niche. Once *Nonna* asked me to help her bake biscotti, a traditional Italian cookie, I was fascinated with baking. It never ceases to amaze me how changing one ingredient can make a completely different dessert.

I found courses in Denver I could take after school, and began selling baked goods from home in high school. I knew I wanted to enroll in a pastry chef program at a local community college, and while my family wasn't rich, my parents made a deal with me that they'd match whatever I was able to save, which ended up being just enough for the program, course materials, and a new-to-me car to drive to and from the campus thirty minutes east of Eternity Springs. The best part about the program was the apprenticeship at the end, which led me to the Eternity Springs Bakery.

I'd known Norma Klein all my life, but had no idea she routinely offered her bakery for an apprenticeship. I was thrilled to learn from her, and she told me early on that she hoped to retire sooner rather than later. Coming straight out of the pastry arts program, I didn't have two nickels to rub together, so I knew I didn't have the money to buy Norma out immediately. She was patient, willing to work with me, and such a treasure to have the years we worked together.

I saved every cent that I could. I lived at home, rarely drove my car to save on gas money, and ate way too much Ramen once I finally moved out. In my spare time, I took on pet sitting opportunities, babysitting, and any odd job that worked with my schedule. I'd have worked myself to death had a massive weekly standing order not come into the bakery. A burly man picks it up every Friday morning, saying no more than five words to me at any given time, and always leaves a fifty dollar bill in my tip jar. Without fail. I gave up asking questions about the order when he ignored me on four straight Fridays. What the hell kind of acronym is RMRRMC anyway? I tried a Google search for it once, and nothing made sense.

That standing order was the game changer for me. Norma was adamant that I receive all the funds from it, as I was the one working two extra hours getting the order ready. Everything on the order fell under the quick and easy, so it wasn't incredibly hard for me to get it all together. It was almost as if they had been told what would take the least amount of time. Muffins, cherry turnovers, cinnamon bread, and coffee cake. I don't mind baking all of these things, but I can do *better* than those. One of my favorite things to make in the spring and summer is a strawberry lemon cake, with moist layers of cake separated by pickled strawberry jam, lemon cheesecake, and milk crumbs. But sure, let me whip up a triple batch of blueberry muffins.

As I stand in what is now my bakery, after finally taking over for Norma over five years ago, I lean over the counter as I plan next week's menu. While I buy as much as I can from big box stores, I try to source tons from local farms and shops to ensure I'm putting back into the community that raised me. I vowed to continue on with many of Norma's recipes, but did make one significant change. Eternity Springs Bakery was too boring. So many aspects of the town are pun-based, and I wanted my establishment to reflect that. Hence, the Bake, Batter, and Bowl Bakery was born.

Six small circular tables dot the exterior walls, and pale yellow paint covers the space. It's soft, comforting, and homey. A very tacky chicken wallpaper adorned the walls of the only bathroom, but I removed that with Norma's blessing very soon after beginning my apprenticeship. Eventually, I'd love to fully own this space, but right now, I'm content paying the rent to whatever commercial real estate person owns the building.

Looking at my watch, I sigh as I see I still have two hours before I can close. Most of my business happens in the first couple of hours I'm open, but stragglers trickle in throughout the day, especially in the summer months. When the bell on the door jingles, I straighten my back, pasting on a pleasant smile, ready to greet new customers.

"Hi, welcome in. What can I get started —" I begin, as a hand comes crashing onto the counter in front of me, right where my head had been only seconds before. I scream in shock as Rick stands before me.

"What did you do with it, bitch?" he seethes.

"With what?" I stammer, clasping my hands together tightly. I hate confrontations.

"Oh, you're gonna act dumb now?" Rick says, his eyes narrowing as he leers at me. "You never were the smartest broad, Izzy, but I thought you were better than this."

"I really don't know what you're talking about," I whisper. His eyes are wild. Hair in disarray, his skin looks clammy, with random sparkles of glitter catching the light occasionally. I bite my lip to refrain from giggling. I also have a habit of laughing when I'm nervous.

Rick leans in closer, and I don't see the hand that quickly snaps up to grab my neck. "When you had your little temper tantrum in my apartment yesterday afternoon? There was a package on the counter. A very important package. I don't know how the fuck you figured it out, but you better give it all back to me. I'll fucking count every goddamn tablet if I have to."

I feel the blood drain from my face. "Tablets?"

His grip tightens. "Yeah, you stupid cunt. Tablets. Pills. The fucking drugs you stole from me."

"I swear I don't know anything about —" I cry out when Rick squeezes enough to cut off the oxygen to my lungs. I see my phone, just a couple of inches out of reach, and as I'm about to lunge for it, a voice stops me.

"Get your motherfucking hands off her."

Chapter 2

SEBASTIAN

I never come to Isabella's bakery anymore. Sure, it's mostly due to my own pride being incredibly beaten up by her consistent refusals to give me a chance. It's become somewhat of a joke with my guys that I can't get over Isabella, and certainly her brothers bust my balls about it on occasion. But it's also because I'd never want to make her feel uncomfortable. So I send my VP, Trace, to pick up anything extra that we need at the Clubhouse if we run out of things from my Bake, Batter, and Bowl weekly standing order.

I've been President of the Rocky Mountain Range Riders Motorcycle Club for well over a decade. I started it after a buddy of mine spoke about how he wished he had a club to ride with. He'd deployed with the Marines a couple of times, and after receiving an honorable discharge, he had difficulty transitioning back into civilian life. Riding was one of the only things that gave him peace.

He took his own life a few months after our conversation.

I'll never forgive myself for waiting to do something — anything — that may have helped him. But I'm determined to make sure no other returning veterans feel they have no one. While I have no military experience myself, I have two things on my side: money and time.

RMRRMC has a fully licensed therapist available via Tele-health, group therapy sessions whenever someone needs one, and we're very active in the community. When asked how I'd describe the Club, I like to say we're a step up from the movie *Wild Hogs*. We're definitely a little rowdier than Tim Allen and his friends, but the camaraderie and friendship is the same.

So here I am, walking into Isabella's bakery, rehearsing the order I intend to place as quickly as possible so that Isabella doesn't find the entire interaction unpleasant. Smile. No small talk. Don't stare at her like a lovesick puppy. Get in, get out, and move the fuck on.

It would really be easier if I wasn't half in love with the woman.

I'd have sent Trace in, but he took a call a moment ago. I promised my *mamá* I'd bring pastries for an event she's hosting. Looking down at my feet as I open the door, I expect to hear Isabella call out her standard greeting. It's been the same phrase since she began working here. *Welcome in, what can I get started for you?* When I don't hear anything, my head pops up, and I fucking see red.

"Get your motherfucking hands off her," I growl. The man holding Isabella by the neck doesn't even turn around, and I quickly fire off a text to Trace, telling him to get his ass in here. He drove, intending on eating at least two donuts before we got back to the Clubhouse. I quietly slide my phone into my pocket as I look at Isabella. Her eyes are wide with panic, and I'm desperate to get her away from this guy. "I'd listen if I were you."

"This doesn't concern you," the dude responds.

I chuckle sardonically. "Oh, it absolutely does concern me. You're better off dealing with me than one of her brothers."

His hand tightens on her neck, and she reflexively tries to take a jagged breath. "You remember what I told you. Get me back that Molly, or you'll fucking pay."

What the fuck? This dipshit must have her confused with someone else. No way is Isabella mixed up with drugs. As I'm about to say something, Trace barrels in through the door. The commotion as he stops next to me allows the man holding Belle a moment to push her backward, then take off into the kitchen.

"Chase him," I command, as we both venture deeper into the bakery; Trace to follow the man, and me to get to Isabella. She fell to the ground when she was surprised by the shove, and I kneel next to her, gingerly placing my hand behind her head. Her beautiful brown eyes, now glassy with tears, latch onto mine, as her hand trembles against her neck. "What hurts, *mi Cielo*?"

"What?" she stammers. Shit. I just called her 'my sky.' It's rare that I use a pet name for a woman, yet here I am laying all my cards on the table — er, floor — with Isabella like I always do. I've been a goner for her for so fucking long.

My parents, along with my grandmother, emigrated from Puerto Rico when my mother was pregnant with my oldest sister. Initially settling in Miami, my father was determined to experience as much of the country as possible. Only a few months after I was born, we began our slow migration to the west. Atlanta, New Orleans, and Albuquerque didn't satisfy whatever feeling my dad was chasing. My mother fell in love with the Rocky Mountains, and we headed north until we arrived in Denver. They opened up a restaurant and bar, *El Puerto Plate*, and shoved my sisters and me into the local school district. After only speaking Spanish for the entirety of our lives, we were thrown to the wolves in our predominantly suburban area.

As a reward for surviving the entire school year, my parents treated us to a night in the mountains at a neat hotel they'd found on a day trip. That's how I met the Santos. Everlasting Inn and Spa became a symbol of good times and successes. Every summer we'd return for one week. I learned to swim in one of the pools, and my two sisters, Elena and Catalina, learned how to do some kind of hair braid from one of the Santo kids. I'll always remember roaming the property, with Luca mostly, and having deep conversations with Dominic about the business he was determined to take over one day. Even at a young age, Dom exuded power, control, and professionalism. Luca made faces behind Dom's back, and I attempted not to give him away.

I failed often at the task.

I don't really remember Isabella during those visits. Maybe she was the one who taught my sisters how to braid. Or, as I suspect is more likely, she stayed away, content in her own bubble. I don't remember her until around ten years ago, when I came into this very bakery, and felt the world tilt on its axis.

She wore a yellow shirt under an apron covered in flour, with a line of flour across her face where she must have absentmindedly swiped at her skin. Black leggings looked painted on the most phenomenal curves I'd ever seen, and I felt the need to fall to my knees and worship them. Good fucking God, the woman was a knockout. And when she greeted me with a soft smile? If my mouth had been able to make sounds, I'd have asked her to marry me right then. Instead, I put my foot in my mouth and said something about her floured face, joking about how management must be on their break, and she bolted to the back of the store. An older woman came back out to take my order, and when I saw Isabella again a week later, a coolness had replaced the sweet innocence I'd witnessed before.

I've lost track at how many times I've asked Isabella out. Well into double digits. Somehow I end up saying things that upset or embarrass her, and I never get a chance to apologize. This woman unravels me. Thirty-six years old for fuck's sake, and I can't seem to get my act together.

Shaking my head, I grab Isabella's hand, and pull her to standing. I gingerly touch the back of her head, asking, "Did you hit your head when you fell to the floor?"

"No, I don't think so," she murmurs. Her wide eyes connect with mine, and I realize this may be the closest I've ever stood to her. This close, I see her brown eyes have speckles of gold in them. The border of her iris is slightly darker, and I get lost in her gaze.

My other hand cups her cheek, and she ever so subtly leans into my touch. "Does anything hurt?"

"No," Isabella responds quietly. Her gaze doesn't veer from mine, and a hundred thoughts fly through my mind. She isn't backing away from me. Her skin is so fucking smooth. So soft. One of her hands holds onto my forearm, and it feels like lightning on my skin. What if I leaned in to kiss her? Does she want me to? Would she kiss me back?

Before I can act on my completely inappropriate thoughts, given the situation, Trace slams back into the bakery, panting. "Couldn't catch him, man. Fucker is fast."

"He runs marathons," Isabella says absently as she steps back from me, and my hands drop from her.

"What was that?" I blurt out. "Who is he to you, and why does he think you have drugs?"

"He's an ex-boyfriend, and I don't know what he was talking about. Didn't he say someone's name?"

"He said Molly, which is another word for ecstasy."

"I swear I didn't take anything," she says, her eyes closing. I watch as her hands ghost the space in front of her, as if she's walking through something. "I didn't see a bag or box on the counter. It wasn't there. I doubt Ari would have grabbed it either."

"Your sister was there too?" I ask. "But he wasn't? What were you doing?"

Isabella sighs as her eyes open. She grabs a rag from the edge of the sink and busies herself by cleaning the counter. "I'm not sure I want to say what we were doing. It's very out of character for me, and if he goes to the police, I'll definitely be in trouble."

"He won't go to the police," I tell her.

"How do you know?"

"If he does, he'll have to explain the missing drugs."

"He won't tell the police about those," she retorts with an eye roll.

"He may not, but you can sure as hell guarantee I will be."

Isabella's eyes whip to mine. "What? How would you even know if I was arrested?"

I cock an eyebrow at her. "Seriously? In this town, and with your family? I'd know before the police even made it to your door."

"Could they even arrest me here? I mean, his apartment is in Denver. I can just avoid going to Denver from now on," she says nonchalantly. "I didn't even do that much that would involve jail time. At least I don't think so. How much time do you think I'd get for glitter bombing an apartment and sticking really stinky shrimp all over the place?"

I can't help the grin that spreads across my face. "What else did you do?"

Her cheeks tinge with pink as her face tilts to stare at the floor. "I may have put laxatives in his protein powder and superglued his shoes to the carpet."

I let out a loud bark of laughter. "I fucking love that. What did he do that necessitated a quick glitter bomb?"

"I caught him with my best friend."

My laughter dies as I take in those words. "The fuck? You caught him?"

"Yup." She smiles bitterly. "Caught in the throes of passion."

I feel anger rising, and I pull my phone from my pocket, ready to set my anger onto someone who deserves it. "Give me his name."

"No."

"Isabella."

"I handled it. Nothing else needs to happen."

I shake my head emphatically. "I disagree. I need to keep an eye on him. Make sure he doesn't come back here."

"You don't need to do anything, Sebastian. You are not responsible for me in any way, and I'm not a damsel in distress that needs you to solve my problems." Her voice sounds one way, but I see the fear in her eyes. She's rattled, but I'm probably the last person she'd ask for help.

"I know that," I say in a huff, reaching up to scratch the back of my neck. Focus, Seb. Think of your words. Don't stick your foot in it again. "I'd never forgive myself if something happened to you, if I knew I could have prevented it. I'd rather you hate me, but be safe, than for you to be hurt at all."

Isabella studies me momentarily. I see the moment she shutters her heart. "I'll be fine. Besides, I can just talk to Alex and get the Eternity Springs police involved."

I sigh. "He just had a baby. Don't involve him. All of your brothers have families. If something else happens, you contact me, okay? Let me handle it."

Silence ensues for a few moments as Isabella ponders my words. I cast a quick glance at Trace, who swipes at his phone, but is very clearly listening to this conversation. Finally, Isabella speaks, and I'm unprepared for the vitriol that oozes from her voice. "Why do you want to help me so much? Did my brothers tell you to keep tabs on me? Am I some kind of bullshit bet? I never understood why you showed interest in me. I'm not a toy, Sebastian."

"Woah, what the fuck?" I blurt out. "I never said you were a toy, and I'm certainly not playing games with you. I've asked you out at least a dozen times. Have you said no every time because you thought it was a game or a bet?"

She shrugs, the tension evident in her shoulders. "If the shoe fits."

I tilt my head back, looking up at the ceiling. "I didn't realize you thought so poorly of me."

"What am I supposed to think?" she exclaims, gesturing up and down my body. "You look like *that*, and I'm me! We are not equal."

My phone vibrates in my hand, and I quickly look at the screen to see a text from Trace.

Trace: Circle back. She's picking a fight to get off the topic of her safety.

Fuck. He's completely right.

I step closer to Isabella, watching as she slowly inches backward until she runs into the counter. Once our shoes touch, I lean forward until my lips are next to her ear. She shivers as my breath skirts over her skin, and I revel in that small victory. "You are not a bet. I would never play games with you, because I'd fucking lose every time. You are an absolute goddess, and if you ever allow me the *privilege* of taking you out, I'll spend every fucking moment worshiping you until you see yourself the way that I see you. You are spectacular, *mi Cielo*. You may not want to tell me your ex-boyfriend's name, but I will find out. Now get your things so I can escort you back to your apartment. I know you're about to close, and I'll feel better if I can see you safely home."

I dip my nose into her hair, taking a deep inhale of roses, vanilla, and a hint of sugar, and hoping I never forget how this smells. How it feels to be this close to Isabella. I honestly can't believe she's allowed me to be in her space this long —

Hands hit my pecs before Isabella pushes with all her might, shoving me six feet back. "I don't know what you think you're doing, Sebastian, but it better be from this far away."

God, I wish she'd let me take care of her. Let me into her orbit. Trust that I've only had eyes for her for as long as I can remember.

Sure, I've scratched an itch here and there when I felt it was needed, but no one truly interested me like Isabella always has.

But if I can't save her, I can at least build her confidence, so she never thinks she's less than. The fear in her eyes only moments ago has been replaced by fire, grit, and determination. And that's the Isabella I know.

Chapter 3

ISABELLA

A loud meow next to my face is followed immediately by one paw patting my nose and I shriek in surprise as my body twitches. Looking over at my ginger cat, affectionately named Butterscotch, I raise an eyebrow. "What?"

He loudly meows again, before burrowing his head between the couch cushion and my shoulder. I sigh loudly, looking toward the kitchen to see the time on the microwave. Eight o'clock. I'm not sure what time I fell asleep, as I rarely allow myself to even sit on my couch, much less nap there. I have no memory of anything after I walked into my apartment.

When I found this one-bedroom space, I immediately knew it was for me. A bright and airy kitchen with two large windows that look out toward a forest. The large island could fit six or eight stools, but my two are perfect for me to eat breakfast while Butterscotch watches, patiently waiting to see if I'll give him some milk. The wall that runs the length of the apartment is red brick, except for a small section in the living room where a wood-burning fireplace is the focus.

While the kitchen appliances have been upgraded, the rest of the apartment has not. Which is why I consider myself so lucky to have an actual claw-foot tub that I use for baths almost every day. I'm on my feet for eight to ten hours a day, and my hands take a hell of a beating making all the pastries, donuts, and cookies I dish out daily. My workload tends to double during the summer months, as the tourist traffic increases exponentially, and I'm able to hire on students on summer break to help out. I typically enjoy summertime, because the extra help means I can relax slightly, but right now, I'm so damn exhausted.

The shit with Rick and Amelia, then Rick showing up at the bakery, and whatever the hell that was with Sebastian — I'm so drained. Did he really say it would be a privilege to take me out? How is that even possible?

As Sebastian drove me home, I felt oddly comfortable in his truck. I typically walk to and from work, as it's only a few blocks, but I couldn't complain once I settled into the passenger seat. His truck smelled divine, with elements of his cologne and the leather in the car, but he kept his arm on the console between the seats. I couldn't help but imagine what it might be like if he slid his arm over to hold my hand. Or better yet, if he rested his hand on my thigh. Usually, I'm not into affection in public. I chalk this odd feeling up to assuming any woman would want to touch him, to stake their claim.

Sebastian is gorgeous. Absolutely breathtaking. I'm not without eyes. He's a couple of inches over six feet, with tan skin and dark brown eyes that sparkle with mirth in almost all situations. His hair and beard, so dark they're almost black, make me want to reach out and touch them. I also want to know what his face looks like without the beard ... but I want to know what his beard feels like all over my body. I bet it hurts so good.

Not that I'll ever find out. Sebastian can talk all he wants. But I'm *me*, and he's well above my pay grade. I bet I could pick his last five girlfriends out of a lineup. Blond, blue eyes, lots of makeup, and at most a size six. Not me, coming in at a size sixteen on a good day. My brown hair is straight as a board, nothing like the beautiful curls my sister Gianna got, or the waves Arianna has. They're both rocking olive complexions, whereas I pulled some random gene out of thin air and look more northern European than anyone else in my family. If I didn't have my dad's nose, I'd think my mom stepped out on him. I know she never would, though. Nick and Sofia Santo love each other passionately, and our entire town knows it.

All around me, I see perfect examples of love. None of my siblings ever thought they'd find love, or felt they deserved it. Hell, we even have this stupid Santo tradition of being carried across the threshold at my parents' house to prove we've found our true loves. I've tried it twice, and both were blatant disappointments. I tripped, dropping my high school boyfriend, and my college boyfriend broke up with me on the spot, saying he couldn't afford to chance throwing out his back because of how much I weighed. I attempted to explain that I had to carry him, but his tires left marks on the driveway before I even got a sentence out.

While it definitely left me down in the dumps, it didn't really change my outlook on my own body. I love my body. I have curves, and I love them. I love food. I love cooking and baking. I'll never force myself to give up the joys in my life because of some stupid archaic thinking about body types and happiness. And who the hell would trust a stick-thin pastry chef? I certainly wouldn't.

It's also why I doubt I'll be bothering with dating for quite some time. I've developed a foolproof way of determining if someone is worth any effort. One of my favorite desserts is creme brûlée. The best I've ever had was at a steak restaurant in Colorado Springs, of all places, and I almost wept with joy as I finished my bowl. I've been fine-tuning a recipe ever since, determined to replicate their version. So, I think about that dessert. If I had to choose between a potential date and a serving of creme brûlée, which would I choose? Yeah, the dessert wins every damn time.

My phone buzzes, and I tap the screen to see what the notification is. A text chain with the Santo women pops up.

Hannah: Okay, who was responsible for picking the book club book this month? I have a massive bone to pick with you.

Kate: That's what she said.

Hannah: Oh shut up.

Arianna: Poor Hannah. She's clearly struggling with her husband's bone.

Hannah: Are you really talking about your brother's dick?

Arianna: Crap. Ignore me.

Natalie: I'm only a couple of chapters into the book, so don't spoil anything!

Gianna: Didn't Nonna pick this one?

Me: If she picked a JT Geissinger book, I'm going to have a heart attack at the meeting.

Kate: It wouldn't be bad if she didn't INSIST on pantomiming one of the spicy scenes with whatever baked goodies you have us make.

Hannah: Honestly, I'm still surprised no man in Eternity knows about our underground Cock Cookie Club. When Luca asked what CCC stood for, I told him Critical Cookie Club. I still can't believe he bought it.

Gianna: Travis knows, but he doesn't care. He benefits from me reading any kind of romance books, whether it involves sexy cookies or not.

Arianna: Stone says the same about the books, but he doesn't know about the baked goods. He's too close with Alex and Dom. Once one of them finds out, they'll all know.

Hannah: What are we making this month, Bells?

Me: It's a surprise.

It's only a surprise because I completely spaced on book club being next week, and I don't have anything planned. My bakery has a small basement that is perfect for an intimate book club meeting. After reading a book by Amy Daws that involved a main character making charcuterie boards that she renamed 'Cocku-terie' boards, I had a moment of inspiration. How often do we see baked goods accidentally turn into phallic shapes because of incorrect ingredients? Why not do it purposely?

That's how the Triple C group came about. I can fit eighteen women in the bakery basement, which only leaves a little over half the seats available for other residents besides my family members. Gianna and Arianna are my only sisters, while Hannah, Kate, and Natalie have married my brothers. My mom and *Nonna* both attend, although *Nonna* embarrasses the hell out of everyone with her antics. While she claims she hasn't been with another man since my grandfather passed away, she certainly has a very vivid imagination.

Or she was a freak with my grandfather.

Me: We'll have a new member joining us since Carol moved out of town, so try to behave, ladies.

Natalie: You better tell Nonna that too.

Me: She won't listen, so why bother?

Kate: God bless Nonna. She's my favorite Santo.

Arianna: You're married to one.

Kate: I said what I said.

Laughing, I turn off the screen and toss my phone onto the chair next to me. Butterscotch takes the opportunity to stand up, stretch, and climb onto my stomach. One slow blink later, and he begins kneading my soft tummy, purring loudly.

"I love you too," I tell him, absentmindedly scratching his neck, before wincing as his claws breach my shirt and dig into my skin. "But I'll only let you have at it for about thirty more seconds. I'd rather not bleed through my shirt."

He chuffs at me as if he's only slightly offended, and jumps down of his own accord. I follow him into the kitchen, where he waits patiently for me to gift him with a small treat. I'm not sure who trained who here, if I'm being honest.

Sitting at my island, I grab a claw clip from a bowl in the middle, securing my hair in a messy French twist, then pull up Pinterest on my laptop. I need to find a suitable dessert for book club.

The first few months of meeting, it was easy to come up with a dessert. But we can only make so many dick and boob desserts before it becomes monotonous. That's when I had to start getting creative. The ladies were big fans of the 'dick on a stick' cookie, where the tip was dipped in melted white chocolate. They also enjoyed the coffle: a waffle shaped like a cock. We even made soft pretzel penises one time.

Finding actual recipes for penile-shaped baked goods isn't an exact science. Usually I skim through my favorite Pinterest pastry boards until I find an idea that strikes a chord with me. My mind takes over, imagining different ingredients, and how easily the item could be shaped. Any cookie can be molded into a penis shape, but ingredients matter. I'm not making chocolate chip cookies here. It would look like the poor penis had a bad STD. But a white chocolate macadamia nut cookie? That could work. An eclair with the perfect cream filing? The book club ladies were simply feral for that one.

At the beginning, we used our hands to shape our creations. They were never perfect, and it bothered me. No one wants a lumpy dick in their mouth, whether a pastry or not. So I found a small custom boutique online that specialized in 3D printing anything and everything. Was the guy who I spoke with slightly confused when I asked for twenty silicone dick molds? Probably. I clearly heard him gasp on the phone when I said they needed to be nine inches in length, though. It's a romance book club. If we're building penises, they need to be above average ones.

I'm sure he's going to love me when I contact him in the future about making vagina molds. While easier to shape with our hands, a proper silicone mold will make everyone happy.

Me. It'll make me happy.

And honestly, as the ringleader for the Cock Cookie Club, that's all that matters.

As I mindlessly scroll through Pinterest looking for any inspiration, my phone rings. I stare at it for a moment, shocked that anyone would call me. Who doesn't use texting as the main line of communication these days? When I see it's my brother Luca, I pick up.

"Normal people text, Luca," I tell him.

"Yeah, well, you ignore me most of the time when I text, so now I'm calling," he replies. "You want to tell me what happened today?"

My spine straightens as a wave of anger courses through my veins. "If there had been *anything* that happened today that required any of my family finding out, *I would have told them.*"

He chuckles bitterly. "You're such a fucking liar, Belle. You wouldn't have told us a goddamn thing, which is why I'm glad I ran into Seb so he could tell me."

"I can't believe him!" I burst out. "It was nothing!"

"Alright," Luca says. "Go look in the mirror and tell me if you have any marks on your neck from that asshole. If it really wasn't anything, I'll apologize immediately. Better yet..."

The phone beeps in my ear as Luca switches to a video call, and I sigh in frustration as I answer. I'm barely on the screen before he swears. I feel the blood drain from my face, as even I can see the fingerprint bruises across my neck. I'd hoped they wouldn't be too noticeable, but I've always bruised like a banana.

"It's not nothing, Belle. A man putting his hands on you is not nothing," Luca says softly. "I'm so fucking glad Seb was there. He said he didn't intend to stop at the bakery. Said he just felt like he had to go. Felt pulled there."

"I could have handled it without him," I mutter. "I was just about to reach for my phone when he barged in."

"Jesus Christ. What the hell is your problem with him, Belle? As far as I know, the guy hasn't done anything to you."

I honestly don't know what my deal is with him, other than I find him exceptionally handsome, and it's unnerving to me. "I don't trust him."

Luca clearly rolls his eyes at me. "You don't trust him, but the entire family does. Hell, he's been one of my best friends for years. You think so poorly of me, then? Do you honestly think I'd bring someone around our family that I didn't feel was a good person?"

I shrug. "I don't know. Maybe."

"He's a good guy, sis. I'd never say that if I wasn't absolutely sure of it. He was so keyed up when I saw him. I had to talk him out of trying to find your ex and beating the hell out of him. He was straight murderous when I ran into him."

"Oh," I whisper, looking down at the dotted pattern on my countertops. I don't know how to process that. Sebastian is no one to me. He's friends with my brothers, and I sometimes catch him looking at me. But then he opens his mouth and stupid shit comes out. Once he suggested he didn't think I could carry empty trays between my car and the bakery.

"You need to let people in," Luca says quietly.

My eyes pop up to meet his. "Why bother when people like Rick are out there? Even Amelia, who I thought was my best friend, totally screwed me over. Well, she screwed Rick, but whatever."

Luca's eyes heat. "She was sleeping with him?"

"Yup."

"I never liked her," he states, and loud laughter bursts from my lips. "Really. I never liked her. She hit on me all the time, and I know she tried to hook up with Dom a time or two."

"Everyone hits on you, so I never thought anything of it. I didn't know about Dom, though."

"Well, good riddance. And had I known your ex had the name Rick, I would have told you to dump the bastard months ago. But with a name like that, he can't be trusted. What parent gives a baby the name Rick? Fucking ridiculous," Luca mutters with a shake of his head.

"Rick is a nickname. His name is Richard, but his dad is also a Richard, so they called him Rick."

"Explains so fucking much. He's a junior," he sneers. I hear a shriek from behind Luca, and he turns to address someone. When he faces me again, he says, "I have to go. Caleb learned how to climb out of his crib, so we moved him to a toddler bed. What one-year-old climbs out of a crib?"

"Sounds just like something his dad would do," I comment.

"Mom told Hannah that I was a daredevil as a kid, and now she brings it up anytime Caleb even looks like he's gonna do something."

"Some kids are hard-headed and have to learn things themselves."

"Like splitting their head open? I'd rather not deal with that. Needless to say, it's not going well."

"For him or for you?" I ask.

"Hannah, mostly. He gives her his puppy dog eyes, and she ends up falling asleep next to him every damn night. He knows I don't put up with that shit," he tells me with a smile. We say goodbye, and I stare at the dark screen on my phone after our call is disconnected. It's so wonderful seeing this side of my brother, where hockey isn't the only thing that he has in his life. Hannah brought him back to life, and watching him become a dad has been phenomenal.

I can only hope that I get to be that lucky as well.

Chapter 4

SEBASTIAN

"You gonna go check on your girl?" Trace asks me as I grab my keys and helmet from the bar. He gives me a knowing look as he takes a slow sip of his draft.

"She's not mine," I mutter as I stalk past him.

"Not yet," he calls after me.

As I enter the parking lot of my bar, Range Roadhouse, I strap on my helmet and throw a leg over my Harley. I don't often ride my hog to the bar, but after a few weeks of forecasts for thunderstorms, I knew I needed to feel the wind against my skin on the first sunny day. Colorado is known for having three hundred sunny days per year, so when we have extended periods of clouds and rain, I get moody. My bike immediately brightens my disposition.

Range Roadhouse is located about twenty-five minutes from Eternity Springs. While I haven't told Trace where I've gone for lunch each day, he's too damn perceptive not to figure it out. I was furious after depositing Isabella at home that day a few weeks ago. I saw how easy it would be to break into her apartment complex, and how blissfully ignorant she was to anything going on around her. I want to pick her up and lock her away, protecting her how I see fit. Isabella won't even let me take her on a date, so I think if I attempt to protect her, she'll be pissed about it.

She doesn't know that I'm the customer who has the massive standing order every week. While I think she'll be upset about that one, she'll get over it. The thing that she'll definitely be murderous over — should she ever find out — is the fact that I own her bakery.

In my defense, I purchased it around the same time Isabella began working there. I intended to sell it to her, but she seemed content to continue paying the rent. Norma Klein, the previous tenant, made me swear I wouldn't raise the rent on Isabella; as if I'd do that to the sister of some of my best friends. I only raised the rent to be on par with other businesses on the same block. I own an LLC, and the bakery was purchased under that. No one in the Santo family knows I own it, and I plan on keeping it that way.

I got into the commercial real estate world in my mid-twenties, recognizing it as a perfect opportunity to invest. My research found that commercial real estate allowed more financial reward than residential properties, and after hearing horror stories about the rental market in Colorado, I was more determined than ever to slowly increase my reach in real estate. I started small, grabbing compact spaces on the far western side of Denver. A hot dog shop and a small ice cream stand were immediate hits. My first big foray into a standalone space, Range Roadhouse, continues to be my favorite. The bakery is the only retail location I own in Eternity Springs, and no one outside of my family and very close friends know that the company who owns the space, SGI, is me. Sebastian Garcia Incorporated.

Slowing to a crawl, I ease down the main drag of Eternity Springs. It's as if every other building falls away into the background as I zero in on Bake, Batter, and Bowl. I smile to myself, loving the ingenuity and creativity of the name. Creeping past the bakery, my eyes strain to find her through the windows, but someone else stands at the helm. Disappointed, I turn around, intending to head back out of town.

And then I see her.

She's by the main square, sitting on a bench with her head tipped back, a soft smile on her face as she enjoys the sun. A parking spot opens near her, and I quickly slide in. Even from here, I can see flour on her cheek again, and I chuckle.

Turning off my bike, I'm surprised the sound hasn't registered in her brain, but it gives me an opportunity to study her for a minute before quietly walking over to sit beside her. "Lovely day for lunch outside."

Isabella gasps, jolting with an exaggerated kick of her legs, and she lets go of her lunch. I watch helplessly as a large slice of lasagna hits the concrete. Stormy eyes focus on me. "I was really looking forward to that lasagna, Sebastian."

Fucking hell. The way my name sounds on her tongue makes my cock twitch. Clearing my throat, I attempt to focus my thoughts. "I sincerely apologize. I thought you heard me sit down."

"You could have been anyone," she retorts, annoyance evident in her posture as she stands. "Normal people don't speak to strangers on a park bench."

"That's probably an incorrect generality, but I digress," I reply, and Isabella growls at me. She legitimately growls. "I'm just saying people talk all the time. I'm sure new conversations between strangers happen on park benches all over the world."

"Well, fortunately for me, this conversation between strangers is over," she snaps as she bends to pick up her Tupperware container, and her ass is right in my face. Right in my face, and I force myself to stifle a groan. Tight legging material covers every inch of her skin from her knees to her waist, but I can almost feel her soft skin. Taste her pussy. My hands itch to reach out and grab her, to pull her down into my lap so she feels what she does to me, and that's when I notice the outline of her thong.

Sweet motherfucking Christ, Isabella wears thongs.

I'm an ass man, but I don't have a specific type. I like 'em all. I also don't care what a woman covers herself with. Style, fabric, cut, whatever. But the thought of a tiny sliver of lace disappearing between her cheeks? I'm immediately rock hard, sitting on a park bench, in the middle of Eternity Springs.

As she attempts to stalk away, I reach out and lightly grab her wrist, before hoarsely saying, "Isabella, wait."

"For what?"

I take a moment, willing my dick to calm the hell down, before speaking. "I owe you lunch."

"It's fine. I have another slice at home, and I can eat it for dinner."

Adjusting myself discreetly as I stand, I gently turn Isabella toward a small sandwich shop I know she likes. "While I know I'll never be able to replace what I assume is your *Nonna's* lasagna, I can at least get you a sandwich. Isn't today the day you stay late to prep for the weekend?"

Her eyes widen as she shoots a shocked glance at me. "How di — how did you know that?"

Because mine is of the orders she preps on Thursday afternoons. "Luca has mentioned it. He's pretty proud of you. Talks about you all the time. Dom and Alex do too."

I see a subtle pink sheen cover her cheeks as she fights to withhold her smile. "They just like the free baked goods."

I stop her immediately.

"What?" she asks.

"Why do you do that?"

"Do what?"

"Why do you write off any compliment? Is it all compliments, or just ones from me? That wasn't even from me, though. It was from your brothers. So tell me why you do it."

"It was a joke." Isabella crosses her arms, staring at me defiantly. God, I fucking love the fire she has inside her that no one but me appears to see. "I'm allowed to make jokes about my brothers."

"Not at your own expense. You're fucking phenomenal at what you do, *mi Cielo*. Own that shit. Don't apologize for having a gift."

"It was a joke about how much food they can eat, Sebastian. Not about my product." Her eyes narrow as she catches on to what I said again. "And stop calling me that. I looked it up, and I'm not your fucking sky."

Oh, but you are.

I chuckle as I place my hand on the small of her back, gently pushing her to walk beside me into the sandwich shop. "We'll see about that."

After grabbing two sandwiches, Isabella hastily mumbles her thanks before scurrying back to the bakery. I watch her go, noting how she attempts to look back at me quickly. As soon as she sees me watching, her head whips around again. I chuckle as she rushes through the bakery's front door.

New Lovebirds?

Anyone who has lived in Eternity Springs for longer than a minute knows we're now down to only two Santo siblings who haven't found love yet. Or maybe only one? Our own baker extraordinaire, Isabella Santo, was seen chatting amicably with her brother Luca's bestie, Sebastian Garcia, over lunch in the park. Has Sebastian finally figured out how to lock down his love interest, or is Isabella just being friendly? We have it on good authority that Ms. Santo holds quite the grudge, and Sebastian should hide the glitter if something goes awry in their budding relationship.

AFTER FINISHING MY INVENTORY AT THE BAR, I HEAD HOME WITH THE SUN and wind feeling perfect against me. Contrary to what most people believe, not every MC President lives at the clubhouse. I've chosen to live in my own home, because I need my own space. My property abuts to the Club property, which is incredibly convenient when I've had more than a couple of drinks.

The guys know not to just show up at my house. It's basically an unspoken rule, although some of them try to get prospects to break it on occasion. Once they know about Camila, however, they understand why.

"I'm home!" I shout as I walk in through the garage door, dropping my things in a decorative bowl beside the door, and toe off my shoes.

"In here, *Mijo*," my grandmother calls. At eighty years old, Rosario Garcia is as spry and outgoing as the day we landed in Florida. In order to make ends meet, my parents worked multiple jobs. My *abuela* was the one who raised us, helped with homework, took us to school, and worked on school projects with us. In turn, we helped her with learning English. While we mostly speak English nowadays, certain words, like *Mijo*, have stood the test of time.

"Hi Daddy!" A blur launches toward me, and I grunt as I stumble back against the counter.

"Hello, Camila," I reply as my beautiful five-year-old daughter stares up at me, eyes sparkling. She may not have been expected, but taking on the single dad role has been an absolute joy.

I meant what I said about my world tilting when I saw Isabella for the first time. But that didn't mean I remained celibate. Camila was the result from a one-night stand, and her mother didn't want to be in her life. There were some thinly veiled threats in an attempt to extort money from me, which didn't fly. Her mother, Beth, had no desire to be a mom. The pregnancy definitely wasn't planned, and one of my swimmers got through the condom. I, however, took to Camila immediately, and haven't regretted one moment since. With dark brown hair and tan skin, she also has my nose and eyebrows. Striking blue eyes are the only trait she took from her mother.

"Daddy, *Abuela* doesn't like the microscope you got me for my birthday," Camila pouts.

"And why is that?" I ask.

"I made her look at an ant."

"Ahh," I sigh. "Did you find a dead ant, or did you kill it first?"

"It was in the name of science!" Camila shouts, her finger pointing as she shoots her arm into the air. Where the hell she learned the saying, *or* the gesture, I'll probably never know. Taking my daughter's hand, I pull her into the living room, where *Abuela* sits on one of my couches.

"She said it was a girl bug," my grandmother snaps. Girl bug?

"Ladybug, *Abuela*. Ladybug," Camila corrects cheerfully.

Abuela shrugs. "Same thing, no?"

I fight to hide the smile threatening to break free. "I don't believe there is an insect called a girl bug."

"She screamed," Camila tells me.

"Oh? Why would a ladybug be any different than an ant? Both insects. Both bigger under a microscope."

"Do you know how big ant eyes are? And it looked like it had hair!" *Abuela* whispers, her own eyes wide. "No more microscope."

"Alright. Camila, save the microscope for me or *Abuelita*. Better yet, *Abuelito*. He will help you find more insects, I suspect." My parents don't spend as much time with Camila as my grandmother, but they'll both be more patient about bug eyes.

"What am I supposed to do after school then, Daddy?" Camila whines, a sullen expression on her face as she follows me back into the kitchen.

I sigh as I pull out the ingredients to make *arroz con gandules*, a rice and peas dish that *Abuela* taught me to make when I wasn't much older than Camila. "There's a swingset in the backyard. You have an entire cabinet full of craft supplies, and two shelves of books. Your room looks like a Barbie factory, and if *Abuelita* buys you any more Legos, you'll be able to cover an entire wall."

"I don't like the big Legos, Daddy. I want the little ones," she pouts.

Crouching so we're eye level, I cluck her under her chin. "But with the big ones, you and *Abuelita* get to build towers so tall that even I can't knock them down."

Camila giggles. "*Abuelito* can't jump that high. Will I be able to jump higher than you when I'm a grown up?"

"I'm sure if you set your mind to it, you can do anything you want, *mi Chiquita*," I tell her fondly. "Now go ask *Abuela* nicely if she'll help cut the plantains for *tostones*."

"Oh!" Camila squeals. "I love *tostones*!"

Who doesn't love a fried plantain?

ISABELLA

Arianna: SOMEONE has finally made her dramatic debut on The Eagle Has Landed, and I am so fucking excited!

Hannah: This better be about Isabella, and not one of our daughters.

Kate: I just saw it! Boy, someone got the scoop up there quickly. Isn't Belle still at work?

Me: I am, in fact, still at work.

Me: Just an article? No picture?

Natalie: Do you WANT a picture, Belle?

Me: I was just curious.

Gianna: She's totally going to the site right now to look.

Me: This had to be photoshopped.

Arianna: Why?

Me: Because I'm smiling. At Sebastian. Today.

Hannah: You're allowed to smile at him.

Me: I didn't smile at him, though! I swear I didn't. At least I don't think that I did.

Me: Did I smile?

Me: OMG. There's FLOUR on my face!

Kate: It's kinda your trademark.

Me: Lovely.

Arianna: See you tonight for girls night, Mrs. Garcia!

Me: Aren't you a funny girl.

Fuck.

"I CAN ONLY STAY FOR ONE HOUR. I'M POOPED," I ANNOUNCE AS I DROP my bag and slide into the booth next to Arianna. Kate and Hannah sit across the table. My sister, Gianna, rarely comes to our girls nights because of her husband's paramedic schedule. "Is Nat going to make it?"

"No," Hannah says with a frown. "Two kids have a stomach bug, and Alex has to work an extra shift tonight. I'm sure she wishes she were anywhere but home."

Yuck. I'd volunteer to help, but I'm not the best with vomit.

I'm also not the best with kids.

I enjoy being an aunt to the constantly growing brood my siblings keep popping out, but I bet if they are honest, none of them would say I'm their favorite aunt. I'm not outgoing like Arianna and Natalie, and I don't have the wonderful southern patience Hannah has from growing up in Georgia. Kate is just naturally good with kids, and Gianna has a peaceful quality that seems to bring everyone happiness.

Then there's me. I'm introverted, rarely sarcastic, and I don't have kids of my own. I'm not even sure I want children. A moot point, considering I'd need to find a man that was willing to participate in the construction of a child. After the Rick and Amelia debacle, I'm taking a break from the dating scene. I'm expecting a package of self-care items tomorrow, so I won't even need a man to satisfy me.

"Why only one hour, Belly?" Arianna asks.

"It was an incredibly long day, and I have to go in early tomorrow to finish up what I didn't get done today."

"Aren't you usually off on Saturdays?" Kate asks.

"Not all the time. It really depends on what's happening in town. I can usually plan accordingly for any big tourist events or celebrations. No one could work tomorrow, though, so it's just me."

The three women share a look, and I sigh. "What is it?"

It takes a moment before Arianna speaks up. "We don't like you being alone in the bakery."

"Why?" I ask, then close my eyes in frustration. "Fucking Luca. No. Wait. Fucking Sebastian."

"Yeah, you should," Kate says with an exaggerated cough.

"What?" I ask, my brow furrowed in confusion.

"Uh, nothing. And it wasn't Sebastian who told us. It was Luca. Well, he told Hannah, and she told us," Kate says hastily. "But I guess Sebastian told Luca? How did he even know anyway?"

"He walked into the bakery," Hannah pipes up when I don't answer. Her eyes dart to mine before continuing. "Luca said when he ran into him right after, Seb was vibrating with anger."

"Did he hit your ex?" Arianna asks with excitement.

"No. He just glared at Rick."

Kate's mouth screws up in distaste. "I can't believe you went out with a guy named Rick. That would have been an immediate deal breaker for me."

"Evidently I'm not so snobbish," I respond defensively.

"I'm sorry. That wasn't meant to come out as a dig on you. What kind of a name is Rick anyway? Is it short for anything?"

"It's short for Richard," I answer, before my gaze swings behind Kate. "Isn't that Stone?"

The four of us turn to look at the doors to the restaurant, as we watch Stone, Dominic, Luca ... and Sebastian walk in. I'm suddenly filled with intense anger. "Is this a set up? Did you guys do this on purpose?"

"No!" Hannah hisses. "They were supposed to go play pool at a bar. I swear!"

Luca notices us, and immediately walks over, sporting a massive grin. "We're not here to interrupt girl time. We changed our minds about what we want to do tonight, and I don't think Hannah ever told me where you were meeting."

"Uh-huh, sure," I mutter.

"While not planned, I'm not mad about it," Stone says huskily as he stares at Arianna. "How about we push two tables together and we all have dinner? Then we can go our separate ways."

"Oh, what a great idea!" Kate gushes, jumping up from the booth. Dom puts an arm around her waist, tugging her into his side.

"Move," Arianna whispers as she nudges my side. "I want to get to my husband."

Slowly standing, I'm acutely aware of how blissful my siblings are with their spouses, and I feel like crying. Regardless of whether this was a setup or not, I don't think I can sit and watch three happy couples throughout dinner. "I'm suddenly not feeling well. I'm going to go."

I don't wait for anyone to speak as I dart out of the restaurant.

I hate this. I hate feeling inferior. I don't want to be jealous of what Hannah, Kate, and Arianna all have, but I am. They have husbands who adore them. They've done the stupid crossing the threshold test that everyone failed until they found 'the one,' and I can't even get a guy to stay monogamous.

Tears fill my eyes as I root around in my bag for my car keys. I keep my head low as I head into the parking lot, hoping I don't run into anyone I know. I hate how often my family is featured on *The Eagle Has Landed*. It was supposed to be a town website touting all the amazing things Eternity Springs has to offer, yet somehow morphed into a TMZ-type site that enjoys breaking news and rumors, whether they're true or not.

Now they're talking about *me*, linking me to Sebastian, and referencing a grudge? What do they know? Is it only about what I did to Rick's apartment, or is there something else?

I squeal when a hand grabs my elbow and spins me around, and I'm so surprised that I don't bother trying to wipe the tears away. I should have known Sebastian would be the one they sent after me. This absolutely was a setup.

"Go back inside," I tell him, attempting to turn away, but his hand is locked around my elbow. "I just don't feel well. There's a stomach bug going around, and I think I might have it. I'm fine."

"You're not fine," he says softly. His deep brown eyes search mine. "Why are you crying?"

"Allergies," I lie.

His lips twitch as he studies me. I hate how I feel like he's seeing into my soul, slowly dissecting the most intimate parts of my heart. "I've heard those six o'clock in the evening allergies are brutal."

"Uh-huh. They are." I'm about to wrench my arm out of his grip when he slowly brings a hand up to my cheek, cupping my head, and wipes one tear off with his thumb. I can smell the leather from his black leather MC cut, and the scent mixed with his cologne is intoxicating.

"Tell me why you were crying," he commands. My hands come up to push him away, but somehow land on his chest, holding the sides of his cut. Sebastian's breath whooshes out in an audible exhale as his other arm wraps around my waist. Butterflies erupt in my stomach. He's holding me. He's literally cradling me in his arms, like I'm the most precious cargo in the world. And suddenly, I'm so overcome that my eyes close and the words fly out of my mouth.

"I can't sit there and watch them all be happy. I just got out of a relationship, and while I didn't necessarily think Rick was my forever, it still hurts to be cheated on. To know you're not enough. And I'm not truly jealous of my siblings, but I am actually envious of their happiness. Why do they all have to be so adorable with each other? Couldn't one of them develop gout, or a hunchback? Or lose the ability to communicate. Something that makes them more realistic. Five years ago we were all single, and now everyone is married with kids, and honestly, it's just not fair." When Sebastian doesn't respond, I open my eyes to find him smiling widely at me. Good God. He's even more attractive with that smile.

"I bet it feels better now, to get all of that out."

Huh. I do feel a sense of relief. "It might."

"Does anyone in your family know how you really feel about ... anything?" he asks, his hand still holding my cheek. It should feel weird, but it doesn't? I don't know how to process that.

"How I feel about anything? Yes, they know how I feel about some things."

"But I bet you placate them often. You'd rather toe the line than rock the boat," he surmises.

"I don't like to fight," I whisper. I'm not a very argumentative person. In fact, the only person I seem to find it easy to argue with is the one standing right in front of me.

"You argue with me," he says, reading my thoughts. "And before you say anything, just know that I like getting the real you, Isabella. I'll argue with you anytime."

"Um, Isabella? Hi," a voice says from behind me. Sebastian's hand drops. I turn to find Amelia staring at me awkwardly, and I'm surprised to find how much I miss his hand on my cheek. She looks perfect, like always, in a sundress and sandals. Her blond locks are swept up in a messy updo, one that I have no doubt she spent at least fifteen minutes constructing so it appeared like she didn't spend a moment on it. "How are you?"

"I'm fine," I answer, equally as uncomfortably.

"I recognize you. What's your name again?" she asks, eyebrows raised as she stares at Sebastian. I see the interest in her eyes, and I'm suddenly pissed.

"Why? You gonna sleep with him too?" I blurt out. I feel angrier about her interest in Sebastian than I ever did about Rick. What does that mean? I have a quick epiphany where I flashback to every relationship — or almost romance — in my adult life. Amelia was always involved. Either she convinced me to break up with the guy, or she'd flirt outrageously with the guy to 'prove' to me that they weren't worth my time. I wonder if Rick was the first guy of mine she slept with.

Amelia's eyes go wide. "No, I mean — is this a new boyfriend? I don't want to sleep with him, I swear. I'm glad you've moved on and you're happy."

"I moved on?" I repeat. "What an interesting way to say that you fucked my boyfriend. Honestly, I didn't realize you had a thing for sloppy seconds."

I hear Sebastian snort as Amelia chokes. "I'm sorry — I just —"

Sebastian interrupts her. "You should walk away now, Amber.

My girl is just getting started, and you don't want to be the target."

"Your girl?" Amelia sputters. "Okay. Um, well. I'm sorry. I'll go."

Sebastian's arms wrap around me from behind as we watch Amelia walk quickly across the street. His breath is warm against my ear as he whispers, "Sloppy seconds? Brutal. Absolutely brutal. Bet that felt good too, didn't it?"

"It did," I confess. His arms tighten momentarily before he drops them. I turn to face him. "I don't believe I'd have been as forceful had I been alone. I appreciated having the support."

He gives me a lopsided smile. "Anytime, *Mami*."

"*Mami*?" I sputter, a horrified look covering my face. "I'm not a mom."

He chuckles. "It's the same as calling someone baby."

"I have never heard that from anyone."

His eyebrows raise. "Have you ever dated a Puerto Rican?"

I shake my head.

"That's why." He walks me to my car, then leans in to kiss my forehead, shocking me into silence. "You let me know when you're finally gonna let me take you on that date, *mi Cielo*."

Sebastian saunters away, and my eyes drift to unabashedly check out his butt.

He has a really nice ass.

Chapter 6

The girls look disappointed when I walk back in alone, probably expecting me to leave with Isabella or drag her back inside. I'd do neither of those things. First, it's not my style to push a woman past her comfort zone. I'm also not one to chase someone who doesn't necessarily want to be chased. For something to work with Isabella, it will take patience, finesse, and a whole lot of luck.

Rapping my knuckle against the table, I wave to everyone. "I'm gonna head out. Let you lovebirds enjoy a triple date."

Dominic stands, coming to shake my hand. "You alright?"

"Yeah. Isabella is on her way home." I turn back toward the door, surprised when Dominic continues to walk beside me.

He lowers his voice, leaning in to say quietly, "I half expected you to take her home. Or at the very least, follow her."

I chuckle. "Debated on it. But any progress I make with her will immediately go backward if I break her trust, or make her feel like I don't respect her. It's slow going right now, but we're moving in the right direction."

"Oh yeah?" he asks, a smile sliding across his face.

"I kissed her head tonight!" I burst out in excitement, then feel immediate humiliation as everyone laughs. I didn't intend for everyone to hear me, and I'm suddenly defensive over them laughing at my reaction. Or worse, laughing at Isabella's feelings.

"It may not seem like it, but it's a big deal. She's barely let me hold her hand."

"Isabella has never been a very touchy-feely kind of woman," Arianna pipes up. "You should probably know that so you're prepared for when she shoots you down in public. She doesn't even like hugging any of us."

Hannah nods. "I immediately hugged her when I first met her, and it took months before the awkwardness disappeared. She definitely won't be participating in a PDA anytime soon."

My heart sinks a little, because I am incredibly tactile in showing my affection for a partner. Physical touch, I learned, is my love language, with acts of service a close second. Shaking my head, I say, "I don't care. I'll do whatever she's comfortable with. I just need her to give me a chance."

Heading home, I'm surprised when my phone rings only a few minutes after leaving the restaurant, and I see it's Luca calling. "Miss me already?"

"Where are you?" he asks strongly.

"Only a mile from you. Why?"

"In what direction? Are you close to Isabella's apartment?"

Ice fills my veins. "Yes, why? What happened? Is she okay?"

"Her neighbor called Alex. She heard Isabella scream, and now she's not answering her phone. No fucking clue why the neighbor called Alex instead of calling the police. Alex is calling his sergeant, and I'm on my way to her apartment, but since you've already left, you're closer."

Blowing through a red light, I speed up to double the limit as I tear across Eternity Springs. I should have fucking followed her home. She's finally getting more comfortable with me, and if something happens to her now ... I should have followed her home.

I peel into the parking lot of her complex, barely slamming my truck into park before tearing down the sidewalk and up the stairs. Panic fills my blood when I see her door slightly ajar, and I cautiously push it open.

Isabella's living room is completely destroyed. Couch cushions ripped open, picture frames broken, and books ripped apart. I can't take it all in because I hear a scuffle in the back of her apartment, and I stalk toward it. I can hear a deep grunt, and I know whoever is in there is male. When I peer through the door and find a man on top of Isabella on her bed, trying to undo his belt, I fucking see red.

I take two steps before grabbing the guy by his hair, yanking him up.

"What the fuck?" he stutters, but I don't let him say anything else as my fist meets his mouth over and over again. I vaguely recognize hearing Isabella scream, but I don't stop. I can't stop.

"Who are you?" I snarl. "Who sent you?"

"What's it to you?" the guy spits out, blood spraying my clothes and face.

I laugh mockingly. "You have the audacity to touch my woman, and you think you're walking away from that? You touched what is mine, and now you pay the fucking price."

Grabbing him by the neck, I push him into the wall, lifting him so only the tips of his shoes touch the floor. His hands grasp my arm as he gasps for breath. I study his face, noting this isn't the same man who confronted Isabella at her bakery. "Tell me who your fucking boss is, or I won't stop until you're dead."

His eyes widen as he attempts to kick me. "Go fuck yourself."

I smile menacingly. "I get to fuck her, so I'm good."

"Fuck ... you ..." he sputters, and I release him. He falls to the ground, taking long draws of air, allowing me the opportunity to crouch down and pull his wallet from his pants.

"Devon Carlisle of Denver." I pull out my phone and take a picture of his license. "Think I'm gonna hold on to your information for a bit, Devon. Got a crew of guys who would just love to meet up with you to tell you in person what a fucking bad decision it is to fuck with a rider's old lady."

"You're MC?" he stutters, his voice labored as he struggles to breathe normally.

I nod, finally looking over at Isabella. Her eyes are the widest I've ever seen, with an expression that is new to me. "I'm gonna let you go, Devon. But you need to realize this as a gift. I held your life in my hands, and I could just as easily take it away. Tell your boss to leave my woman alone, or you'll be dealing with wrath like you've never experienced before. You understand?"

Devon nods frantically as he rubs his neck. Before letting him go, I pop him in the nose, enjoying the crunch of broken cartilage as I watch bright red blood stream from his face. Nodding toward the bedroom door, I say, "Get out of here before I change my mind."

Devon spider crawls out of the room, finally standing and running as fast as his lungs will let him, and I turn to Isabella as I stand.

"Are you alright?" I ask quietly, dragging the hem of my shirt up to swipe at the splatter of blood across my face. I'm not prepared for her to launch herself at me, wrapping her arms and legs around me. "Fuck, *Naranja*. I'm so fucking sorry."

"You don't need to apologize," she mumbles, her face buried in my neck. Her arms tighten around me, and I turn to sit on the edge of her bed. I force myself to breathe evenly, focusing on slowly rubbing up and down her spine.

"I should have escorted you home," I admit. "I knew your ex was out there, and I shouldn't have left you alone." I tighten my arms around her, acutely aware of how close I'd been to losing her ... when she's not even really mine. Yet.

"Shit," I hear muttered from outside, before Luca charges into the apartment. He stops when he sees us, and his eyes widen dramatically. "Belle ... fuck. What do you need?"

Isabella shakes her head against me, a ragged inhale against my neck making me relax a little.

Luca drags a hand through his hair, then grips his neck in obvious frustration and helplessness. "Alex is waiting for a police buddy of his outside. He can't take your statements because —"

"No!" Isabella shouts, her head popping up, watery eyes whipping to mine. "No cops. He said if I got cops involved he'd come after everyone."

"Everyone?" I ask quietly.

She turns to look at Luca. "He named your kids, Luca. Everyone's kids. He said they'd disappear, one by one."

Luca's eyes turn murderous, darker than I have ever seen them. "Do we know who this guy is?"

"I took a picture of his license. Name's Devon," I tell him.

"If that's even his name," Luca says as he pulls out his phone. "I'll tell Alex to send the cop away, at least for the moment. Hopefully we can figure out who this Devon guy is, and who he's associated with."

"Oh, I'll find him," I say with a deep voice. "Don't you worry about that."

Isabella puts her head back on my shoulder, sniffling quietly. Luca watches me, and we have a silent conversation. "You're coming home with me, *mi Cielo*."

I watch as Luca mouths "*mi Cielo*?" Assuming the Italian word for "sky" is something close to the Spanish word, I shrug. I'm sure he'll look it up. "Um, Belle, you can stay with me and Hannah if you'd feel more comfortable."

Isabella shakes her head as she exhales. "I can't bring this into your house, Luca. I'd never forgive myself if something happened to any of you."

Luca approaches us, leaning down to kiss the top of her head, before looking at me. "Keep my sister safe."

"I will *never* let anything happen to her," I vow. As Luca walks out, I hear him speak quietly with someone. Assuming it's Alex, I pat Isabella softly on her back. "Let's get some things together for you to bring back to my place."

"I don't want to stay with a bunch of guys," she admits. "I can get a hotel. I just didn't want to involve any of my siblings."

"I don't live with a bunch of guys," I say with a snicker. "We use the Clubhouse for events and meetings, and some guys stay there from time to time. But we all have our own housing. My property abuts the MC property, but the guys know never to show up unannounced. You'll have privacy, and you'll be safe there."

Isabella sighs as she sits up straight, but her head hangs. "How did I get here? How is this my life now?"

I drag a finger across her forehead, pulling her hair to behind her ear. "I meant what I said. I'll keep you safe."

"I don't think this is going to end well for anyone," she whispers, before climbing out of my lap. I immediately miss her closeness, the feel of her skin under my palms. The fact that she sought me out when she needed solace. I watch as she silently walks to her closet, carefully grabbing the few clothes still left on the hangers that Devon didn't toss around the room.

"Seb." I look toward the sound to find Alex beckoning me into the living room.

"I'll be right outside the door, okay? Shout if you need anything," I tell Isabella, but she doesn't acknowledge me. I can sense her walls closing, with new brick being built to keep everything — and everyone — out, but I won't push. This extraordinary woman needs someone who recognizes her, who values her exactly as she is, and I'm determined to be that man.

Walking to the living room, I find Alex, Luca, and Dominic. The fury emanating from the three Santos is palpable. Dom opens his mouth, but I hold up a hand. "My guys and I will handle this."

Alex's eyebrows shoot up to his hairline. "That's our sister, man."

"Exactly," I answer. "You're too close to this, and you all have families. I've got a couple dozen men with military experience, and most have connections all over the country. Some have friends in prison too, so we've got a lot of avenues we can start with. And if something goes south … I'll do whatever it takes to make sure Isabella stays safe. You have my word."

"Did he really say she couldn't involve the cops?" Dom asks.

"I don't believe she'd lie about that," I answer.

Alex scoffs. "I told my buddy to go, but I'm not leaving it alone. There's no way this is a coincidence. It'll be off the record, though. ESPD will step up patrols by the bakery, and I plan on asking some contacts in other precincts if they want to take on some off-duty patrols. I'll make sure there isn't any paperwork to track."

I nod. "All I know is Devon has to be associated with her ex-boyfriend. I don't know much yet, but I'll get a guy working on it. So far, Rick seems clean."

"Never liked that guy," Luca sneers. "I only met him once, and thought he was a pretentious douchebag."

Alex nods. "I never told Belle my opinion, because she seemed happy. She's watched so many of us fall in love, and I think she was sad about being single."

"I'd like to go now," Isabella says quietly from behind me. Eyes downcast while holding a bag in one hand and her purse in the other. My girl looks so broken.

I clear my throat, but my voice still cracks. "Anything else you need from here?"

She shakes her head, refusing to make eye contact. "Just my cat, and then I want to leave."

I grab her bags in one hand as Luca picks up an orange cat, handing it to Isabella. I had no idea she had a cat, but it doesn't surprise me. It fits her. I place my other hand on the small of her back. Each one of her brothers gives her a hug as we walk past them. As Isabella slowly walks through the apartment door, her eyes catch on a framed image of her family. I recognize the picture from an event only a few weeks ago, because Alex and Natalie's new son is featured in the center. I quickly reach down, grabbing it from beneath the broken glass. I look back at the guys, and point around the room. "Grab anything not broken or damaged, and bring it to my place."

All three nod as I close the door.

I'd love for Isabella to move into my home and never move out. But if that can't happen, she sure isn't coming back here.

The ride back to my house is silent.

Isabella stares sullenly out the window, her hands gripping her cat tightly against her chest. I don't know if I should talk to break the tension, take her hands in mine to give her support, or let her alone. I've crushed on her for so long, but I don't actually know how to help her when she's struggling.

"What's your cat's name?" I ask quietly.

"Butterscotch," she answers.

"Boy or girl?"

"Boy."

"Is he friendly?"

"For the most part," she answers. I tentatively reach out my hand, letting Butterscotch sniff it, and he immediately begins purring as he butts his head up against my fingers.

"Where do you live?" she blurts out suddenly, making me jump slightly.

"About twenty minutes outside of Eternity. I wanted a lot of land for my guys. Some really struggle with transitioning back into civilian life after being active duty. Many admitted that they felt more peace when they didn't feel claustrophobic."

"I'm not following. Your guys?"

"The guys in my MC."

She's quiet for a moment before continuing. "So everyone is prior military? Is Alex part of it? Or Leo?"

"No, neither of your brothers are. They don't ride."

"I think Leo used to. Or maybe he just talked about wanting to get a motorcycle? Well, before ..." she trails off. I know what she was about to say. Before his injury overseas. I still haven't gotten the full story about what happened to Leo. He's close-lipped about it, and none of his family seems to know. If I find out he used to ride, or if he has any interest in learning, I'm definitely inviting him to one of our events. It sounds like he could use some of the services my MC provides.

Turning onto my winding driveway, we pass by the Clubhouse where I can hear music playing somewhat loudly. The guys mostly keep it down after sunset, knowing sometimes sound can really travel here, and Camila has a routine bedtime of eight o'clock. Tonight she's with my parents, who occasionally have her over for special sleepovers. I haven't had time to text my parents to let them know about Isabella coming to stay with me, but I need to do that before morning.

I've never had a woman in my home before. Well, one that isn't related to me. Sure, I've dated. But we've always stayed at the girl's place instead of mine. But from the moment I met Isabella, I haven't had a serious relationship.

The only woman I've ever wanted here is about to step foot inside for the first time, and I fucking hope she stays.

Chapter 7

ISABELLA

As the long driveway curves around what I assume is the Club-house, I'm surprised to see a basketball court, what looks like a sand volleyball court, and an area with covered picnic tables. "Is that an ice rink?"

"In the winter, yeah. We remove the ice for the rest of the year, so anyone can use rollerblades there. We've even done some fun races with puppies that the guys have really enjoyed."

"How do you race with puppies?" I ask, intrigued.

Sebastian looks over at me and winks, and my stomach does a somersault. "With food, obviously. One person holds the puppy at the starting line, then another is at the finish line with a treat. They're puppies, so they have short attention spans. It's pretty comical to watch the chaos."

"And this is done just for fun?"

"Keeping up good morale, and showing how fun life can be, are important to guys struggling to find a place in civilian life. I'll do just about anything to ensure that my guys know they have all the support they need. I refuse to lose —" he stops abruptly.

"Lose what?" I ask.

He sighs, scrubbing a hand over his beard. "I don't want someone else to think they don't have anyone. I can't lose another friend that way."

It takes me a moment to realize what he's saying, and I gasp. "You lost someone? To suicide?"

He nods as he turns around another corner, but doesn't elaborate. I look out the windshield as a home comes into view, and I immediately forget the conversation. What stands before me is quite possibly the most beautiful home I've ever seen.

It's not massive, ostentatious, or elaborate. But it is spectacular. Cream stucco meets stone accents with large windows around a bright blue door. One room has a bay window, and a large chandelier is centered above the front door. The home faces east, and as the sun begins to set behind the Rockies, I can only imagine the breathtaking views from the back of the home.

When Sebastian pulls into a four-car garage off to the side of the home, lights immediately flicker to life inside the space. The walls are lined with shelves, meticulously organized. Besides his truck, there's another car and his motorcycle, plus an extra space he appears to be using as a construction area. He has sports memorabilia hanging along one wall, including Denver Wolves items from Luca, and the Colorado Coyotes, our football team in Denver.

As soon as the engine is turned off, I open my door, but Sebastian puts a hand on my arm. "Wait until the garage door is closed."

"Why?"

"In case we were followed. I highly doubt someone would be dumb enough to follow past my Clubhouse, but you never know. Better safe than sorry, *mi Cielo*. I won't play with your safety."

Why does my heart skip a beat each time he calls me his sky?

Once the door is closed, we both exit the car. Sebastian retrieves my things from the trunk and motions for me to follow him into the house. He stops at a security panel, quickly punching in a code to turn off the system. "The code is one-one-zero-nine-nine-four."

Holy shit.

"Is that —" I stop, swallowing roughly. "That's my birthday."

Sebastian looks over his shoulder, a soft smile on his face. "I know."

What the fuck?

"That's — but — Sebastian!" I sputter, audibly panting as my heart rate increases.

"Come on. Let me show you to the guest room."

"Wait! I — just wait. Why the hell is my birthday your security code?"

He steps closer to me, so close I have to tilt my head to look up at him. He cups my cheek tenderly as he smiles. "You're not ready for that yet."

"What the hell does that mean?" I ask exasperatedly.

Sebastian chuckles. "You're getting there. I'm pretty patient, so I'm cool with waiting you out."

"This is ridiculous. Just tell me why."

"In due time."

"When will that time be, exactly?"

"That is all up to you."

"What is?"

"When you see."

"What am I supposed to see?" I snap.

"What I see."

I throw my head back in frustration. "You're talking in riddles."

He smiles goofily at me. "I'm not. You aren't ready. But you will be."

"I am so pissed at you right now," I mutter, stepping back from him, immediately missing the warmth that emanated from his nearness.

"No, you're not," he says with a chuckle. Another wink as he continues, "I'm not the one in control here. You are. So you're actually pissed at yourself."

He's not completely wrong, as I'm definitely irritated that I can't figure out his stupid riddle. For some time, my entire family has said that he's got a thing for me. He's flirted with me here and there, but also said some really stupid things in my presence that have made me think he doesn't have the highest opinion of me. He's asked me out, said it would be a privilege to take me on a date ... but I've been burned so many times that I don't know who I can trust anymore.

"Come on. Let's get you settled in the guest room," he says, grabbing my hand, being careful to avoid jostling Butterscotch in my arms, and walks through the house. With no lights on, I can't make out any room specifics, but I can tell there's a large kitchen, and a living room that seems to have a two-story ceiling. We quickly coast up a curved staircase, and Sebastian points to a double-door entry. "That's my room. Just in case you need anything."

I cough to cover a snort. I may not truly understand his intentions, but even I got the undertones on that comment.

We cross a hallway overlooking the first floor, then Sebastian enters the first room on the left. Turning on the light, I see a large four-poster bed with mounds of fluffy bedding covering it. Beautiful hand-painted mountain images bracket the bed, and dark wood nightstands sit on each side. He pulls me across the room to another doorway, swatting a light switch that illuminates the en suite bathroom. "I texted ahead and had someone put a litter box in here for Butterscotch. I hope that's okay. There are some toiletry items in here if you need anything. Unused, of course. I mean new. New things. But anything you can't find I probably have in my bathroom. I keep everything I can think of on hand. You know, for emergencies."

"You bring a lot of women here after their apartments are

trashed?" I ask, a sharpness to my voice I didn't expect. I have no reason to be jealous of anything Sebastian does, yet I am.

His face pales, and he looks remarkably horrified. "Fucking hell, *no*. I have sisters. And a mom. And a grandmother. She's the worst, because she asks for the oddest things. So I just started grabbing anything that seemed even remotely female. Now her requests are getting even more outlandish. Last week she asked for a purple wet brush."

"Okay?" I ask. A wet brush isn't that out of the ordinary. My sister Gianna has incredibly curly hair, and I know she uses a wet brush.

"She doesn't have curly hair, Isabella. She barely has any hair at all. The hair she does have gets done by a professional every week. The fuck does she need a wet brush for?" he asks, deadpan. I can't help the laughter that bursts from my mouth, causing Sebastian's gaze to snap to my lips. He grins, but doesn't say anything as he reaches up, ghosting his thumb over my bottom lip.

I inhale sharply as he presses down in the center of my lip, my mouth opening slightly. My breath quickens as I imagine what it would feel like if his thumb slid between my lips. How his skin would feel. Taste.

"One day," he murmurs. "You'll be ready one day."

Removing his thumb, he leans in to kiss my forehead, then turns and walks toward the door. When I call out his name, he stops. "What will I be ready for?"

Sebastian stands still for a moment before giving me his one-word answer.

"Me."

Four hours later, I'm wide awake. I have to be up in a few hours to be at the bakery, and I can't calm my mind down. I just keep reliving what that man — Devon — did. What he told me he was going to do to me.

I wish I had a therapist. I've never been one to think about my emotional health too much, but right now, I could use the help of a professional. I debate on texting Arianna, but I just *can't*. It would freak her out, and then she'd tell Stone. I know he would immediately tell Sebastian or my brothers, and they'd stop at nothing until Devon was dealt with. I can't have that on my conscience. Even with the lewd and appalling things Devon claimed he'd do, I won't tell anyone.

"Gonna fuck your ass first," he'd grunted as he attempted to rip my pants off. "Then this pussy. I was only supposed to rough you up a bit, get you to work with us and tell us where the drugs are."

"I don't know anything about drugs!" I'd wailed as he'd jammed his hand down my pants, roughly cupping my sex.

That was when Sebastian roared into the room.

He literally roared, like a lion protecting his mate.

I'd never seen Sebastian so angry and fired up.

And now, sleeping in his guest room, I can't settle down because the only place that has felt even halfway peaceful over the past couple of weeks was in his arms.

I'm up and opening the door before I truly even realize what I'm doing.

Tiptoeing down the hallway toward Sebastian's room, I make it all the way to his doorway before noticing it's wide open. He left the door open for me.

Moonlight casts a glow through open windows right onto the bed, and I see Sebastian turn his head my way. Without a word, he throws back the comforter for me. I don't question it, immediately climbing into the massive bed and straight into his embrace.

I've been so closed-off with him. So mean. And he's patiently waited, never judging me for my behavior. A different man would have locked the door, but Sebastian lets me right in.

We both sigh as we sink into relaxation. My left hand rests on his chest, and I throw my left leg over both of his. He lays his right hand over mine on his chest, clasping it firmly against his skin. I feel Butterscotch jump onto the bed, finding a spot between our legs. The feel of Sebastian's heartbeat under my palm is steady, and lulls me into sleep.

I only vaguely remember him whispering to me as finally fall asleep.

"This is where you belong, *Naranja*."

I WAKE UP DISORIENTED BUT INCREDIBLY RESTED. IT TAKES ME A MINUTE to remember where I am. Not only am I at Sebastian's house, but I'm in his bed. Sunlight streams in through large windows with slate blue curtains falling along the sides of each one. My head swings to the side, checking for Sebastian, and I let out a small, relieved breath when I find I'm alone. Now I can continue my perusal of his space.

The room positively reeks of Sebastian. A dark walnut dresser and a deep brown leather chair sit across from the massive bed. I'm surprised to discover there isn't a wall-mounted television, and also that there is no clothing out of place anywhere. Spotting an open doorway, I quietly climb out of bed and tiptoe over to peer into a large bathroom. The largest soaking tub I've ever seen occupies the corner, with two gigantic picture windows meeting in the middle. A walk-in tile shower is next to the tub, and when I can't see the shower head, I step inside to find the space wraps around a wall. Multiple heads cover the walls — and the *ceiling* — and I'm taken aback at how luxurious and opulent it is.

Don't get me wrong: Sebastian has an aristocratic way about him. He carries himself proudly, almost regally, and treats women with reverence and respect. But the juxtaposition between that and the Sebastian I've experienced with my brothers is so dramatically different. I hear about the Seb who owns a bar and runs an MC club. I've witnessed the first Sebastian, but my mind is finding it difficult to marry the two together.

Exiting the shower, I see the closet is open, and I can't stop myself from peeking inside. The space smells like Sebastian's cologne, and when I notice a bottle on a shelf, I snatch it up, taking a big whiff. The Tom Ford cologne is phenomenal, with a perfect mixture of oakwood, cardamom, and sandalwood. I already know it's well out of my price point, but I'm tempted to sneak it into the guest room and spray it on a pillowcase or one of my sweaters. This scent has to be remembered.

As I'm placing it back on the shelf, I sense I'm being watched. I hang my head as I imagine how Sebastian will react. "I'm sorry. I know, I should ask first. This is your space, and I'm being so disrespectful by snooping."

"What's snooping?"

That's not Sebastian. That's a child's voice. What the hell?

Spinning, I find a little girl, no more than five, watching me with interest. "Uh, hi."

"Hello," she says. "What's your name?"

"My name is Isabella," I tell her carefully. "What's yours?"

"Camila. Why are you in my Daddy's closet?"

There's a ringing in my ears as I process that information. Sebastian has a daughter? How have I never known about her? Where was she last night? And more importantly, where is her mother?

"I got lost," I lie. "I was staying in the other bedroom and couldn't find the bathroom."

"That room has its own bathroom," Camila says, her expression so similar to her dad's that I'd have known she was his even if she hadn't announced it.

"Oh. You're right. I forgot about that," I tell her sheepishly, suddenly aware I'm wearing a tank top and tiny sleep shorts. "Can you show me back to that room? I need to get dressed. I should have already gotten to work by now."

"Why are you staying here?" Camila asks. She doesn't move from the doorway, crossing her arms exactly like Sebastian does. Two dark chestnut braids hang down her back, and she chews on her bottom lip. Spectacular blue eyes peer up at me as she waits for my response.

"I needed a place to stay, and your dad offered me one," I tell her simply. Stepping toward her, I motion for her to move, and she reluctantly does. I know where I'm going, but allow Camila to guide me back to the guest room. She immediately jumps on the bed.

"You didn't sleep in here last night," she says matter-of-factly.

"Yes I did," I answer defensively.

"Did you get scared? Sometimes when I get scared, Daddy lets me sleep in his bed too. It's okay if you did. I promise I won't tell anyone," she whispers. "Why did you need a place to stay?"

"My apartment needs some work done, so your Dad said I could stay here while that happens," I answer finally. I'm not telling this kid anything. I'm still shell-shocked that I'm getting grilled by a preschooler at seven o'clock in the morning.

"Are you staying more nights?" she asks.

"I believe so, yes."

She immediately claps her hands in excitement. "Daddy never has girls here! Well, other than *Abuelita* and *Abuela*. And my *Tías* come stay here. But they're all family. You're new. Can we have a sleepover?"

Before I can answer, Sebastian bellows from downstairs. "Camila!"

"Uh-oh," she whispers. "He told me I was only allowed to go to my room. I'm gonna get in trouble. I always wanted a cat. Is that cat yours? He's never gonna let me get a cat now."

"Camila Isabelle! Downstairs, right now!"

Oh for fuck's sake.

Stomping to the door, I hit the top of the stairs and glare down at Sebastian. That can't be coincidental, can it?

"Seriously? Isabelle? What the hell, Sebastian?"

Camila gasps before whispering, "I can't say that word."

Crap. I look down at Sebastian, and he raises an eyebrow at me. "Um. I'm sorry. You're correct. I should have said something different."

Camila nods, giving me a pleased grin, then looks down at her father.

Sebastian has the most breathtaking smile I've ever seen as he shrugs. "You probably don't want to know what's on her birth certificate."

Chapter 8

I was only slightly teasing. Camila's middle name is actually Isabelle, but it's twofold. My grandmother's middle name is also Isabelle. And, yeah: it's for Isabella as well.

My sisters both had a field day with that. They know how I've felt about Isabella for years. My parents are either in denial, or blissfully ignorant.

Abuela just wants me to have more babies, she doesn't care who the mother is. She'd prefer I be married in a proper Catholic ceremony before my wife pops out her great-grandchildren, but she's even willing to compromise on that if I deliver a chubby newborn wrapped in muslin.

"Daddy," Camila whines as she prances into the kitchen.

"Yes, *Mija*?" I reply, taking a big sip of coffee.

"Is Isabella my mother?" Camila asks bluntly, and I immediately choke, spewing coffee all over the table.

"Daddy! Are you okay? You made a big mess!"

"Oh my. Are you alright, Sebastian?" Isabella asks innocently as she rushes into the room, patting my back as I cough.

"Went down the wrong pipe," I croak. Jesus. I did not think Camila would connect her name and Isabella's so quickly. It's only recently that Camila has begun to ask about her mother after seeing classmates picked up by their own moms after school. I'd explained that Camila's mother chose to move away and leave her in my care.

I'd have liked to tell Camila the truth; that her mother was a selfish bitch who could rot in hell for all I care, but on the rare chance the woman comes back into Camila's life, I don't want to start things off poorly for Camila.

"Well, is she?" Camila asks impatiently, her foot tapping against the floor. Wearing pink shorts with bows on the sides, a purple shirt with a glittery unicorn, and her hair in perfect braids courtesy of my mother, I can't help the small grin that slides across my face. My daughter is, without a doubt, the best thing I've ever done in my life.

"No," I answer simply, hoping she'll drop the subject.

"Oh," Camila responds, her shoulders dropping in defeat. She slinks to the furthest stool at the island, sitting down and resting her head on the counter.

"What was that about?" Isabella asks.

Before I can come up with a reply, Camila states, "I asked if you're my mom. But he says you're not. I'm sad. I thought you'd be a good mom, I guess."

Silence.

Shit.

"What Camila means —" I stammer, but Isabella holds up a hand to stop me.

"I think it's clear what she means. You have a very smart girl on your hands. Your Daddy is right, Camila," Isabella says, turning to walk toward my daughter. "I'm not your mom. I can be your friend, though. Would that be okay?"

Camila studies Isabella, chewing on her bottom lip nervously. "Can we still have a sleepover? And do you do braids like *Abuelita*? What about making cookies? Daddy makes the worst cookies. Uncle Luca says they're like hockey pucks."

"Uncle Luca?" Isabella asks softly, her eyes finding mine.

I put my hands up in mock surrender. "I swear, I didn't start that. Luca did."

Isabella quietly sits beside Camila. "As long as your dad says it's okay, we can have a sleepover. I can do braids, but I think your *Abuelita* may have better skills than me. I can, in fact, make excellent cookies, and I definitely don't create hockey pucks. As Uncle Luca is actually my brother, he knows what a good cookie tastes like."

"He's your brother?" Camila whispers incredulously, her eyes as wide as saucers. "How come I've never met you then?"

Isabella laughs awkwardly. "I'm not sure. That's a question for your Daddy and Uncle Luca. I own a bakery, so I will be sure to leave a good recipe for cookies with your Daddy so the two of you can make them in the future."

"You own a bakery?" Camila squeals, clapping her hands in delight. I beam at her happiness.

"Well, I don't own it outright." Well, fuck. My good mood just fell insanely quickly. "But I run it, and I bake everything that I sell each day. In fact, I'm really late today, and I have to get going."

"Can I go with you? I wanna see how a bakery runs," my daughter asks.

"No, *Mija*. Not today. You're with me all day," I tell her with a frown. Camila has her yearly checkup after lunch, an eye appointment right afterward, and a play date with the daughter of another single dad from her kindergarten class. In between the excitement, she'll be hanging with me at the bar while I check payroll and inventory reports.

And damn it all to hell, but I'm furious that I can't be protecting Isabella today.

As Camila skips away, Isabella turns to me, her eyes full of questions. "Why didn't I know about Camila?"

I shrug. "Luca is the only one who has met her. Dom knows I have a daughter, but he knows I keep her private."

"Why hasn't she come to any birthday parties? She'd probably fit right in with my nieces and nephews."

"I haven't been to a Santo birthday party in quite a few years," I confess, rubbing the back of my neck sheepishly. "Maybe I subconsciously stopped attending because of her, but I think it was also a safeguard for my own heart."

"Why?" she asks quietly.

I sigh, the weight heavy on my chest. "Because I feared how you might react, and I knew I couldn't take it if you were upset. If it impacted how you treated me."

"Oh. I guess that makes sense," Isabella whispers, her gaze pinned on the ground. Before I can say more, she swivels, turning to walk toward the garage. As she gets closer, she stops with a gasp. "My car isn't here!"

"It is, actually," I tell her, reaching around her to grab her keys from a hook by the door. "Trace and Zee went back to get it so you'd have it here."

"Zee?" she asks.

"His name is Zach, but he goes by Zee."

"Is that like a club name?"

"No, we have never really bought into the club name thing. Some of the guys have nicknames. But we call everyone what they choose to be called. I don't feel like we need to issue a new name or identifier just because they're part of the club."

"Do the guys have nicknames from their time in service?" Isabella wonders.

"Some do. It depends on the career field. Pilots definitely do, and some of them are weird as hell."

"So not all Maverick and Goose?" she says with a smile.

"Nope. One guy had the call sign Tater. I never did get an explanation as to how that came to be."

I reach around Isabella again to open the door, holding it for her as she breezes through. Following her into the garage, she stops when she sees her car is in place of mine.

"I don't want to displace you, Sebastian. This isn't right," she murmurs, her eyes seemingly zeroed in on her license plate.

"I'm not leaving your car outside where anyone can reach it. I've debated on dropping you off so your car isn't a sitting duck in town."

Her eyes whip to mine, horror evident. "Should I be worried?"

"No," I tell her quietly, grabbing her hand and bringing it up to my chest. Placing it against my heart, I wait until she feels the steady beat, and I visibly see her relax. "I promise I will never take your safety for granted. Everything I do is in an abundance of caution. Trace and Zee will be taking shifts keeping an eye on the bakery until we have more information on who is pulling the strings here. You'll never be alone."

Isabella's lower lip trembles slightly as a sheen of tears over takes her pupils. I don't even think, I just yank her into my arms. I'm not sure who is more surprised when she willingly circles her arms around my waist, but I'm not about to ask. I worried last night was a one-off, her needing to sleep with me in my bed. Burying my face in her hair, I relish how her body lines up perfectly with mine.

"If it's all the same to you, I'd like you to leave your car here. I'll drive you to work today." I wait, holding my breath, for Isabella to respond.

I feel her relief before she answers, "Okay."

"I wish I could be there with you all day today," I admit softly, running a hand up and down her spine.

"Me too," she whispers, and I think my heart stops.

"Seriously?" I blurt out with a laugh.

Her head tilts back as her eyes find mine. "Is it that surprising?"

"That you'd want me to be around you? A little, yeah."

Isabella shrugs as she snuggles back into my embrace, and I bite back a groan. Good fucking God, she feels perfect. Her voice is quiet when she speaks. "You make me feel safe. There aren't many men who make me feel that way, but you … do. I know I haven't been the nicest to you over the years, Sebastian, but I find comfort with you. I'm struggling to undo the damage in my brain that tells me all men are jerks, but I'm trying."

"I'll always keep you safe, *mi Cielo*," I say reverently, and I feel her arms tighten around my midsection almost imperceptibly. A tremor wracks her body, and I assume she's struggling. In an attempt to break the tension, I joke, "Besides. Your brothers would straight up murder me if anything happened to you on my watch. And I expect Leo and Alex would make me suffer for the fun of it."

Isabella giggles. "They absolutely would. They definitely fall under the safe category, but they're slightly feral when family is involved."

I chuckle, pressing my lips to the top of her head. "I fully support a feral family. Wait until you meet my sisters."

✦ ✦ ✦ ✦ ✦

"Update," I bark into the phone.

"Jesus, man. I just gave you an update ten minutes ago. Nothing has changed," Trace says with an exaggerated sigh.

"I don't fucking care. I said updates every ten minutes. If you don't text me, I'm calling. If you don't answer, I will hunt your ass down until I get the fucking update."

I hear a rustling and the jingle of the bell on the front door of the bakery. "Look, Seb, she's fine. Business as usual. Seems like only regulars have come in today, and definitely not the douche who had her by the throat earlier. But you gotta calm the fuck down."

I find myself growling as I grip the wooden bar beneath my hand so tightly my knuckles turn white. I reply back with every ounce of sarcasm and snark I can find in the depths of my body. "Look, *Trace*, I'll react any fucking way I want to when we're talking about my woman's safety, and you don't get to tell me to act otherwise."

"Yours, huh?" he says with a laugh. "She know about that?"

Fuck. "Not exactly."

"You know, I may be more single than you, but I'm fairly sure that it's frowned upon to keep women in the dark about their own relationships."

"She's not in the dark." I pause, wondering just how far gone Isabella really knows I am for her. "Maybe she's *mostly* not in the dark."

Trace snorts. "How is that any different?"

"It's a work in progress. She's like a baby deer, and I'm scared she'll either get spooked and run, or ..."

"Get run over by a car," he finishes.

"Something like that," I mutter. "I've had a lot more time to think about a relationship with her. I don't think she's ever really believed that I've had a thing for her."

"Why?" he asks incredulously.

My brows furrow as I contemplate how to explain my thoughts. Why is Isabella so surprised at my interest? Why has she turned me down every time I've asked her out? Did she really think it was a bet with her brothers? It can't be that. All of her siblings know about my feelings, so why hasn't she believed any of them? "I honestly don't know. I'm not sure if she's lost trust in all men, or if she's wary of just me. Maybe she thinks it's a fun time for me, but she doesn't understand I'm playing the long game here. So I'm patient. Gonna wait her out, show her that I'm a guy she can trust."

Trace is silent, and when I'm about to joke that he's being too quiet for my liking, I hear a bunch of noise as he blurts out, "I'll call you back."

"What? Why? Did something happen? Trace? Fuck!" I pull the phone away from my ear to see he's ended the call. My heart rate shoots through the roof as I grab my keys and take off running. Shoving open the door to my bar, I'm almost to my car when my phone vibrates with an incoming call.

"I'm fine, don't freak out. It's fine. I'm fine," Isabella says breathlessly.

"What happened?" I shout as my feet slide on gravel in the parking lot.

I hear another commotion as the phone jostles between hands before Trace answers me. "I heard a crash, then Isabella shrieked. A cabinet fell off the wall."

"A cabinet fell off? How the fuck does that happen?" I ask.

"Well, from what I can see, there don't appear to be suitable brackets holding up any of the upper level cabinetry in here, and —" Trace abruptly stops, and I hear Isabella murmuring in the background, "— and she just admitted she's known about the cabinets needing to be replaced, but hasn't had the money to do so."

"You know what I'm about to say," I state.

"Yup. Limits?"

"None. Whatever the fuck it takes to make that the safest damn kitchen in the entire state."

"Got it. You want to talk to your girl?"

"Yes."

I hear her mutter, "I'm not his girl," and both Trace and I reply in unison, "yes you are."

"What?" Isabella snaps as she takes the phone back from Trace.

"Are you alright?" I ask quietly.

"How do you mean?"

"Did anything hit you, *mi Cielo*? Are you hurt?"

She sighs, her voice noticeably softer. "No, nothing hit me. I'm fine."

"Physically, yes. But I imagine it frightened you."

"A large cabinet coming at me? Yes, Sebastian, I was a little unprepared for that."

"Anything broken in the cabinet? Dishes? Glassware?" I ask, as I slowly walk back into the bar. My bartender looks at me quizzically, after watching me bolt only moments before, but I don't acknowledge him. Heading into my office, I grab my tablet and Google bakery necessities.

"A bunch of cheap plates. Nothing too important ..." she trails off. "Sebastian, what are you doing?"

"Hmm?"

"Right now. Right this very second. What are you doing?" she asks impatiently. I can almost imagine one hand on her hip, tapping a foot in aggravation.

"I'm at my bar. Doing inventory things this week," I answer innocently.

"That's not what I asked."

"I'm sitting at my desk in my office."

"And you're not doing anything else? Like looking up the cost of cabinetry, or buying me replacement plates?"

"I'm not buying anything right now." I'm adding a ton to a cart on a wholesale restaurant website, but again, she hasn't asked that specifically.

"Don't you dare replace this kitchen, Sebastian," Isabella says loudly.

"Do you really see me as the type to hang cabinets?" I tease.

"I think you can do almost anything you put your mind to, and being a knight in shining armor is absolutely up your alley," she replies.

"You see me as your knight, *Mami*?" I coo, knowing I'm effectively redirecting her. "Unrelated question. Are you attracted to men in knight costumes?"

"Sebastian," she sighs in exasperation, but I can hear a smile in her tone.

"I'll have you know, I look good in silver."

"Your modesty knows no limits," she replies, deadpan. "Women must line the streets, just trying to get a piece of you."

"Don't fucking care about any of that, sweetheart," I answer huskily. "I only want you."

Chapter 9

ISABELLA

"I could have just gotten a rideshare," I mumble as Trace opens his truck door for me.

"Nah. I'm headed back to the Clubhouse anyway. Besides, I'm pretty sure Seb would cut off my balls if I allowed you to go in a car with someone neither of us vetted," Trace says with a shrug, before wincing. "Fuck. Now he's really gonna have me by the balls for saying 'cut off my balls' to his old lady."

My mouth drops open in shock. "I am not old!"

Trace throws back his head in raucous laughter. "I know that. Damn, darlin'. You've gotta be a decade younger than me. The term 'old lady' is an MC thing. It means your woman."

"I'm not —" I say, but he cuts me off as I slide into the seat. One hand on the top of the truck and the other casually draped across the door, Trace looks at me seriously.

"It's a status thing. A sign of respect, and also a sign that no other club member can fuck with you. Whether you think you're Seb's or not, he'll let everyone know that you're off limits. Although in my opinion, you could do worse than Sebastian Garcia." With that, he closes the door and walks around to the driver's side. Sliding in, he turns on the ignition and buckles his seatbelt. "I don't know a more honorable man than Seb. He'd take the shirt off his back and give it to just about anyone. You could tell him you have no interest in him romantically, and I know he'd still have us looking after you, because even if he couldn't have you, he'd want you safe."

I don't reply as I let Trace's words marinate. I know Sebastian is honorable. My brothers wouldn't respect him if he weren't. They certainly wouldn't allow me to stay at Sebastian's home right now. I got a couple of strongly worded texts from Dominic this afternoon, threatening to come and remove me from Sebastian's if I didn't answer him about the status of our relationship, but then got texts from his wife Kate, telling me she'd calmed him down. She also encouraged me to 'ride the sexy motorcycle man,' but I chose not to acknowledge that text.

Speaking of texts, the sibling group text has been overly active today. Honestly, all the group texts revolving around my family have been busier than normal, and usually the chat with the girls is complete bedlam. Today, however, my brothers are out for blood.

> Alex: I've got a buddy who is Denver PD, and he's staking out Rick's apartment.
>
> Dominic: Hypothetically speaking, how easy is it to dispose of something that weighs around two hundred pounds?
>
> Leo: Depends on a variety of factors.
>
> Arianna: Didn't someone threaten to drop my ex in a lake in the mountains?
>
> Alex: Your husband did, and he roped me into it as an accessory.
>
> Luca: How is no one asking Leo for more information? We need to know what Leo knows, and if he's used any of this knowledge before.

Gianna: How am I the only one who thinks this entire conversation shouldn't be in text form? Paper trails, people!

Dominic: She's right. At this point, we're all fucked. Leo, whatcha got?

Leo: Does the person really weigh exactly two hundred?

Leo: Body weight on land is higher than in water.

Leo: Body fat percentage?

Leo: What object is being used to weigh the body down?

Leo: Some items are denser under water, so different items may "weigh" the same, but weigh a body down differently.

Leo: Are we dumping the body — I mean, the object — in a landfill? Underground? In water?

Leo: Ocean or freshwater?

Alex: ...

Dominic: Jesus Christ.

Luca: I fucking LOVE this family.

Gianna: Travis is going to enjoy the play-by-play of this chat when he gets home from work.

Arianna: You can't tell him! Isn't that like some kind of cardinal rule, like Fight Club?

Luca: First rule of Siblings for Hire Club: don't tell your spouses.

Luca: Second rule of Siblings for Hire Club: come up with a better name for the club.

Alex: Bad Boyfriends Club.

Alex: Taking out the Trash.

Dominic: Boyfriend Butchering.

Gianna: Can we not name this never-gonna-happen club, please?

Luca: Ho-ho-homicide House.

Dominic: The Slaughter Saloon.

Arianna: Guys.

Luca: Club Carnage. Where fun becomes deadly.

Leo: We're not naming any kind of club where we may or may not off Belle's ex-boyfriend. Hypothetically.

Leo: And I'm unavailable for the next few weeks anyway.

Leo: Since I know you all will expect the majority of the covert bullshit to fall on me.

Leo: So don't.

Luca: Unavailable for a few weeks?

Dominic: What's going on?

Alex: Where the hell are you anyway, Leo?

Arianna: Gia, he's your twin. Use that twin voodoo crap and pin down his location.

Gianna: Last time I checked, sharing a womb didn't make me a human Find My Friends GPS, Ari.

Gianna: I know where he is. And he told me not to share, so I'm not saying a word.

Dominic: As head of this family, I find that answer unacceptable.

Alex: How the hell did you become head of the family? First of all, I'm the oldest. Second of all, Dad is still alive?

Dominic: Please. You really think I don't run everything already?

Alex: Fucker.

Dominic: That's what I thought.

Me: Can I leave?

Arianna: Don't you dare, Belly, I'll add you right back in!

Me: I DON'T WANT TO BE HERE FOR THIS SHIT.

Arianna: You don't get to unsubscribe from siblings. If I have to suffer through this testosterone-fueled group text, we all do.

Luca: You're my favorite sister, Ari.

Arianna: Fuck off, Luca. I'm only your favorite because Isabella hasn't brought you any desserts lately.

Luca: This is true.

ISABELLA HAS LEFT THE GROUP

TRACE CLEARS HIS THROAT, AND I LOOK UP FROM MY PHONE TO FIND Sebastian staring intently at me from inside his garage. I was so engrossed in the chaos of my siblings that I didn't realize we'd made it back home. I mean, to Sebastian's home.

Holy hell, I cannot think of this man's home as being my home.

"He gave me the all clear. You can get out," Trace says quietly.

My eyes dart a glance at his profile. "The all clear? You think someone might be hiding out there?"

"It's a precaution. Seb doesn't take chances on those he lo — the people he cares about," Trace stammers. "Zee will be with you at the bakery tomorrow. And then you're off the following day, correct?"

"Yes," I answer, my eyes widening. "How did you know that? The bakery is open every day."

"You switch your off days every week, but you've been adhering to the same schedule for over a year. You flip-flop Tuesdays and Thursdays, then the third week of the month, you take off Sundays."

"I didn't realize you'd kept such a close eye on me," I tease.

Trace chuckles. "I think you know who has kept a close eye on you, and it sure as shit wasn't me."

I feel heat spread up my neck as I giggle awkwardly. "Thanks for being there today, and helping me clean up after the cabinet catastrophe."

"My pleasure. Now get out before Seb stalks over here and demands a duel. I can see the steam coming out of his ears from here."

I look up quickly, and notice Sebastian's eyes trained on me. He definitely looks unhappier than he did when we originally pulled up, but I find it hard to believe it's solely because I spent a minute speaking with Trace. Thanking him again, I exit his truck and approach Sebastian slowly. "Is everything okay?"

"What were you talking to Trace about?" he asks.

"My schedule," I say slowly, watching as Sebastian's eyes dance along the horizon as he pulls me into the garage. I hear Trace drive away as Sebastian closes the door. "And how apparently you gave him a look that told him I could get out of the car?"

"I did." His hand finds mine as we walk between his motorcycle and my car.

"Do you really think some sharpshooter is just hanging out on MC land, waiting for the fat baker to come home from work?"

Sebastian stops, turning so quickly I run into him. His eyes narrow as he steps into my space, and I subconsciously back up until I hit the side of my car. He crowds against me, his hand finding my neck, and I shudder. "I don't know which part of that sentence I need to address first, or which part pisses me off the most. Don't ever speak about a sharpshooter possibly staking you out. You think I'd actually let one fucking inch of my property go unsurveilled right now? Even taking you out of the equation, Isabella, I have a child here. I would never put her safety at risk."

Blood drains from my face. "I'm sorry. That was so uncouth of me. Of course you wouldn't."

His thumb rubs against my pulse point, and his eyes drop to my lips as he lines his body up with mine. "And do you really think I'd put your safety at risk? Now that I finally have you close to me? Now that you might actually be seeing what I've been saying all along?"

I don't answer as his hand slides up to my jaw, and his thumb pushes against my lower lip. With enough pressure, my mouth opens slightly, and I watch as Sebastian's eyes become hooded. His other hand drifts down my side, latching onto my thigh, lifting it. I gasp when he lines himself up with my core, and I feel every inch of him. "Do you feel what you do to me, *mi*

Reina? I haven't even touched you. Tasted you. Fuck, I haven't even kissed you. But I'm hard as steel just being in your orbit. I dream about your body, Isabella. Every inch of you is perfection. I've wanted you for years. *Years.* I crave you, exactly as you are. And the word 'fat' shouldn't ever be used to describe your exquisite body."

I'm absolutely panting, on the verge of an orgasm just from his words. Each word was spoken with such clarity, his hot breath breaking across my skin like fire, and I'm overcome with desire unlike anything I've ever experienced before.

"What's *mi Reina*?" I ask breathlessly, as my core clenches in wanton need. How many different names has he called me so far? Each time my stomach flips, and I wonder if that will change.

His eyes close as he rests his forehead against mine, and his answer is spoken directly onto my lips. "It means 'my queen.'"

Before I can respond, or lose my head and press our lips together like I desperately want to, I hear a door whip open. "Daddy! I found a kitten!"

"Fuck," Sebastian whispers, squeezing my thigh before dropping it from his hand.

"I'm sorry, *Mijo*, but we couldn't leave a kitten on the road. Now come inside so I can meet the woman your daughter hasn't stopped talking about," a woman calls.

I gasp. "Who is that? Do you have a girlfriend?"

Sebastian groans as he steps back from me, hurt evident in his brown eyes. "Seriously? Everything I just said and you still don't believe me? For fuck's sake, Isabella. It's my mother."

Shit. I feel awful. "I'm sorry. I wasn't thinking, Sebastian."

I attempt to shuffle past him, but he grabs my hand. "I'm a patient man, sweetheart. I can wait until you're ready for me. For us. But one thing I will not be patient about is you consistently assuming I'm a liar. The only women in my life are all related to me by blood. I will not stand by and let you accuse me of hiding another woman from you. Now let's go meet my mother, and I bet my grandmother is here, too."

Two minutes later, I'm standing in front of three Garcia women, lined up on Sebastian's living room couch, and I've never been more nervous as he introduces me. His mother, Gabriela, has the same smile as Sebastian, but his grandmother, Rosario, studies me with pursed lips. "*Ella tiene buenas caderas.*"

"Jesus Christ," Sebastian mutters, rubbing his hand across his forehead. "English, *Abuela*. It's rude to speak in Spanish in front of others."

I turn to him as my mouth drops open. "Why is your grandmother commenting on the size of my hips?"

"How did you know that?" Camila asks. "Are you Puerto Rican too?"

"No," I tell her. "My family is Italian."

Rosario scoffs, rolling her eyes. "*Italiano no es lo mismo.*"

"*Abuela!*" Sebastian shouts in frustration. "English!"

"No, it's not the same thing," I answer with a chuckle. "But I took eight years of Spanish growing up. I may not know everything you say, but I can get the gist of it."

Except for the different terms of endearment Sebastian keeps tossing my way, it seems. As if reading my mind, he leans over to whisper, "You just wanted to hear me call you a queen in English, huh."

I feel heat flush across my cheeks. "I actually didn't know that one. And there's another one you said, but I don't think I heard you right, because it sounded like you called me an orange?"

Sebastian clears his throat, rubbing at his beard. "Oh, must have heard me incorrectly then."

"Sebastian!" Gabriela, says with a gasp. "Really?"

"*Mamá,*" he murmurs, and I find myself smiling at the way he looks at his mother. "Drop it, please."

"For now," Gabriela replies, but I see the glint in her eyes.

Whatever this is about, Gabriela Garcia does not plan on dropping it. "Isabella, I planned to make dinner for us. Is there anything you're allergic to, or don't like?"

"No. I love food," I tell her with a smile.

"Isabella," Sebastian growls. "We just talked about this."

"What?" I ask, my eyes dancing between mother and son. "That wasn't a dig at my weight, if that's what you're insinuating. I just really love food. I love trying new recipes, getting to experience new cultures. I love learning how recipes are passed down, and how people create dishes within their families. I honestly love experiencing new things in the kitchen. Really."

Sebastian watches me, a soft smile growing as he listens. "Is that how you began to bake?"

"Some of it, yes. My mom and grandmother have taught me things, but as soon as they realized I was enamored with baking, they encouraged me to learn however I could. My family always supported my desire to be a pastry chef, and as a child, I took any cooking class I could find. I can cook anything, but my true love is pastries."

"Have you ever made *tembleque*?" Rosario asks.

"No, I'm not sure what that is," I confess.

"It's a coconut pudding, but it has a texture like ..." Rosario trails off, her brow furrowed in concentration. *"Comó se dice gelatina?"*

"Jello," Sebastian answers with a grin.

"Ahh, yes," Rosario says with a nod. "I show you how to make."

"Uh, now?" I ask.

"No. Now we make *arroz con pollo*, because Camila asked for it." Rosario stands, grabbing Camila's hand. "We'll let the lovebirds talk."

"What's a lovebird?" Camila asks as she follows her great

grandmother into the kitchen. "Wait! Daddy, the kitten is in my room! Go see!"

Sebastian looks at me and sighs. "I really don't want a kitten."

"Are you prepared to tell her that?" I ask pointedly.

"No," he says with a chuckle. "Any chance you'd be willing to take one for the team?"

"I'm not part of that team, Daddy," I tease, my voice accidentally dropping quite a bit. I step toward the stairs, but Sebastian wraps an arm around my waist, pulling me against his front.

"If you don't want to continue calling me Daddy, I suggest you figure out a way to say it without that sexy as fuck rasp, *mi Cielo*," he whispers against my ear. "Better yet, you can call me *Papi*. Now get your ass upstairs."

Daddy Sebastian does have a nice ring to it, though I'll never tell him that. But *Papi*? Why is that so sexy?

Chapter 10

With every passing day, I can feel Isabella's walls slowly crumbling away. I'm not exactly thrilled with what — or who — has brought us closer together, but I'm not mad about it either.

It's been a little over a week of Isabella living in my home, and while her apartment has been completely fixed up, wired with every fucking security measure I could get my hands on, and ready for her return, neither of us have brought it up. She hasn't come back into my bedroom again, but I've left my door open just in case.

I knew living with Isabella would be difficult for me, only because I'd have to consciously change my natural instincts while around her. A few years ago a therapist did a workshop for my guys about love languages, and I learned mine is physical touch. I'm having to sit on my own fucking hands to keep from touching Isabella. I find myself leaning toward her in an attempt to get into her space. Reaching into her space subconsciously. Brushing up against her whenever I pass, letting the backs of our hands touch, just for a little skin-on-skin contact.

I have never — nor will I ever — force myself on a woman. I'd never want to make a woman feel uncomfortable or unsafe. I feel even more unsteady with Isabella because I've been falling for her for years, and being this close to her day after day is like a drug.

Just being in her proximity is giving me a high I didn't anticipate. But I'll be damned if I push her away by touching her before she's ready to be touched. Isabella is like an injured butterfly, slowly fixing her wings so she can confidently fly.

I just hope she chooses to stay.

"Yo, Prez," I hear called as I step into the Clubhouse on a Saturday afternoon. Following the voice, I find our newest probie, Luke, with two men, one who looks vaguely familiar. "Got two prospects for us."

"Oh?" I go over to introduce myself, staring the one guy down. I know him, and I can't figure out from where. Trey Mathis is tall, with wavy blonde hair and hazel eyes. Rico Delgado, on the other hand, is a couple inches under six feet, with buzzed brown hair and beady dark eyes that never leave mine. The men shake my hand, and Trey launches into explaining their back history that feels very ChatGPT-coded. I'm only half paying attention as I wrack my brain over where I know the other guy.

"So we met while we were stationed overseas," Trey continues.

"Where?" I interrupt, watching as Trey's eyes widen almost imperceptibly. As he stammers, Rico takes over the conversation.

"Al-Asad Air Base," Rico says smoothly. "In Iraq. There are only a couple thousand troops left there."

"And you were both honorably discharged?"

Trey nods. "I thought about doing the full twenty years, but I was sick of deploying."

I turn to Rico. "Rank upon discharge?"

His eyes narrow. "Staff sergeant."

"E-seven?" I ask.

"E-six," he corrects.

"My mistake. MOS?" MOS is the acronym for Military Occupational Specialities. It's how the military puts a specific number on a job type.

"Eighty-nine B," Rico answers.

"Ammunition," I muse. "I bet that wasn't dull in theatre."

He chuckles, but there's no heat behind it. "I deployed a lot."

"And how did you hear about Rocky Mountain Range Riders?"

Trey interrupts. "Luke here. We go to the same church in Denver."

Luke nods excitedly. "Trey approached me a few weeks ago, wanting to know if I knew of any neat places to ride. Just moved here and saw me get on my bike after service one day. Then he told me about a buddy who also rode, and I invited them here."

Luke is twenty-three and like a happy puppy who just found a massive bone under the Christmas tree. His energy levels rival those of a six-year-old boy, and we routinely have to remind him to be quiet whenever we have speakers, or meetings of any kind. He regularly jostles his legs while sitting, as if his energy is just zooming around his body trying desperately to get out. His glass isn't half-full, it's almost always overflowing. The kid doesn't have a negative bone in his body, but at times I can only handle him in small doses.

"Well, take a look around, and I'll give you a schedule of upcoming speakers and events. If you're interested in joining, we can discuss the steps for moving forward," I explain. Pulling out my phone, I send a two word text to Trace.

Me: Find me.

Trace: Clubhouse?

Me: Affirmative.

Less than a minute later, Trace bursts through the door, slightly breathless. I motion for him to approach. "Trace is my VP. He'll show you around and answer any questions."

Trace looks at me, and we have a silent conversation as he

nods. He knows to watch these men like a hawk. I notice Trey shuffling around uncomfortably, like he knows they're here to do something nefarious, and suddenly he's worried about his task. I watch as the four men slowly walk toward the kitchen, Luke animatedly telling them about our last meeting where an active player on the Harlem Globetrotters stopped by for a visit, and I immediately Google the two men's names.

Fuck.

Trey Mathis comes back mostly innocent. As I expected, absolutely no military service is listed on his LinkedIn professional profile. Rico Delgado, however, is more concerning. He does show a few years in the Army as Rico. But when his middle name is searched, Diego Delgado, I see an arrest record that sends a chill down my spine. Multiple arrests and suggested ties to *La Milla Roja* gang, known as The Red Mile. I've heard of the gang, but I don't have any firsthand experience with them. They've got a reputation for drug trade, fierce loyalty to their brothers, and way too many times with blood spilled over territorial boundaries.

Checking my photos, I find the name of the guy who attacked Isabella in her apartment. Googling known connections, I see if Devon has any connections to Trey or Rico/Diego. When nothing comes up, I don't know if I feel relieved or restless. In my gut, I know there's a correlation. Maybe it's not the dastardly intentions my mind keeps thinking up, but I know it's something.

As the men finish up their tour, I get a notification from one of the outdoor security cameras that motion has been detected between the Clubhouse and my property. Assuming it's an animal of some sort, I nonchalantly open my security app and do a double take when I see Isabella walking with my grandmother. Isabella seems to be carrying something, and their direction suggests they are heading toward the Clubhouse.

I make it to the front door at the same time as the women, but

I hear whispered conversations behind me coming from Trey and Rico. Fuck.

"*Mojo*, Isabella made you something," *Abuela* says proudly as she waves to all the men. My grandmother loves hanging out in the Clubhouse with the guys. They all call her *Abuela*, and she preens with joy every time. She waves at me with a wicked glint in her eye as she turns around to walk back to my house. It's only around one-eighth of a mile, but a quick glance toward one of my men, and he immediately follows her to ensure she makes it back in one piece.

"I'm sorry for interrupting," Isabella says hastily, her eyes darting in every direction, "but *Abuela* said I should bring these while they were warm and fresh."

"My boys must eat them while hot," *Abuela* announces, turning her head to look at us, and I hear more than one snicker. I've never been able to confirm if *Abuela* consciously chooses to make most of her statements sound overtly sexual, or if it's coincidental how her mind translates the words, but my guys absolutely love what she says.

"Did you know Prez had a woman?" I hear whispered.

Shit. Leaning into Isabella's space, I whisper against her ear, "I need you to pretend we're together, please."

"What?" she breathes.

"Act like you like me. Put your arms around me," I tell her as I grab the platter of pastries that smell divine, then slide one arm around her back, pulling her against me. Isabella's arms come around my waist hesitantly, but within a few seconds she snuggles into my embrace. She smells like vanilla, sugar, and sunshine. "Agree with whatever I say for the next few minutes, okay?"

"Okay," she says softly, and the feel of her warm breath against my neck is exquisite. I forcibly tense to fight the shiver that threatens to course down my spine as I step away from Isabella, grabbing her hand.

"Range Riders," I state clearly.

"Hooah," they shout, jolting Isabella against me, before she giggles.

"What did they just say?" she murmurs.

"Hooah. It's like a battle cry," I explain quietly, before straightening to peer at my men. "This is Isabella. She's staying in my home, and is to be respected at all times. She's off-limits."

"Is she yours?" someone shouts.

Turning to look down at the beautiful woman beside me, she gives me a sweet smile that is so full of trust, I'm momentarily speechless. Her eyes, so full of innocence and longing, tell me she's falling for me as quickly as I've already fallen for her. For a long second, I have a vision of our future. Isabella holding a baby to her chest as she watches Camila playing in the backyard at sunset. Her arms wrapped around me while riding my motorcycle on a rare date without our children. Isabella formally adopting Camila. Holding my woman as I fill her, watching her come as she's wrapped around me.

I know with every fiber of my being that Isabella is meant to be mine, and I don't care who knows.

"Fuck yeah, she's mine," I murmur as I slide one hand into her hair and bend down to press my lips against hers. I feel her shocked intake of breath before she sighs against my mouth, and she melts against me.

This isn't a sensual kiss. It isn't erotic in nature. It's a man claiming a woman. A possessive, territorial, non-sexual kiss with no tongue and barely any lip movement.

But it's with *her*, and it's the best fucking kiss of my life.

Breaking apart, I look down at Isabella as pink floods her cheeks. She buries her face against my shoulder, and I have a moment of sheer panic as I worry about whether or not I overstepped. I've been so careful around her, thinking about respecting her boundaries. Leaning down, I say quietly, "I can't tell if you're embarrassed, or regretting agreeing to this."

"I'm not entirely sure I know what 'this' is, Sebastian," she confesses as her eyes find mine.

"This is me protecting you, and I'll explain why in a few minutes. Okay?"

She gives me a nod, chewing on the inside of her cheek as her eyes dart around the space. When her eyes land on Rico and Trey, I notice a subtle widening. I turn us so she isn't visible to the potential recruits, pulling her against me again. "What's wrong?"

"The shorter one has been into the bakery twice this week," she whispers. "Never stayed long, but I found it odd. I've never seen him before, and suddenly he's there twice in the same week?"

Fuck.

There's no way these coincidences aren't related. Now I know I need to dig deeper into Isabella's ex-boyfriend and any potential ties to *La Milla Roja.*

"Prez, I'm gonna walk them out," Luke says, and I look over my shoulder to see him ambling over with Trey and Rico.

"Hey," Rico says, staring intently at Isabella. "I know you. You work at that awesome bakery in Eternity Springs."

"I do," Isabella says nervously, her hand finding mine. I squeeze it reassuringly, and notice Rico's eyes darting down to our joined hands.

"My girl has the best bakery around," I state, bringing her hand up to my lips. My head is turned toward Isabella, but my eyes are on Rico. "I'm there as often as I can be."

"Oh?" Rico challenges. "I haven't noticed you there yet."

Wanting to get Isabella out of direct contact, in case anything goes bad, I pull her hand around my waist, turning her slightly so she's behind me, with her front to my back. I internally celebrate when her other hand naturally slides across my abdomen to link up. "I may not always be there in person, but rest assured, I'm always there in other ways."

Rico looks like he's going to continue the conversation when Trey steps in. "It's good that you're protecting your girl. Can't be too safe these days. Listen, we gotta go. Just got a family emergency come up."

Uh-huh. Sure.

As I watch the potential recruits leave with Luke, Trace approaches. "That tall one is about as smart as a box of rocks, but that little guy is looking for a fight. He asked way too many personal questions about security for the Club, how you got started, and wanted to know what side of the law we stay on."

"Nice," I mutter as Isabella drops her arms, stepping away from me. I reach out and snag a hand, desperately needing the connection. I'm relieved when she doesn't fight me, and I wonder if she senses how fired up I am right now. I can keep a calm exterior, but inside, my blood is fucking boiling.

Whoever this group is, they've not only come after my woman, but they've walked right into my world. I have no doubt Luke explained the dynamics of the group, and how I live on the property. I've made it abundantly clear to everyone that they're never to mention Camila, but I wouldn't put it past him to reference her vaguely, and Rico would catch it. He's a slimy bastard, that much I can tell.

"What's the plan?" Trace asks.

"Definitely Bravo for the time being." I chose to keep a lot of the military terminology within the Club that the guys are used to hearing and understanding. There are five basic levels of security for the military: Normal, Alpha, Bravo, Charlie, and Delta. Normal is the baseline for operation. Alpha is an increased risk, which we'd jumped to when Isabella's apartment was ransacked and she was attacked. Knowing these assholes are gutsy enough to walk right into the Clubhouse, I have to raise it to Bravo immediately.

I'm tempted to go to Charlie, which insinuates some kind of attack is imminent, but I have no evidence of that as of yet.

"Alright. I'll send out the alert. You hanging tonight?" Trace asks, his eyes darting between me and Isabella. Usually once a week, I stay to spend time with the guys. I don't drink a lot, but having a couple of beers with them is for morale and connections. But tonight, I'm suddenly so damn weary.

"Nah. I'm beat. I think we're gonna head home." I could have worded it differently, but I want Isabella to know that I'm thinking of the future. That maybe my house will become hers as well.

I say goodbye to my men, then slowly begin walking the short distance back to my property. Isabella silently walks beside me. I can almost hear her mind working as she tries to come to terms with the evening.

"Should I be worried?" she finally asks quietly.

"I don't know," I admit. When she gasps, I stop walking to turn to her. Catching her face in my hands, I continue. "Let me rephrase. I'm not sure what we're up against here. There has to be a connection between those guys and what's happened at your apartment and with your ex."

"I don't like the unknowns." Her voice is barely a whisper, and her eyes glaze over with tears. "I don't do well with gray. I'd rather have black and white."

"I know, *mi Reina*," I reply tenderly. "It's why you like baking. The measurements either work, or they don't."

"How am I supposed to go on working like nothing is happening?" Isabella's voice cracks as her emotions take over. "Hi, welcome to Bake, Batter, and Bowl. Would you like an apple turnover? I made them this morning after being threatened by my ex-boyfriend. Oh, you'd rather have a red velvet cupcake? Those are on the docket for this afternoon, when I'll undoubtedly get roughed up by the gang my ex apparently got involved with. No, sorry, I don't make donuts here. There's a donut shop down the street, and I bet they don't have to fear for their lives while working." Her voice rises, bordering on hysteria.

"Isabella," I say, resting my hands on her shoulders. "Have I ever lied to you?"

"What?" she asks, confused.

"It's a clear question, sweetheart. Have I ever lied to you?"

She pauses to think, her eyes going over my right shoulder. "I don't think so, no."

"I've been asking you out for years. Yes?"

She nods, almost shyly.

"Do you still stand by your previous statement, that I haven't lied to you?"

Her eyes widen. "Well, I wasn't thinking in terms of you asking me out."

"How is it any different?" I ask.

Isabella shrugs. "It's just you're ... you."

I stare at her incredulously. "So?"

"I've seen the women you've been with before," she retorts. "I bet Camila's mother is all-American, skinny, and absolutely beautiful."

Jesus Christ.

"I don't know, maybe she is," I say flippantly, and I see the flash of pain that crosses Isabella's face. But I'm so fucking angry I can't even feel guilty. This woman still doesn't think she's enough.

"See?" she says, but the slight tremor in her voice gives away how Isabella feels. She's hurt, even though she basically brought it on herself.

"No, I don't fucking see," I say angrily. "But maybe it's about time you see, *Naranja*. If I were forced to pick Camila's biological mother out of a lineup, I'm not sure if I could do it. Yeah, it's been years since I've seen her, but also because she's a dime a dozen.

Fucking forgettable. I might have slept with her, but it wasn't serious, and she was never someone I saw myself settling down with."

Isabella crosses her arms, forcing her breasts to sit higher, and the fabric of her shirt strains to hold them in. With only a quick glance, I see her erect nipples, and I fucking salivate so badly I have to force myself not to drop to my knees and suck one into my mouth.

"You, however," I finally say, my voice thick and husky, "I could pick out of a lineup no matter what. The curve of your waist. That ass that I've dreamt about more than once. Your hair that I desperately want wrapped around my fist. The legs I've visualized hooked around my body."

"S — so you've thought about sex," she stammers. "That's a physical reaction. It's chemical."

I grab her left hand, bringing it up to my chest, but my eyes don't leave hers. "I've thought about how it would feel to wake up with your hand on my chest. I've thought about the freckle on your ring finger more often than I care to admit," I tell her with a quiet chuckle, and Isabella takes a quick breath as her eyes whip down to look at her hand. "I've thought about whether or not you like to cuddle, and if just being in your presence would lull me to sleep faster than any medication ever could. I may have thought about sex, *Naranja,* but I'm so far past that with you."

Chapter 11

ISABELLA

I've thought about all of that too.

There isn't a soul in the world who knows what my thoughts have consisted of in regards to Sebastian Garcia.

Ever since my sister, Gianna, found love, my entire family has been pushing for all of us to find our person. I'm one of the most introverted in the family, and have never felt confident to take what — or who — I wanted. Arianna had no problem letting Stone know she wanted him. Luca fell so hard for Hannah that he was ready to walk away from hockey in the middle of the season for her. Dom and Alex were slightly more stubborn about their love stories, but now they're so obsessed with their wives that I can barely remember a time when Kate and Natalie weren't part of our family.

But all of the married women are mostly bubbly, extroverted, and ready for anything. Honestly, I could probably tell my sister-in-law Natalie about everything going on with Rick and whatever drugs he thinks I stole, and I bet she'd know someone who could make all the problems disappear. A couple of years ago, she'd have probably taken care of things herself, but as a new mom, I'm not going to bother her with my problems.

In any case, I've never told any of the ladies in my family that I've harbored a secret crush on Sebastian for a couple of years. The first few times he'd asked me out, I'd chalked it up to some weird friend-of-a-sibling challenge. He's close with three of my brothers, so I figured they'd made a weird bet. Ridiculous? Yes. Why I thought so poorly of my brothers at that time in my life, I'll never know. We might poke fun at one another, but we'd never be intentionally vicious. And getting a hot guy to ask me out, only for it to be a joke, would be unspeakably cruel.

But it garnered some interest in Sebastian. I began to look for him while out. If he came to a family function, I'd keep him in my peripheral vision. I looked for any detail that might explain his apparent interest in me. He'd left me alone for well over a year — which I now know is when he first had Camila — but then started asking me out again. I just couldn't comprehend his interest. Why me? A beautiful man who rides a Harley, and has a successful business, is gold. He could have anyone.

But as I stare at him, with sunlight glinting across his forehead as the rays cast through the trees, I'm wondering why I fought so hard to keep him at bay.

"Daddy! Hurry up!" I hear Camila call. Looking toward the house, I see her waving excitedly at us. Sebastian's father stands behind her, and appears to be slowly rubbing his temples.

"Uh-oh," I say with a nervous giggle. "Did she wear him out?"

"My beautiful daughter asks a lot of questions, and apparently *Abuelito* has a numerical limit before he taps out," Sebastian says wryly, casting a quick glance with a wink my way. Taking my hand in his, he pulls me toward his home.

I really like how my hand feels surrounded by his. Warm and strong. Steady.

"Daddy, Isabella promised I could help make dinner!" Camila says proudly, her energy palpable as she bounces in her bright floral shoes that apparently are scented. I thought she was joking until she shoved one shoe in my face, and I smelled a vague scent of blooming florals. She's wearing jean shorts covered in sequins, and a rainbow colored shirt that matches two bows in her hair. The braids tell me Sebastian absolutely didn't do Camila's hair this morning, because his hairstyles tend to stop at pigtails.

Sebastian's father nods at the two of us before quietly stepping away, heading back inside Sebastian's house.

"She did, did she?" Sebastian asks, cocking an eyebrow at me. A perfectly shaped eyebrow with a symmetrical arch of black hairs. How have I never noticed how perfect his facial structure is? Sure, I've always known he's attractive. But now I'm suddenly acutely aware of just how damn beautiful he is. "Isabella? Are you okay?"

"You're pretty," I blurt out, then slap a hand over my mouth in complete shock. My eyes widen as Camila giggles uproariously, and Sebastian grins at me.

"Thank you, sweetheart. It's nice to know I'm not the only one here catching feelings," he says. Before I can reply, he stoops down to pick up Camila. "What are we making for dinner?"

"Are you gonna help too?" Camila squeals. "Isabella said spaghetti and meatballs is an easy recipe she can teach me."

"Ah. A nice Italian dish," Sebastian says as he shifts Camila onto his hip, again grabbing my hand.

"It's actually not Italian," I pipe up, then explain more when I see Sebastian's confused expression. "It's more of an Italian-American dish. For the most part, meatballs aren't served in sauce in Italy."

"Really? Why?" he asks.

"From what I understand, it became popular when Italians emigrated to the United States. There was a bigger selection of meat here than in Italy, and the dish we know as spaghetti and meatballs was born. Any meatballs in Italy are served in a different course."

"Huh," Sebastian says as he motions for me to go in the door.

"Learn something new every day. Camila, go wash your hands if you're helping to make dinner."

As Camila dashes off to the bathroom, Sebastian grabs my waist and pulls me back against him. "I'd like to ask you something, but I don't want an answer right now."

"Okay?" I reply quietly.

He rests his chin on my shoulder, his lips close to my ear. "I want — no, I *need* you to stay with me tonight. Please. I'm not asking for anything else. I just want to hold you."

This man.

This sweet, sensitive, and beautiful man. I wonder how many people know this side of him, and I find I'm hoping it's reserved just for family. And me.

"Don't answer. Just think about it," he says, applying the lightest of kisses against the skin where my shoulder meets my neck, and I audibly moan at the touch. Goosebumps bloom as he steps away from me, and I don't have a moment to revel in his touch, because Camila bounds out of the bathroom, ready to tackle dinner.

I SHOULD HAVE PICKED SOMETHING WITHOUT MEAT.

And definitely something without a red sauce.

"How did she get meatball on the ceiling?" Sebastian murmurs, as we survey the completely destroyed kitchen. A dusting of flour coats half of the counters, and a line of red sauce dances down one upper cabinet. "And the sauce?"

"She lost her footing on the step stool, and didn't let go of the spoon. I thought I got it all," I tell him sheepishly.

"And the flour?"

I sigh. "I don't even know. I turned away for one minute, and the flour had appeared."

"I wasn't aware we owned flour," he admits with a chuckle, rubbing the back of his neck and making me pause as I stare at the veins on his forearm. Arm porn really is a thing.

"You didn't. I bought it, and I guess I forgot to put it away. I'm sorry," I whisper sadly. I'm mortified that this mess is due to my attempt at bonding with his daughter, and in turn, I was basically a negligent adult. I'm lucky Camila didn't find any knives to terrorize us with.

"Nothing to be sorry for, *amor*. Kids are messy, and they're quick little jerks when they want to be. I have no doubt Camila had a great time, and she'll probably ask you to cook again."

Oh, good God. A new one. How many names now? Why are all the names he calls me hot? I know *amor* means love. But with the others, he slaps a "mi" on there. My queen. My sky. So why only *amor*? And why the hell am I so damn focused on this?

"How about you handle the counters, and I'll tackle the cabinets and walls," Sebastian says with a laugh as he places his hand on my lower back, guiding me into the kitchen. The heat from his palm sears through my shirt, and I feel like he's branding me.

I'm silent as we get to work cleaning up the mess. Dinner was lovely, and it was nice watching Camila scarf down every last bite. Sebastian's parents and grandmother stayed, and they were polite, but slightly awkward, with me. I think they're equally as confused as I am about the dynamics with Sebastian.

As I start on the dishes, I think back to every smile he gave me throughout dinner. I'd been at a loss in the moment on how to describe the smiles, and now I know. It's adoration. He smiles at me like he's completely enamored with me.

I've never felt adoration before. Never felt like a man would burn down the world for me. And while I do believe Sebastian would set fire to things if I needed him to, I can't help but wonder when the other shoe will drop.

"I think I got all remnants of dinner off the surfaces they

shouldn't be on," Sebastian announces as he jumps down from a chair. "I'm going to go give Camila a bath. I think she got more sauce on her skin than in her mouth at dinner, but I know she enjoyed the hell out of it."

"Oh, okay," I murmur as he passes by me. "When I'm done, may I use your bathtub? I'd really like to relax in a bath myself."

Sebastian stills, tilting his head back so his face looks up at the ceiling. His voice is much deeper when he replies, "Of course."

"I don't have to if you don't want me in your space," I say hurriedly, second-guessing if I've overstepped his hospitality. "I don't want to step on your toes. You have been so gracious, and I'm fine just taking a shower in the guest bathroom."

He whirls around, his eyes intense as he stalks to me. I subconsciously back up until I run into the counter, and he cages me in. "What gave you the idea that I don't want you to take a bath?"

"You looked aggravated, or frustrated, I guess," I stammer.

He chuckles. "Oh, I'm definitely frustrated, but not for the reasons your mind has conjured."

"I don't understa —" I break off with a gasp as Sebastian leans in, his body aligning with mine. I feel his hard length against my lower abdomen, and I clutch onto his shirt with both hands. My heart rate speeds up, and my breathing is labored as I take in his hooded eyes and plush lips. I resist the urge to lean forward and nip at his bottom lip.

"If you take a bath, you'll be naked, Isabella. Naked in my bathroom. In my tub. In my space. And all I'll want to do is break down the fucking door so I can join you, or at least watch. The thought of you covered in bubbles makes me so hard I think I could come without a touch. Do you have any idea what you do to me?"

His nose touches mine as he tells me this, and I struggle to stay standing upright. I wonder if he can feel my heart beating against his chest. Butterflies erupt in my stomach as he drags one hand up my arm, sliding across my shoulder until he brackets my neck. "Sebastian ..."

"What, *mi Reina*? What do you need?" he murmurs, rubbing his stubble against my cheek. "Do you want to know what I want? What I need?"

I nod quickly as my hands find purchase in his waist, my thumbs on the edge of his obliques that make the beautiful V-line I've seen on him only a couple of times when he's been at Everlasting to enjoy the hot springs. Sliding my thumbs only an inch more, I touch his bare skin, and Sebastian lets out a low groan.

"Fucking hell, baby," he grunts. "Answer my question."

I'm not sure how to answer him. My brain, heart, and vagina are all shouting different things at me. My brain is telling me to steer clear, to keep things professional. Sebastian is my protector and nothing more. I can't fuck this up, because he'll always be around my family, and I don't want anyone to feel like they have to choose.

My heart is dancing in a field full of wildflowers, picking out wedding dresses and asking which flavors of wedding cake I'd like.

My damn vagina is just screaming, "dick, dick, dick, we need the dick," so clearly I know how she feels about this current scenario. Honestly, it's been a while since I've had great sex. Sex with Rick was okay. Good, even. Mind-blowing? No. Life-altering? Absolutely not. But somehow, I *know* sex with Sebastian would destroy me, in both a good and a bad way.

"You're at war in your mind, Isabella," Sebastian says, dipping his head down to press light kisses against my shoulder. I lean my head so he has better access to my skin, and it isn't until I feel a hand under my thigh that I even realize I lifted my leg to shamelessly grind against him. Sebastian drags his tongue along my collarbone. "I want you so fucking bad, and I know you want me too. But I won't pressure you into anything you aren't completely sure you're ready for. Because once we take that step, *Naranja*, the game is over. You'll be mine."

"Why are you calling me orange?" I say breathlessly.

He laughs against my skin, sending a shiver coursing down my spine. "That's not what it means. Well, it does mean orange, but not in this case."

"What does it mean?"

He leans up, smiling softly as his deep, dark eyes watch me, and he lets go of my leg. "I'll tell you when I know you're ready."

"Ugh," I groan. "Not this 'when you're ready' crap again."

He shrugs as he steps back, and I immediately miss the warmth of his body against mine. "You aren't ready, Isabella. And that's fine. We're taking this at your speed."

"What if I'm never ready?" I whisper, closing my eyes as I wait for his response.

I hear him sigh. "Then I'll accept that."

As he begins to walk away, I call out to him. "You said I'd be yours. Does that mean you'd be mine?"

He gives me a breathtaking crooked smile. "Baby, I've been yours for years."

To Faux Date or Not to Faux Date

Yours truly was genuinely surprised upon hearing that Isabella Santo had recently moved in with Sebastian Garcia. While residents are hearing reports the relationship may be a little more on the fake side than not, I can report that Mr. Garcia has been seen more than once leaving Isabella's apartment with many of her things in tow. An anonymous source claimed a break-in happened at the apartment complex the same night she was moved into his home, but his consis-

tency with moving her things leads me to believe he has no intention of letting her go that easily.

It's been a few days, and while we haven't really spoken again about where my feelings are, I can sense the awkwardness whenever we're together. After Sebastian asked me to stay with him that night, I struggled with sending mixed signals, choosing instead to stay locked in the guest room. Just like he said, my mind is at war with my body. I didn't sleep a wink, weighing the pros and cons of allowing myself to lean on Sebastian when my life is basically a dumpster fire. The following day, I was incredibly crabby, and Sebastian's knowing smile was icing on a shitty cake. That's when the texting started, and I realized much later that he used it to establish rapport with me. Sebastian Garcia was slowly whittling away at every single wall I'd built, one text at a time.

Sebastian: What's your favorite movie?

Me: Why?

Sebastian: Are you always this defensive?

Me: No.

Sebastian: So I just bring this out in you?

Me: A little, yes. I have a lot of favorite movies. I need you to narrow it down a bit. It's like picking a favorite book.

Sebastian: Ah. I bet you have favorites for every trope.

Me: You know about tropes?

Sebastian: I have sisters, Isabella. Romance book tropes are brought up at least once every couple of months when we're together.

Me: I've never met your sisters. Do they live around here?

Sebastian: Elena lives in Loveland. She comes around fairly often, as she has a daughter only a few years older than Camila. Catalina moved down to Albuquerque over a decade ago, but she comes home to visit as often as she can.

Sebastian: Now answer the question about movies. I'll narrow it down: your favorite rom-com.

Me: Can I have two?

Sebastian: Of course.

Me: The Holiday and Sweet Home Alabama.

Sebastian: I'm pretty sure I've watched Sweet Home Alabama at your house. Luca made me sit and watch it. I assume you were there.

Me: I totally forgot that! My parents wouldn't let me watch it until I was ten. I was completely enamored with the southern accent and the small-town atmosphere.

Sebastian: From what your brothers have told me, it's pretty similar to Eternity Springs, with kooky residents and odd traditions. Of course, in the movie, they don't have a rogue rodent meandering around and snatching people's belongings.

Me: I'm relatively unbothered by Mason. It is odd that he hangs around our town, though. Marmots typically live above the tree line.

Sebastian: Maybe he's rabid.

Me: He seems pretty calm when he trots up to front doors, looks directly into the doorbell cameras, and thieves things.

Sebastian: Did Luca ever find his Stanley Cup hat?

Me: I don't think so, but Hannah was prepared with extras. They have one locked in a safe. Honestly, if a marmot can crack open a safe, I think he deserves the loot.

Sebastian: How did you find out Mason is a male?

Me: We don't actually know. I think it was just the alliteration of the M's. Mason the marmot. Sounds better than Chad the marmot, or Becky the marmot.

Me: What's your favorite movie?

Sebastian: Why don't I get it narrowed down?

Me: Fine. What's your favorite action movie?

Sebastian: A Christmas classic.

Me: Don't you dare say it.

Sebastian: Die.

Sebastian: Hard.

Me: IT IS NOT A CHRISTMAS MOVIE.

Sebastian: Agree to disagree, sweetheart. It begins on Christmas Eve, his wife's name is Holly, and a huge chunk of the soundtrack is Christmas music. Plus, one screenwriter said it's a Christmas movie.

Me: Christmas movies should be ABOUT Christmas.

Sebastian: Says who?

Me: Says me.

Sebastian: Well, I say a movie taking place during Christmas also counts.

Me: Your opinion doesn't count.

Sebastian: Why?

Me: Because it's different from mine, and now I'm mad about it.

Sebastian: You just made me laugh so hard I scared the bartender working for me right now.

Me: Why are you asking me about movies anyway?

Sebastian: A couple of reasons.

Sebastian: I told the jerks at the Clubhouse that we were dating. Even if it's fake, I figure it's a good idea to know a little more about you.

Sebastian: I also just really enjoy talking to you and seeing what you like. You've never been open to dialogue before, and I'm liking this side of you. But most importantly …

Me: What?

Me: Well aren't you a tease.

Me: Sebastian, this is just mean.

Me: Fine. I don't need to know your last reason.

Sebastian: Teasing is excellent foreplay, baby.

Sebastian: And you just teased yourself right into my hands.

Sebastian: Bet you're wondering what I can do with my hands now, aren't you?

Dammit. He's absolutely correct.

Chapter 12

SEBASTIAN

Wasn't even a little surprised when Isabella went radio silent. Honestly, that conversation lasted a good ten minutes longer than I thought it would. We've texted a little here and there since I found her with that man at the bakery, but her responses were monosyllabic and mostly vague. I don't want to get my hopes up, but I think I'm making real progress in breaking down the walls Isabella erected years ago.

"When you asked me to meet you for lunch, I didn't think you'd be texting my sister the whole fucking time," Luca drawls, his arm slung over the back of the booth as he studies me with a smirk. The entire Santo family knows I've had a thing for Isabella, and other than Mr. Santo growling at me from time to time, no one has given me any shit about it. In fact, they all seem to have embraced it.

Nonna, the Santo matriarch, whispered in my ear that she hoped I could "loosen the stick" by "giving it to" Isabella. And she did this as she pinched my ass.

Nonna is as scrappy as my grandmother, and I wasn't surprised to find that they have a monthly book club together, and regularly meet for lunch.

Small towns, man.

Even living well outside Eternity Springs town limits, we're here enough that we're considered to be residents. My mom and Mrs. Santo get together from time to time, swapping recipes, and my father helped out at Everlasting a few years ago when part of the hotel flooded after heavy rains.

Our two families have become a little intertwined, and I can only pray that things don't go south with Isabella. I don't know what might happen in that case.

"Sorry," I tell Luca sheepishly, turning off my phone and pushing it to the edge of the booth. "She was actually talking to me. I had to take advantage."

"She doesn't talk to you?" he asks, a surprised look on his face. "I mean, I get it. Belle isn't the chattiest person out there. Too many extroverted assholes in my family. Belle was content to quietly hang in the background."

"Did you really just call your family a bunch of assholes?"

"Yeah, but I meant it with love," he jokes. "You know how it is with siblings. You can say whatever you want about your sister, but if I were to say the same things —"

I cut him off. "I'd slice you off at your knees."

"Exactly. That still stands for my sister, man. I'm in full support of you trying to be with her, but if you fuck with her, it won't just be me coming after you. It'll be all of us," Luca says lowly, the smile dropping from his face.

"I know."

"Do you, though?" he asks. "Do you really know what my brothers can do?"

I roll my eyes dramatically. "Are we really having the 'we'll bury you in the woods' conversation, Luca? I get it. You'll all come after me. I'm not sure why you're telling me this, because you and I both know I've been gone for her for *years*. If anyone is walking away from this, it's going to be her."

"You're probably right," he sighs. Our food arrives, and I gawk at the triple cheeseburger and fries he ordered.

"How can you eat like that?" I ask.

He smugly pats his stomach. "I'm a growing boy. Besides, I chase after high school kids on the ice every damn day. I could still play in the NHL if I wanted. I burn a shit-ton of calories every day, even at home." His smile gets wicked. "Mostly at home."

"Nice."

He shrugs. "You're just jealous you aren't — fuck. Never mind. I can't even finish that sentence because I'd be talking about my sister."

Now it's my turn to smile devilishly. "Well, just the other night, we —"

"Nope," he yells, cutting me off as he drops his burger and sticks his index fingers in both ears. "Nope, nope, nope. Don't you dare give me any details, man."

I throw my head back with a loud bark of laughter. I try to get his attention, but Luca's eyes are tightly shut, and he's quietly humming what I think is ESPN's NHL theme song. Reaching across the table, I grab his arm and yank it down. "I won't tell you any details. Hell, nothing may happen with her, so it's moot."

"Oh, it'll happen," he says surely.

"Why do you say that?" I ask.

Shoving a fistful of fries in his mouth, he chews for a moment before swallowing. "I've seen the way she looks at you when she thinks no one is watching. She's interested."

I'm not sure how much I believe Luca, but I hope he's right. "Can I ask you a question?"

"As long as it isn't about anything to do with banging my sister, yes."

I chuckle. "I get a vibe from Isabella that she doesn't have a lot of self-confidence. Like she's been beaten down time and time again, so she's just given up."

He nods. "That's somewhat correct. She's had a couple of boyfriends who were complete jackasses. You know that stupid superstition my family has about crossing the threshold at my parents' house?"

"Yeah," I say. "I was there when Alex dropped his first wife."

Luca winces. "I fucking forgot about that. Then he sailed right through with Natalie. Actually, all of us have done it, except for Belle and Leo. In Leo's defense, he hasn't tried. His high school girlfriend wouldn't let him, afraid of failing it. And every time they reconnected since, it's been hush-hush, so she hasn't been to the house again. But Belle has tried. And failed both times."

"Seriously? She tried twice?" I find myself suddenly irrationally angry that she thought she found love with two men that are clearly not me, and that they failed getting her over the threshold. How fucking hard can it be? "You just pick her up and walk across, right?"

"Not entirely correct. The first time, the guy tried to carry Isabella over, and he dropped her —"

I cut him off. "Give me his fucking name right the fuck now."

Luca laughs. "He's a non-issue."

"I'll be the judge of that."

"Really. He got caught in a string of armed robberies. He's in prison down in Cañon City for a twenty year sentence."

"Oh." I feel sheepish. "Continue."

"So after that, Alex had an epiphany, and realized the reason it didn't work was because the Santo kid should be carrying his or her beloved across the threshold. So, Isabella has to carry *you*, not the other way around."

"Damn. So Arianna carried Stone across?" I ask.

"Yup. They both just closed their eyes and charged through the doorway. Pretty sure Hannah closed her eyes when we did it too. She almost hyperventilated with fear over us not making it."

"So the second guy that Isabella dated, she tried to carry him across but couldn't?"

"No, he didn't even let her try. The fucker misunderstood, spouted off about her weight, and hightailed it right outta there. Isabella was completely crushed," Luca says angrily.

"Can I have *his* name, then?" I ask hopefully, making Luca laugh.

"No need. We took care of him," he says proudly.

"Oh? How so? Hypothetically, of course."

"Well, hypothetically speaking, there may have been a man who showed up at a Denver police precinct with half his head shaved, the other half bleached, his nipples pierced, and a tattoo that says 'I eat ass' as a tramp stamp. Oh, and the men who took him may have each taken a couple shots to his face and dick. Hypothetically."

"Jesus. You Santo kids are creative, I'll give you that."

"And that's why I said you better not fuck over my sister. That fucker only dated her for less than a year. You've been trying to date Isabella for well over five years. Close to ten, right? So this better not be some scheme just to get in her pants. If that happens, there's no telling what my brothers will come up with as a punishment for you." Luca's expression is deadly, but he brightens immediately as he looks behind me toward the door. "Pixie!"

Turning my head, I see Luca's tiny wife walk in, holding a toddler, and dragging her daughter behind her. Not even looking at me, she thrusts the kid toward me. "Here. Take this. I need a minute."

I stare into her son's eyes, and he grins at me, a gummy grin as drool drips over the finger he's chewing on. A grin identical to his dad's across the table, as he scoots over and lets Hannah sit down.

"What's his name again?" I murmur. I know his name, but I

can't get over how cute Melanie is when she proudly tells people her brother's name.

"Cay-web," the girl answers, making me grin. She drags a hand over her forehead, attempting to push her dark brown hair away. With Luca's hair color, matching skin tone, and Hannah's bright blue eyes, Melanie is an absolutely adorable child, and I have no doubt she'll grow up to be quite beautiful. Those Santo genes are remarkable. I haven't met a Santo yet that isn't attractive.

"Caleb," I say softly as the youngster reaches out to grab my cheeks. I vaguely hear Hannah telling Luca about how Melanie accidentally knocked over the entire display of apples at the grocery store, then something about opened containers of animal crackers, but I zone out as I look at Caleb.

In this moment, I realize how badly I want more children.

I love Camila. I adore being her dad. I'm in no way suggesting that she's not enough. But I want her to experience having a brother or sister, and I want to experience a full pregnancy with a woman that I love, then us being an entire family together.

I want that with Isabella, and I have no idea if she even wants kids. I've seen her with her nieces and nephews, and she's amazing with them. Hell, she's great with Camila too. Watching her with my daughter as they cooked dinner together was exquisite. It was like I had a brief glimpse into what my future could be.

Caleb rubs his eyes, and I naturally snuggle him against my shoulder. He lays his head down, and I get a whiff of that wonderful baby powder scent that all babies have.

"Oh, um, hi," I hear from a few feet away, and I see Isabella walking toward us, apron still on, and a little bit of flour dots her forehead. The bakery is a block from where I met Luca, and I imagine she had no idea I'd be here. "I was just coming to grab a drink while I finish up my muffins for tomorrow."

Her eyes are zeroed in on Caleb, then they dip to where my arm holds him in place. I flex my hand, and watch as her pupils dilate.

"You wanna join us, Belle?" Luca asks.

"No, but thanks. I have a lot to finish, but I need a little caffeine to do it," she explains, tearing her gaze from me to look at her brother.

"You sure? Seb can scoot over," Luca says with a smirk. Asshole knows exactly what he's doing, baiting both of us.

"No. I need to get back to work," Isabella says. She grabs the large fountain drink the server left for her on the counter, and waves to us awkwardly.

Nope.

"I'll walk you," I announce, carefully sliding out of the booth and depositing Caleb into Hannah's arms.

"You look good with a baby," Hannah whispers. "You think she'll want to be the momma?"

"Say a prayer for me," I murmur as I wink at her and wave at her husband. Turning, I expect to find Isabella, but see she's already through the door and speed-walking down the street. Damn, she wants to avoid me that badly?

I take off at a jog to catch up to her, calling her name. She turns, and at the same time, I notice her ex-boyfriend loitering outside the bakery entrance. Shit. I turn Isabella slightly so I'm blocking the angle, and whisper, "Do you trust me?"

"Why?" Unblinking, I see the immediate fear she feels.

"Yes or no, *mi Cielo*."

"Yes," she whispers.

"Good." And with that, I bend down and take her lips with mine.

This is nothing like the kiss at the Clubhouse where I basically marked territory. This kiss is a fucking branding. This kiss is full of every ounce of desire I've felt for this woman over the last decade.

Pulling her to me, I slide one hand to the back of her neck and an arm around her waist. I grip her braid, pulling lightly, moving her head the direction I want so I can take the kiss deeper. Isabella gasps into my mouth, and I take the opportunity to slip my tongue between her perfect lips. I groan as her tongue sneaks out to tentatively touch mine, and her arms come around my waist.

God dammit, this is the best kiss of my life. I fucking knew it would be like this with her. I knew it. It's perfect. Her taste explodes on my tongue, and I can't help but think about how she tastes elsewhere. I need this beautiful woman in my bed.

Her warm vanilla scent covers me like a quilt, the scent I've come to know as something so inherently Isabella that I think no one else should ever smell this way. Sugary sweet, a juxtaposition of her quiet and reserved personality.

I hear a catcall from somewhere, forcing me to focus before I do something subconsciously like grab her ass, and I break off the kiss. We're both breathing heavily, and I look down to find Isabella's pink lips gloriously plump from the kiss. I slide my hand along her jaw, then gently rub my thumb against her bottom lip.

"Why?" she whispers breathlessly.

"Your ex was watching," I murmur. Her eyes widen as she attempts to look beyond me, but I tighten my arm around her waist. "If you look for him, he'll know it was a show for him. Leave an arm wrapped around me as we walk back to the bakery. Now look up at me, and pretend you really *do* like me."

She laughs lightly, and buries her head against my chest. I can't resist the opportunity to kiss the top of her head, and we begin walking back to the bakery. My phone is vibrating incessantly in my pocket, as I'm sure Luca watched, and I bet the Eternity Springs phone tree is already working overtime. Hell, I bet an article on *The Eagle Has Landed*, the stupid city website that turned into a TMZ-inspired gossip site, is getting approval as we walk.

"Just so you know," I whisper so only Isabella can hear, "I didn't just kiss you for him. I kissed you because I've wanted to know what you tasted like for years, *mi Reina*. Years. And when you finally accept that this is happening, I plan to taste every perfect inch of your body."

"I don't know how to respond to that," she stammers, but her arm tightens around my waist. We pass the spot where her ex was, and I stop right outside the bakery. Turning her, I look into her eyes.

"You know exactly how to respond, but your brain is fighting you on it. You want this as much as I do. I know it," I tell her strongly. Looking in the bakery, I see Trace skulking around the back, and Isabella's part-time associate standing behind the counter. How the hell Isabella snuck out without Trace knowing is beyond me, but Trace will be getting an earful about the whole situation later today. "And the next time you want a drink, you send whichever one of my men is in there, or you call me."

"That's ridiculous. Why would I call you for a soda? You'll undoubtedly be at least thirty minutes away," she scoffs, rolling her deep brown eyes.

I bend down so we're eye level. "If no one can get you a drink, I will happily drive here to get you one. I told you I'd never lie to you, and this is no different. You have my word. Now please promise me you won't go by yourself again."

She studies me momentarily. "This is my town, Sebastian. I think I'm safe here."

"There are only two places you're safe, Isabella. One is in my house, and the other is in my bed. Preferably underneath me. Promise me you'll call me if you need a drink."

"In your bed," she repeats.

"In my bed."

"Underneath you," she whispers, not realizing her hand holding my shirt has tightened into a fist, anchoring me to her.

"Underneath me."

Isabella bites her lip, hesitating momentarily before blurting out, "*Only* underneath you?"

A wicked smile blooms across my face. Finally, my sweet girl wants to play.

Chapter 13

ISABELLA

Could I be any more out of control?

Who the hell asks their faux boyfriend about sex positions on the sidewalk outside their business establishment?

Me, apparently.

I think that kiss may have broken something in my mind, because now I'm questioning everything. Because that kiss — that kiss — was unlike anything I've ever had the pleasure to experience. I felt it in my toes. My hair may have been standing on end, but I don't know. My scalp was buzzing, and I couldn't get close enough to Sebastian.

Is this how kissing is supposed to be? If that's the case, then I definitely need to kiss him more often.

Which is why I asked my question.

I haven't had that many sexual partners, and they were all similar in bed. One or two positions. It was always fairly quick, and I rarely had an orgasm. If Sebastian can kiss like that, I know sex would be out of this world. But is he vanilla like every man I've ever been with? Missionary for a minute? If so, I'll pass. No thank you.

Please don't be boring in bed, Sebastian.

What the hell am I thinking? I may never find out.

"How about we discuss this after dinner, *amor*? You can think of more questions in the meantime." His tone is low, seductive, and a shiver dances down my spine.

"I think I need that answer right now," I say timidly. I won't be able to focus until I know. I watch porn. I know what's out there, but I'm so scared to speak up that I never tell my partner what I'd like to try. But I'm not like that with Sebastian. In my soul, I know he won't think less of me when I ask him questions.

As a family walks past us, joyfully commenting on how cute the town is, Sebastian grabs my hand and pulls me off to the side. He crowds me against a brick wall on the side of the bakery, his thumb finding my lower lip again.

"Are you worried about how things might ... go in the bedroom, Isabella?" he asks softly, and I nod. His lips twitch as he smiles. "Are there things you may want to ... try in the bedroom, and you're worried I'll think less of you?"

I nod again. I should be worried about how well he sees through me. Yet somehow, all I feel is relief that *finally*, someone is thinking about me and my feelings.

"My sweet girl," Sebastian murmurs, dragging his thumb along my lip before he dips it inside, pulling my jaw open. Hooded eyes watch as my tongue darts out to lick the tip of his thumb, and the answering growl is all I need to hear before I'm circling his thumb. "I will never demean or condemn you for asking questions of a sexual nature. You can always trust me. In regards to whether or not you'd always be underneath me, that's entirely up to you, and what you're comfortable with. We don't need a bed to be intimate. Hell, this is intimate as fuck right now, because all I'm thinking about is you dropping to your knees and taking me as deep into your throat as possible."

Good God, I'd totally do that if I didn't know I'd be arrested.

Sebastian chuckles, his gaze telling me he knows exactly where my mind went. "Love that you're into that, Isabella. Sex isn't a one-way street. We both have input, and we both have to be comfortable. If there are things you want to try, tell me. I'll make it happen."

"Really?" I whisper.

"Really. And there is no rush. I'm playing the long-game, *mi Reina*. I want you, but only when you're ready."

Mind whirling, I head back into the bakery. I'm almost done with my large Friday morning standing order. I usually don't take orders this big, but I couldn't turn this profit away. I bring in extra help on Thursdays so I can prep as much as possible. Every day I drop off baked goods for Everlasting, and on rare occasions, I'll bake a cake for someone in my family, but other than that, I don't take special orders. I simply don't have the time. And as much as I love this bakery, I already spend too much time here.

"What the hell, Isabella? Where have you been?" Trace shouts. "Sebastian is gonna kill — oh. Hey Prez."

"Yeah, we're gonna have words later," Sebastian drawls, folding his arms across his chest as he leans against the door frame. The lighting makes him look borderline evil, dressed almost entirely in black, as rays of light cast an eerie glow around him. His eyes catch mine as I walk behind the counter. "You good, sweetheart?"

"I — I'm good," I stammer, clearing my throat. It's not like I can tell him what I'm really thinking. Hey, Sebastian, can you lock us in the bathroom and do all the wicked things that I apparently need more than life itself? That wouldn't be embarrassing to say in front of Trace at all. I'd never be able to show my face in the Clubhouse again.

I watch Sebastian glower at Trace before stepping backward, closing the door as he goes. I sigh as I blatantly check him out as he walks away. The man has an amazing ass.

"Wow. Subtle," Ava, my employee says, a glint in her eye. Ava is nineteen, and working a couple of odd jobs this summer while home from college. When she leaves in a few weeks, I'll need to hire someone who only wants a few hours a week, which is diffi-cult. I can only pay minimum wage, and certain times of the year mean we're busier than normal. Ava has been a godsend this summer.

"What?" I attempt to reply innocently, but my voice betrays me. It's all high pitched and borderline squealing.

Ava snorts. "Do you remember the list you gave me this morning of things I could do around here if there was a lull in customers?"

"Yes?"

"One of them was cleaning the interior side of the windows."

"Did you finish? Oh shit. You saw." I cover my face with my hands. "God, I'm so mortified."

"You shouldn't be. It was hot. I'm low-key jealous. Sebastian Garcia is one fine looking man," Ava says, appreciation written all over her face.

I gape at her. "You're nineteen!"

She shrugs. "And?"

"He's thirty-six!"

"It's still legal. Besides, he gives strong Daddy vibes."

"Ew. Gross. Just ... no." I screw up my face in distaste. But there's an element of anger simmering beneath the surface. How dare this twit waltz in here and make these comments about Sebastian. He's mine!

Wait.

He's mine.

Holy shit.

He's mine. Sebastian Garcia is mine. It's like the heavens just opened up, shining every light known to man onto me as I have this epiphany. Why have I taken this long to realize this?

I look at Trace, who gives me a knowing look. "We're closing early."

He nods. "You cool if I take what you've got for our order for tomorrow? It'll save our regular guy from driving out here to pick it up. I figure you'll be up most of the night with Seb anyway, so you'll want to come in later tomorrow."

"What order?" I ask, confused.

Trace stares at me as his mouth drops open. "Oh, fuck. He's really going to murder me now."

I'm perplexed. I only have one order. RMRRMC.

Oh my fucking God.

My eyes closing, I keep my voice level and controlled as I ask Trace one question. "What's the name of your MC club?"

"Shit," he mutters.

"Tell me," I demand.

"Rocky Mountain Range Riders MC," he confesses. RMRRMC.

"I am going to murder him!" I hiss.

Trace puts up his hands in surrender. "Listen, I can't let you actually kill the guy. He was trying to support you, and he knew you'd be pissed if he did it himself."

"Your last statement is why he shouldn't have done it in the first place!" I shout. Tearing into the kitchen, I grab my bag out of the safe, ushering Ava out. "Everyone, out. We're closing early."

A quick glance at the cute cupcake clock one of my brother's gave me a few years ago tells me I'm only closing an hour early, which is fine with me. I push Trace out the door, stopping to flip my open sign to closed, then turn off the lights and close the door. Absolutely seething, I put out my hand. "Give me your keys."

Trace has the decency to look guilty. "How am I supposed to get home?"

"Not my problem," I say, thrusting my hand impatiently at him.

"You know what? No. I'm not giving you my keys. I drove you, so either get in the passenger seat, or you can walk home." He looks at me defiantly, crossing his arms and widening his stance. Trace is moderately attractive, standing a couple of inches taller than Sebastian, but has a leaner build. Light brown hair with a slight curl to it, his blue eyes always light up with wickedness, like he knows a secret, but he'll never say what it's about. Worn blue jeans with holes in the knees flare slightly at the bottom, adjusting to his black combat boots, and the leather cut he wears covers a plain white tee-shirt. I bet he's a wet dream to a lot of women.

But right now, he's just pissing me off.

"Fine," I tell him. "I will walk."

"Jesus," he moans. "Isabella, I can't let you walk. Please. Just get in the damn truck."

"Um, I can take her," Ava offers, waving her keys at the two of us. I grin triumphantly at Trace.

"See? Problem solved. Send someone different tomorrow, Trace, because I'm likely to accidentally shove you in an oven," I call out as I skip over to Ava.

"I'd like to see you try!" Trace yells back as he gets into his truck. Waiting for Ava and me to climb into her tiny two-door car, he motions for us to pull out first.

"Thank you, Ava. You're a lifesaver. I want to throttle him right now, but I want to hurt Sebastian even more," I grumble.

She giggles. "I thought it was pretty dreamy. Pretty romantic, right? How long have you had the Friday morning order? Didn't you tell me it's been a few years? He's down bad for you, girl."

"He could have been honest about it. Especially now. He told me he'd never lie to me, and that I could trust him. How is this trustworthy?" I ask.

Ava turns onto the main road heading out of Eternity Springs. "I don't think this is a lie. For it to be a lie, you'd have to have asked him if he was behind the order, and he'd said no. Omission, yes. But it's with your happiness in mind. He's trying to support you any way that he can. Trace is right behind us. Do you want me to lose him?"

I swivel around to look at Trace, ten yards behind us. "You can lose him?"

"Oh, easily," she laughs. "You don't get carsick, do you?"

"Uh, no? Wow!" I shout as Ava hits the gas and we take off. Trace is momentarily shocked, and it takes a moment for his big truck to pop into gear before he tears after us. Ava whips into a neighborhood, tires squealing as she shouts with glee.

I grab the door handle and the seatbelt, close my eyes, and pray for survival.

"Dang! I thought he was a goner that time," Ava says. I peek my left eye open to see her frowning at her rearview mirror, while we're still traveling top speed down a residential street.

"Ava, focus," I finally hiss.

"Oh. Sorry. Let me think. What road should I take? Oh, I got it!" Tires squealing again as we whip back onto the main road. I hear her put her window down.

"What are you doing?"

"Shh. Listening."

"For what?"

"Isabella, be quiet!"

I sit silently, eyes tightly closed, until Ava says, "Yes! There we go!"

"What?"

"I heard a train. Sounds like it's coming across the Aspen View Trail crossing, which means it'll be to the Oakwood Lane crossing in about two minutes. And if I time it perfectly --"

"We can lose him because of the crossing signals," I finish. "That might work. Unless he barrels through anyway. Can he fit between the crossing poles?"

"Doubtful. Plus that crossing is only two lanes, whereas the other crossings are four. More space to work with." More tires squeal as we turn onto Oakwood Lane. She speeds up as we approach, and I hear a train horn signaling its approach.

"There are the lights," I tell her, turning around to see Trace a football field length behind us. "We should be good."

"Better safe than sorry. Hold on!" Ava shouts as she pushes the gas pedal again, crossing the tracks right as the poles come down. We both scream as the car goes completely airborne, slamming down on the other side with a rattle. "Shit. Hope that didn't hurt Darla too much."

"Darla?"

She smiles sweetly, like we didn't just break multiple city and county laws. "My car. Her name is Darla. She's perfect."

"Okay," I murmur, suddenly a little wary of Ava.

"So you wanna give me directions to Sebastian's place? I just know he lives outside of town," Ava says.

"No. I think I'm going to stay at my apartment tonight. I'm not ready to confront Sebastian. A night away will help clear my mind. I should probably move back anyway. No reason to still be at his house if my apartment is good as new."

"I thought you were there because of the scary guys your ex-boyfriend was associated with," Ava says with a worried look. "You should keep staying with him, Isabella. That's more important than some stupid fight about a bakery order."

I don't answer her. It's dumb. I know it is. But I feel like every man I've ever cared for has lied to me about one thing or another. Yes, a bakery order seems trivial. But it always starts small like this. Then he'll lie about who he met for lunch, or what that text message is about that he just deleted. Then he'll come home late from something. And suddenly, I'll find him in bed with another woman.

Even angrier now, I look down as my phone rings. Sebastian. I decline the call, and it immediately rings again. Fucking Trace, the damn tattletale. Five texts come through simultaneously, letting me know Sebastian is furious. Great.

I decide to power down my phone. Juvenile? Yeah, a little. But

I need a break from all these men deciding my life for me. Lord knows as soon as my brothers hear about this, they'll be full of opinions as well.

Sighing, I resign myself to the fact that I'm probably never going to fully trust another man, and will end up a spinster with eighty-seven cats.

MY APARTMENT LOOKS DIFFERENT.

It doesn't look like me anymore, and I don't know how to process that.

Every other day, more of my things have appeared at Sebastian's house, leading me to believe the man is slowly moving me into his home. Like a covert operation, where he thinks I wouldn't notice.

My stand mixer sits on his counter.

My throw pillows dot his couches.

My family pictures are randomly placed throughout the space.

How would I miss all of that?

But even if all those things were here, it still doesn't feel like home.

In only a few short weeks, Sebastian feels more like home to me than this place ever did.

Sighing as I lock the door, I sit on the couch and pick up the remote. Looks like it's a perfect opportunity for me to catch up on all the chaos of this season's *Love Island*.

As I'm beginning the second episode, I hear the exterior door to the complex open with a loud thwack, and I know. I just know it's Sebastian. Standing, I look around the apartment, trying to decide if I should hide, barricade the door, or open it and deal with him head-on.

Fuck this. I'm ready for a fight.

I open the door at the same moment he's sliding a key into the keyhole, and I gape at him. "Why do you have a key to my apartment?"

He glares at me. "Who the fuck do you think cleaned this place up? And keeps bringing your shit home?"

My internal girl — as quiet as she is — screams. He referred to his home as mine, and I actually love that.

"Has it ever occurred to you to ask me before doing things, asshole?"

"Has it ever occurred to you that a lot of what I do is for your fucking safety? And that I will take care of your safety However. The. Fuck. I. Want. Because I'd rather die than have anything happen to you? Has that ever occurred to you, Isabella?" His eyes are wild as he slams the door closed and pushes me against the wall. "You were alone in this apartment for ten fucking minutes — TEN MINUTES — and a dickwad got to you. I've never been so scared. Why don't you see that? Don't you see how gone I am for you?"

He brings his hands to my head, cradling it gently, even though his body vibrates with adrenaline and emotion. Closing his eyes, he rests his forehead against mine, and I grab onto his arms as tears fill my eyes. I feel awful.

"I fell in love with you the first moment I saw you," he confesses, so quietly I almost don't hear him. The words are spoken slowly against my lips, like he hopes the words go directly to my soul. "I knew you were it for me. I was willing to wait until you were ready. Until you finally saw me as I saw you. Until then, I protected you the only way I could, by ordering from your bakery. I knew you'd never accept it from me directly, so I did it through the MC and had other people pick it up weekly. Even if you didn't want me, or my love, I could give you financial peace."

"I'm sorry," I whisper, not sure what else to say. Tears cascade down my cheeks as I study him. Sebastian looks completely heartbroken and miserable. I hate that I did that to him.

"Instead of asking me about it, you take off with your psychotic employee — who, by the way, really should get her license taken away for all the laws she broke today, — almost get hit by a train, and then hide out at your old apartment. Instead of coming to me. Instead of trusting me. Fuck," he lashes out as he steps away from me. His hands drop from my face as he stares up at the ceiling. "I can't keep doing this. I can't."

My stomach drops as I take in his words. "Can't keep doing what?"

"This." He gestures between us. "You and me. I can't keep waiting, desperately hoping you'll finally see me. That you'll *trust* me. You're never going to see me like I see you. Hell, you're never going to see yourself like I see you. As an exquisite, gorgeous, breathtaking creature who steals the breath straight from my lungs. I have to stop waiting for you. I have to move on."

"No," I whisper brokenly as he continues backing up, and I reach out blindly to him as tears block my vision. "No. Wait."

"I can't wait anymore, *Naranja*. I can't. It's not fair to me or my daughter. I want a partner. A family. And if you aren't willing to give that to me, then I need to move on and try to find someone who will." His face is laced with pain as he smiles sadly. "If you feel you are comfortable moving back here, I'll have the men transfer your things back, and I'll keep someone on watch outside your door night and day until we find the bastards that came here."

"Sebastian," I say, sniffling. "No."

"It's okay. You can't help how you feel. Neither can I. Goodbye, *mi Amor*." As the door closes behind him, I fall to the floor as sobs wrack my body.

He just gave up on me!

Wait. No. I will not continue blaming others for what I caused.

I pushed him away.

I gave up on him.

This is absolutely my fault.

As soon as the tears stop falling, I head to the bathroom to clean myself up, before making a series of phone calls.

I have a bunch of apologies to make, and a man to save.

Chapter 14

SEBASTIAN

One step forward, a billion steps back. And I just can't do it anymore. I'm done waiting for Isabella. Praying for her. Wishing she'd let me in. I have to let go and force myself to move on.

I've told her so many times that I was patiently waiting. But I think today I reached my breaking point.

I don't remember the walk from Isabella's apartment to my truck. For one fleeting moment, I thought she'd come after me, but I should have known better. She's fought me tooth and nail from the beginning, and it's my own damn fault for thinking I could change her. Make her fall in love with me. I was so fucking far gone for her that I convinced myself I could persuade her that I was the one.

Shaking my head in both disbelief and bitterness, I pull up Trace's contact and call him.

"You got her?" he asks, and I can hear the smile in his voice. When I peeled out of my driveway, he gave me a thumbs up. I know he assumed I got to Isabella's and probably turned her over my lap for her behavior, then fucked her six ways to Sunday.

"No, man. It's over. I'm done."

"What?"

"She's never gonna see … never gonna feel the same … and I

just can't anymore. I'm done trying to convince her to want me," I admit, and a sob forces me to cover my mouth. Trace can't hear me cry. I can't even remember the last time I cried.

"No fucking way. There's no way, Seb. I've seen how she looks at you. She's right there! You can't give up when you're this close to the finish line!" he yells.

"It isn't a race or a competition. She doesn't fucking trust me, and she never has. It's never going to change, and I can't live like that. I need my woman to know I'll never do anything to disrespect her. That every decision I make will be for her safety, security, and happiness. But Isabella doesn't want to believe that." I sniff hard, wiping my face with the bottom seam of my shirt, before putting my seatbelt on. Putting the truck into drive, I pull away from Isabella's apartment, refusing to look back. "Send someone to her place for the night, please. And round-the-clock surveillance until we catch the fuckers who came after her. And please get someone to clear out all of her things right now, at least from my room. I can't look at them. You and a few of the guys can take everything back to her apartment tomorrow."

"Are you sure? Maybe sleep on it and make decisions in the morning," Trace says quietly.

"No. It needs to be done now. I'm the dumbass who thought I could make her fall in love with me, and she made it clear from the beginning that she wasn't interested. It's my fault. I'm taking the long way home, so you've got an hour to make it seem like she was never there."

"Alright, but if you want my opinion —"

I interrupt him. "I don't."

"Well you're getting it anyway. You're going to regret this. You had an argument, and you gave up. Bullshit if you ask me. You've been waiting for the other shoe to drop, for her to doubt you for even a second, so you could cut ties. Because you, my friend, have more to lose than she does."

"How do you figure?" I ask angrily.

"You're already in love with her, so any ending involves your heart being broken. She isn't there yet, and you got impatient."

"It's not about being impatient!" I shout, my anger and sadness and frustration just exploding out of me. "She doesn't fucking trust me! She tells me she does, but obviously that isn't the case. She thinks I'd risk her safety, and that I haven't had her best interests at heart. She ran back to her apartment because she was mad, and turned off her phone so I couldn't even contact her. It was a fucking temper tantrum and I couldn't find her! What kind of person does that?"

"A scared woman, Seb. That's the person who did that," Trace states quietly. "A woman who has no control over her fate, who has to live in someone else's home because an unknown assailant is after her, and she knows you want her. I bet you told her tonight that you're in love with her, didn't you?"

When I don't answer, he continues. "She's scared and alone. She probably hasn't told her parents anything, and her brothers undoubtedly squashed any rumors about things. All she has is that damn cat and the bakery. And she had you, but you just yanked that out from under her."

"Her parents know," I state offhandedly. "Her dad came to talk to me. He wanted her to move into the hotel, and I said no."

"Why?"

"Because our men could do a better job of keeping her safe."

"Yet now you're just dropping her back off at her apartment without a thought. Fucked up, if you ask me."

"I didn't ask you," I say irritably.

"What if Isabella follows you home tonight and asks for forgiveness? What will you say?" Trace asks.

"That's moot, because it'll never happen."

"Not what I asked, man. What would you say if it happened?"

"I'd forgive her, I guess. But I'd ask that she trust me to keep her safe, and never to turn off her phone when we have an argument. And to let me love her as I see fit, because I know what she needs, even when she won't admit it to herself." I always did. I can read Isabella Santo better than anyone, even her family. I always felt like our souls were tied together, but she couldn't translate the connection.

"Take the night, Seb. Make decisions in the morning," Trace says. "Drive safe. I'll get her things cleared out of your room for the night."

"Thanks," I mumble, then end the call.

I drive aimlessly for over an hour, going over every interaction I've ever had with Isabella. Wondering where exactly I went wrong. Is Trace right? Was I basically waiting for the first time she pushed back to abandon ship?

Thankful I had the forethought to have Camila spend the night with my parents, I pour myself a double shot of rum as soon as I get home. Taking it upstairs, I walk into my bedroom to find absolutely nothing has changed. "What the fuck, Trace?"

When I'm not surprised his phone goes straight to voicemail, I slam my glass down onto the nightstand with a roar. Stalking around the room, I grab anything of Isabella's. A throw blanket, a pillow, a framed picture of me with her brothers. A sweatshirt of mine that she wore once last week, and I haven't wanted to wash yet, because it smells like her.

Walking into the hallway, I chuck it down the stairs. I hear the glass of the picture frame break against the hard floors, but I don't care. I'll clean it up in the morning.

I think about taking a shower, but decide against it, because I know all of her bath products are in there, and I'll probably throw those down the stairs too. I'm pissed off, but I'm at least enough of a realist to think about how difficult it would be to clean up bubble bath and Epsom salts. Laying back against my pillows, I throw an arm over my eyes and will sleep to take me into darkness.

I JOLT AS SOMETHING SOFT SLAMS AGAINST MY CHEEK. "WHAT THE FUCK!"

"Did you throw my stuff down the stairs?" Isabella shouts.

I force one eye open, noting a blurry figure standing on the other side of the bed. "My dreams are getting worse and worse."

"This isn't a dream, asshole. You broke my picture frame!"

My eyes pop open as I realize she is here. Isabella is in my bedroom. Slow to stand, I take my time turning to face her. "What do you care? You got what you wanted, right? You got me out of your life for good."

"I never said —" Isabella's eyes fill with tears as she covers her mouth with her hands. Still wearing the same clothes she had on earlier, with a streak of flour across the right knee of her black leggings. "I never said I wanted you gone, Seb. I never said that, and you left so fast I couldn't even say anything. Why didn't you let me talk?"

"Because I knew what you were going to say," I tell her wearily, rubbing my eyes. "It's the same song and dance. I've been trying to get you to fall in love with me for a decade. I should have taken a hint more than once."

"I didn't think you were in love with me," she whispers. My eyes clear, and I take in her face. Eyes swollen and red, like she's been crying for some time. Hair in disarray, and my fingers twitch with a need to smooth them over the strands. "I assumed it was a challenge to you. A game. I didn't want to be a conquest, and then have to be around you again. I knew I couldn't survive that. It would hurt too much."

I stare at her incredulously. "When have I given you the impression that it was just a game to me?"

Tears fall as her face screws up in pain. "You didn't. It was in my head. Every man I've ever cared for has either cheated on me or lied to me. Or both! And I assumed you'd be the same way."

"You realized that now? Tonight? That it was in your head?"

She shrugs as she nods. "Yes and no. I called Luca. Went to his house, and Dominic showed up. Then Alex. The three of them read me the riot act about how I'd treated you, and how the entire family knows you're in love with me. They lambasted me for not trusting my instincts, and not trusting them, because they'd never agree to me living with you if they didn't know you're a stand-up guy." Head hanging low, Isabella refuses to look at me as she continues. "I explained why I was upset, and they agreed you should have told me about the bakery order as soon as I moved in with you."

"Honestly, I forgot," I admit. "And then you were finally opening up to me, and I didn't want to rock the boat. I hoped you'd give me some grace once I told you. I certainly never thought you'd outrun Trace with Speedracer and rack up a couple of felonies in the process."

"A couple of felonies? Oh, now you're going to be dramatic. Great," she snaps, her blazing eyes finally finding mine. "Let's talk about your behavior tonight, shall we? You decided I couldn't love you back. You very firmly stated that I should move out. You never let me talk, and you determined, incorrectly, might I add, that I didn't want to be a wife or have a family. And worst of all, you claim I couldn't see myself the way you see me, or see you in the same light. You're all I see, Sebastian. Maybe you're the one with the blinders on, not me."

"I need some clarification," I breathe, taking a hesitant step toward her. "What exactly do you see?"

Isabella's eyes soften. "You made me see myself. You gave me confidence that I never knew I could have. I began to trust that not all men are assholes, because you weren't. I knew my brothers were in your corner, and boy did they lay into me tonight about my lack of trust. I hate that I caused you pain because of that. My family is full of these remarkable love stories, with glorious pairings of individuals who match each other so well. I couldn't see our matching. You're bigger than life, and I'm just ... me. It's not about physical appearances or weight —"

"Your weight is fucking perfect. Your body is perfect."

Her lips twitch as she fights a smile. "I know. I love my body. I always have. I'm fine with not being a size two. I love food, and I love to eat. I won't be apologetic about that. But your interest in me made me doubt my own confidence about my body initially. How could someone as gorgeous as you want a plain Jane like me? I couldn't see it."

"You are not plain," I tell her, taking another step in her direction. "You're perfect. I dream about your curves, baby. Do you believe me now?"

"I do," she says with a nod. "It took me longer than it should have, though. Every woman in my family is smaller than me, and while no one has ever made me feel like I'm less than because of being curvier, I think I subconsciously put that on myself. And the last few weeks, as you've been slowly filtering into my soul, I realized that I don't care about what anyone thinks about me. I only care about what *you* think."

"Do you want to know what I think right now?" I ask.

She nods, but I see the apprehension in her gaze. "Only if you want to tell me, Seb."

"I love that you've called me Seb twice tonight, because you've never called me that before."

"Your close friends call you that, and it just seemed too ..." she trails off, exhaling deeply.

"What?"

Isabella's eyes meet mine as she continues. "It seemed too intimate, somehow. And I was too scared to take a step in that direction with you. If something changes, you're still around my family a lot. I don't know how I'd handle that, so stopping it from happening seemed like the best option."

"Okay. What did you mean when you said I'm all you see?" I ask, almost scared of what she might say.

She smiles slightly, just the corner of her lips pulling up a tiny bit. "I've caught myself thinking about you almost constantly. Wondering what you'd think about a new dessert I was debating on trying, or if you'd like one of my perfumes. I'd almost have make-believe conversations in my head with you, which seems ridiculous now that I've said it out loud."

"Not ridiculous," I say, shaking my head. "You're in my thought conversations too."

"Really?" she asks softly, hope finally blooming in her eyes for the first time since she barreled in here.

"You've been the center of my heart, Isabella. Everything I do is with you in mind. You are it," I tell her huskily, stepping close enough to pull her into my arms. Burying my head in her hair, I ask her a final question, that bears the most weight. "Do you see that you're not a game to me?"

"I do," she whispers as her arms slide around to hold me tightly. "I'm so sorry to have doubted you, even for a moment."

"I'm sorry I didn't handle the bakery order better. I promise I'll talk to you about things from now on. Except for the keeping you safe stuff."

"Wait —" she interjects, but I palm her head and shove her face into my chest.

"No. This is where I draw the line, and you need to listen to me before you blow up and yell at me. Okay?"

She mutters something against my chest that I don't under-stand, but finally nods her agreement.

"Good. There are six women in this world that don't get to tell me how to keep them safe. My daughter, my sisters, my mother, and my grandmother. You're the sixth. If something happened to any of you, and it was due to negligence on my part? I'd never forgive myself. Every decision I make about your safety is done so with painstaking finesse. I don't decide something just to piss you off, or make you uncomfortable. I do so because I will not be able to live with myself if something happens to you." My body tenses as I think about her being hurt, or taken, and Isabella squeezes me in response.

"Seb," she whispers, nuzzling her cheek against me.

"Here are the things that I will not compromise on. I will be able to track your location, from your phone and your car, and you'll check in when you arrive somewhere. If I'm not with you, someone I've personally chosen will be around you. We aren't any closer to finding the guys who your ex is associated with, and until that happens, I'm not taking any chances with your safety. Once things settle down, and I know the threat is over, we'll change this expectation."

"Okay," Isabella replies.

"And no more riding with your NASCAR employee with the goal of losing your tail. I don't care how pissed you are at my guys. If they drove you to work, they drive you home."

"Alright."

"Lastly, if we have a fight, which I have no doubt we will have because we're us, and it's probably been a decade of foreplay at this point, you don't go back to your apartment to hide from me. If we argue, we talk it out. Then we have make-up sex, because that's what couples do. Also, get rid of your apartment. I've been moving you in here for weeks, *mi Reina*. You live here now. Accept it."

"Okay," she says with a giggle, and the sound is like a perfect melody. "Can I ask a question now?"

"Of course."

Isabella props her chin on my chest, looking up at me, her chocolate brown eyes shining. "Is this the part of our fight where we get to have make-up sex?"

"Fuck, yes," I say, crashing our lips together.

About fucking time.

Chapter 15

ISABELLA

I didn't know how things would go when I made it to Sebastian's. I knew I had a lot to apologize for. I've handled things so badly with him. My brothers did not hold back once I explained what happened. Luca was incredibly pissed. He admitted that Sebastian first approached him quite a few years ago asking about me, around the time Luca met Hannah, and joked that he couldn't wait to see how long I made Seb wait.

Dominic said he's known about Seb's feelings since before he married my sister-in-law, Kate, and Alex claims he recognized interest six or seven years ago. He said Sebastian would always have me in his sights whenever he attended a family function.

All three of my brothers feel Sebastian is one hell of a stand-up guy, and they believe he's the perfect partner for me. They also very quickly told me they completely despised Rick, which was also news to me. Granted, I didn't exactly get warm and fuzzy feedback from them the first time they met Rick, but they've never been the warmest to any man I've brought around. I assumed it was a brotherly thing to do.

For them to wholeheartedly root for Sebastian says a lot, because my brothers are excellent judges of character. They were clear to state that, should Sebastian end up hurting me, they have no problem helping Leo bury a body.

They gave me the confidence to come to Sebastian's and grovel. In true Isabella fashion, however, I saw the busted picture frame and forgot what I was there to do, choosing instead to hurl a pillow at Seb's head.

Considering he's now kissing me as his hands seem to be everywhere at once, I think it's all ending exactly as it's supposed to.

"Are you sure? You want this?" Sebastian murmurs as he licks down my neck and nibbles on my collarbone.

"Yes," I moan. "God, yes. Please."

He chuckles against my skin, grabbing my ass and pulling me flush against him. "I'm not God, baby."

"You can be whomever you want to be in this moment, Sebastian. Just please put me out of my misery." Sliding one hand into his hair, I wrap my fingers around the strands and pull. The groan that emanates from his lungs is guttural.

"I only want to be yours, Isabella."

Well, hot damn. I'm soaking wet now. "You want to be mine?"

His head pops up as he gives me a smirk. "Did you think I'd settle for anything else?"

I shrug. "You said you had been patient, so I didn't know —"

He interrupts me. "You misunderstood. I was patient waiting for your feelings to catch up to mine. I was patient as you finally saw that I was here. That had nothing to do with my feelings, sweetheart. I told you before that I've always been yours. Now you're ready to accept that."

A wide grin breaks across my face, and he matches it. "So you've always been mine?"

He nods. "Always, *mi amor*."

"I guess the real new information here is that I'm yours?"

"Are you ready to be mine?" he asks, and I nod. The responding smile is downright feral. "I hope you're not tired."

"What? Why?" I ask with a breathy giggle.

"Because you aren't sleeping much tonight," he says, as he picks me up and tosses me onto his bed. I bounce once with a laugh, before he pounces.

"Wait!" I shout, and I see the wince before he schools his expression. "No, not about sex. We're having sex tonight. But shouldn't you shut the door? I don't want Camila walking in."

Sebastian lets out a relieved breath as his forehead drops to my shoulder. "Fuck, you scared me for a second. She's at my parents' house. While the interaction at your apartment didn't go as I expected, I had every intention of the evening ending in this bed. After that kiss on the sidewalk today, I knew we'd at least be making out tonight."

"Making out?" I cackle. "Aren't we too old to be making out? If you ask me to go steady, Sebastian, I'm leaving right now."

"The fuck you are," he huffs, grabbing both of my wrists and pinning them above my head. "I don't care what you call it, as long as a lot of our skin touches and I get to taste multiple parts of your body."

The hand that isn't holding my wrists trails up my ribcage, covering my breast. He groans as his lips find mine again, and I writhe against him, desperate to feel his skin. I need my hands on his body. "Please let me touch you."

"You wanna touch me, baby?" he whispers huskily against my lips. "By all means. Have your way with me."

Sebastian lets go of my wrists, but before I can get my hands on him, he sits up on his knees, straddling my legs. Wearing a white button-down shirt, the top three buttons already undone, and a gold chain swinging from his neck, he looks like sex person-ified. Dark hair hangs over his forehead, and I realize I've never seen him look so relaxed and happy.

I scoot up so my back is against the headboard, and tentatively reach out to touch his shirt. When he doesn't move, I unbutton his shirt slowly. With every inch of skin exposed, tattoos weaving an intricate design across his chest, my hands shake a little more. Sebastian senses my discomfort, taking my hand and pressing it to his chest. "Feel this?"

I nod.

"It's for you, Isabella. My heart beats for you. There is nothing you can say or do that will change that. I already know you are going to be the best I've ever had. There is nothing that could ever possibly top tonight, because it's you, and I've never wanted anyone as badly as I want you."

I sigh as my thumb strokes across his pectoral muscle, watching it twitch. Reaching with my other hand, I slide it underneath the shirt, across his clavicle and onto his shoulder, and revel in how his muscles pulse underneath my touch. He's so strong, and I honestly can't believe he's mine. And that I'm about to see him naked.

"You're wearing my shirt," he rasps, drawing my gaze up to his. He points to the shirt I'm wearing. "I bought that for you three years ago for your birthday."

"What?" I look down at the simple white shirt I'm wearing, with a V-neck and ruffles along the sleeves and hem. "I thought one of my brothers gave me this."

He shakes his head. "I've gotten you something for the last few years, and had Luca give it to you. I knew you wouldn't accept it from me, but I needed to see you wear something of mine."

In disbelief, I ask, "What about last year?"

He moves my hair, thumbing my ear, and the simple cupcake earrings I wear every day. "These earrings."

Emotion clogging my throat, I choke out, "And the year before that?"

He leans down, caressing my cheek. "The mixer that is downstairs right now."

I gasp. "My stand mixer? That was from you?"

He nods. "I told Luca to tell you he'd gotten it super cheap from somebody who worked at a store going out of business."

"But," I say, tears filling my eyes, "I've never given you anything for your birthdays."

"You're giving me everything I ever wanted right now, *Naranja*. There is no comparison."

Unable to verbalize a response, I pull him down and press my lips to his. Sebastian immediately takes over, his tongue sweeping between my lips to tangle with mine. I take great pleasure in allowing my hands to roam over his shoulders and back, feeling the muscles ripple in the wake of my touch. When I tug on his shirt, Sebastian briefly sits up, reaches over his shoulder and rips the shirt off. As he's about to stretch out on top of me again, I put both hands on his chest, stopping him.

Sebastian doesn't say a word, but a soft smile tugs at the corner of his mouth, telling me he knows exactly why I stopped him.

The tattoos. A few I've seen parts of, like an elaborate tribal tattoo around his bicep that now continues onto his chest, and a couple initials Luca told me are of some of Sebastian's friends who have passed away.

But this close, I see dates in Roman numerals. Lightly tracing the first one, he smiles knowingly. "Camila's birthday."

"And this one?" I ask, moving down to one on his ribcage, where the Roman numerals are written within a cross.

"My grandmother's birthday." He takes my hand, dragging my finger across his skin to another tattoo. "I've hidden the date my parents were married within this tattoo. It's called a Taino tattoo, for the indigenous people of Puerto Rico. The spiral one on my arm and shoulder is also a Taino tattoo, representing energy and vitality."

Captivated, I lightly trace the tattoo, finding the hidden

numbers within a tattoo of what appears to be an animal or person. "What is this supposed to be?"

"It's for abundance. And the one here," he points to a figure that is part of the elaborate swirling on his shoulder, "is essentially like a witch doctor. It's for *Abuela*. That mysterious woman can solve every health scare known to man with a sewing kit, an amulet, some herbs, and a drum."

"Why is this one slightly red?" I ask, my fingers dusting over an intricate design in the shape of a mandala. Tilting my head, I see a cupcake. Then a cookie. And a cake. Then the letters BBB.

"Bake, Batter, and Bowl," Sebastian says quietly. He takes my finger, placing it lightly underneath the circle of cupcakes. "And this part is pink because I added your initials."

Emotion clogs my throat as I try to find my voice. "But no birthday in Roman numerals?"

He chuckles, then sits higher on his knees. As he begins to take off his belt, he says, "I lost a bet with your brother. I'm not telling you which one —"

"Luca," I interrupt, deadpan. I know my brothers, and this has Luca written all over it. Whatever 'this' is.

"The bet was we had to get a tattoo, but the other person chose the location. So, to get back at him, I got your birthday tattooed." He unzips his pants, dragging them down with his underwear, and I see the Roman numerals tattooed within a heart. Right between his happy trail and that delicious V leading to his groin.

"Did he know that's what you were doing?" I ask, reaching out to touch the most intimate tattoo I've ever seen, directly above the most intimate location on Sebastian's body, that I'd really like to become acquainted with.

His breath catches as he stares down at my hand. "He knew."

I watch as the bulge in his pants grows, and I'm emboldened knowing I'm doing this to him. With my hand so close, I decide it's now or never, and quickly plunge my hand beneath his cloth-ing, wrapping around his length. Sebastian lets out a choked moan, falling forward. "Jesus Christ, baby. You gotta warn a man first."

I giggle lightly. "I like this idea better."

He groans when I squeeze him, then I slowly stroke from the base to the tip. "Goddamn. I've dreamt so many times what it would feel like to have you touching me."

"Oh yeah? And how am I comparing to your dreams?"

"So much fucking better," he grits through his teeth. "But you have to stop. I'm too close already, and I refuse to come unless I'm inside you."

He grabs my wrist, pulling my hand up and out, before slam-ming his lips down on mine. The kiss is passion personified, bordering on violent as he rolls us so I'm on top. I flip my hair to one side, and Sebastian immediately wraps it around his fist. I gasp when he pulls, and his answering smile is wicked. "I can't wait to fuck your mouth while controlling your head this way."

Sebastian surprises me by pulling my shirt up, sucking the tip of my breast into his mouth, and laving it with his tongue through the lace of my bra. It's rough, dirty, but oh so delicious. I gasp as his hand finds my other nipple, tweaking it with his thumb and forefinger, and my hips mindlessly gyrate as I grind on his cock.

"Wanna fuck these tits too," Sebastian murmurs, almost to himself, as he lets the tip pop out of his mouth. Pushing them together, he sucks the other nipple into his mouth, and I can't help the breathy moan that leaves my lungs. Sitting up, I pull my shirt off, watching Sebastian's already dark eyes turn to midnight. I feel more sexual, more confident, than I ever have. Glancing through my lashes at him, I run both hands up to cup my breasts, my thumbs slowly circling the areolas. Sebastian smiles. "My perfect seductress, blooming right in front of me."

It's all because of him. I know I'm not ugly. But when your

sisters are more glamorous than you, and your brothers pair off with beautiful women, one by one, it's hard not to play the comparison game. I'm average, and fairly plain. You won't find me shopping at high-end boutique stores, or carrying an expensive wallet or purse. I like my comfort. Most guys have rolled their eyes at me when I've told them I'm not into makeup or designer things. They assume I'm lying during the honeymoon phase of our relationship. Sebastian is the only man who sees me for who I really am, and doesn't expect me to change.

"Do you know how perfect you are?" Sebastian's words are so soft I barely hear him.

"I'm not perfect. No one is," I answer.

He shakes his head. "You're perfect for me, and that's all that matters."

A smile creeps across my face as my hands dance up my décolletage and around my neck to pick up my hair. "You make me feel like I'm perfect for you."

His hands have found my hips as he slowly drags me across his hard length. "I'm the lucky man who gets to have you. But just so we're on the same page, I'd like to know what kind of sex you prefer."

"What?" I burst out with a laugh. "What kind of question is that? If I have to explain how sex works, Sebastian, I really don't understand how you have a child."

He flips us so he's back on top. "Sex isn't just one way, Isabella. If you've only experienced humdrum sex, than I both love and hate your exes for that."

"Why love and hate?" I ask.

"I love that they're so fucking stupid that they didn't show you how mind-blowing sex can be. And I loathe and despise them because they had you first." His eyes don't leave mine as he answers quickly. He always answers me with his eyes on mine. In fact, I don't think I've ever felt like his attention wasn't solely focused on me in a conversation. "Now. You have a few options, and we can revisit all of these. This isn't a multiple choice question where you pick one and that's how it is forever."

"Okay," I say warily. Where is he going with this? I swear if this is his way of asking if I'll do anal, I'm gonna be really pissed.

"It's worth mentioning that sometimes I think I can read your thoughts," Sebastian says with a chuckle. "And while I know you'd like that too, I'm not talking about anal."

My mouth drops open. "How did you do that?"

His smile is bemused. "You suddenly looked like you wanted to stab me. It was an easy assumption to make."

I harrumph. "Well, you're wrong. I've tried it before, and I don't like it, so that's off the table."

He tilts his head to the side as he studies me. "Let me guess. The guy barely got you ready, lubed himself up, and slammed into you so fast you couldn't relax. He probably did some damage not prepping you, too."

"I couldn't poop for a week," I whisper, my eyes closing in humiliation. I'd been really intrigued by anal, and my college boyfriend was game to try it. The pain seared through me so quickly that I didn't realize when he was done.

"*Mi Reina*," Sebastian says softly, his fingers stroking my cheek. "That's not how it's supposed to be. Sex of any kind is a two-way street, and know that I'd never enter you before I knew you were ready. If you ever want to try again, I know I can make it a better experience. In fact, I think I'll make it so good you'll consistently want me in this gorgeous ass. But until that point, if and when you're ready for it, anal can be off the table."

"Okay," I tell him. "Have I ever told you that I love all the names you call me?"

"Yeah?" He asks, and I nod. "I thought so. I could see it in your eyes. What's your favorite?"

"*Amor*," I answer.

"Well," he says huskily, leaning down to give me a quick but steamy kiss, *"mi Amor*, I need to know what kinds of sex you like. Do you like it romantic, where it feels like our souls are so connected that we have an out-of-body experience every time we come together?"

Fucking Christ.

"Or," he says as he applies light kisses down my neck, then sucks on my pulse point, "would you prefer the sex to be slow? So painstakingly slow that you feel like you're going to lose your mind if I don't make you come? Where I keep edging and edging you until you have the most explosive orgasm of your entire life?"

I whimper, my body taut with need and adrenaline.

"What about good old-fashioned fucking? Where it's so intense, so passionately violent that I don't just send you over the edge; I catapult you into a vicious orgasm that makes your legs shake for hours?"

"That one, that one, that one," I shout. "I choose option three. Please."

"Good girl," he growls, and my eyes roll back into my head.

Sebastian's lips take mine again in a kiss full of intention and promise. His velvet tongue darts into my mouth precisely, circling my tongue before he sucks it back into his mouth. His hand reaches between our bodies to cup my sex, giving the perfect amount of pressure against my clit to send a wave of pleasure coursing through my veins. "Can I taste you?"

"God, yes, please," I moan. It's been a while since a man went down on me, as Rick claimed he didn't like it. I don't think there's a better way for a woman to have an orgasm, but my man-led orgasms have been lackluster at best.

Sebastian pecks my lips once more before scooting down the bed to peel off my pants, socks, and underwear. "Look at this pretty pink pussy. Do you have any idea how many dreams I've had about being camped down here, making you come over and over again? God, Isabella. I've wanted you so fucking bad that I almost feel like this isn't real."

I reach down to brush a lock of hair that has fallen across his forehead. "It's real. Now lick my pussy."

He grins wickedly. "Like I said. Perfect seductress, blooming right in front of me."

Chapter 16

SEBASTIAN

If I were to be asked what my proudest moments were in my life up until this point, I'd have a variety of things about Camila, getting the MC off the ground, and buying my bar.

But watching Isabella trust her own femininity, and lean into it? Besides the birth of my daughter, I'd say Isabella's confidence ranks right up there. Six months ago, had we had an opportunity to be together, I highly doubt she'd have told me to lick her pussy. But now, she's confident about her sexuality, and I'm so fucking here for it.

Looking at her beautiful thighs, I want to wear them like earmuffs. I want her to sit on my face and cover me in her desire. I want to be fucking buried with her taste on my lips. And as soon as my tongue touches her core, taking one long lick from bottom to top, I loudly groan as her sweet and salty taste hits my taste-buds. "Fucking delicious."

Isabella's hand has made its way into my hair, holding the strands tightly as she maneuvers my head to where she wants it. I try to get my tongue inside her, but she yanks me back to her clit. Wondering if she's pushing me toward the place that will get her off the fastest, I try an experiment. Slowly circling around her clit, but only barely touching it, she gets restless as she tries to move my head. As soon as I suck her clit in between my lips, she stops moving.

I back off, hearing her whimper of dismay, and cover a chuckle. Lightly pressing my tongue to her clit and vibrating it against the bundle of nerves, I do another experiment by slipping one finger inside her. Her breath catches as I massage the rough patch of skin I find, and the sound that comes out of Isabella is part moan and part sigh. Adding a second finger, I crook my fingers to press harder against her G-spot, then suck harshly on her clit. She clamps her thighs around my head as her back arches. I feel the walls of her pussy flutter as she comes, and the gush I feel against my chin as I work her through the orgasm is eagerly lapped up.

As soon as her breathing evens out a little, I attack her clit and G-spot simultaneously again, and her cries of pleasure fan the flame of desire currently stewing at the base of my spine. Her second orgasm hits faster, and the walls of her pussy tighten so much I can barely move my fingers.

"Jesus Christ, Sebastian, no more," she pants, and I appear from between her thighs with a fake pout.

"No fair," I say dramatically. "I could have easily given you another."

"Three in a row makes me lose the feeling in my legs, and I prefer not to feel my heartbeat in my vagina," she says wryly. "I definitely don't think I could handle any more than that."

I shrug. "I bet you could."

Her eyebrows raise as she looks at me while I slide up her body. She asks, "Not that I really want to discuss actual numbers of partners or anything, but exactly how many orgasms have you given in one sitting?"

I think for a moment before answering. "Eight."

"Eight!" Isabella screeches. "Did she live? Need medical attention? Could she form a coherent sentence afterward?"

I chuckle. "No, but I do think I remember her being basically comatose for a little bit, then making me help change her sheets before I left. Eight is ... messy."

"Messy," Isabella repeats calmly, but her eyes twinkle and her lips twitch as she fights a smile. "Did she send you an award? I feel like there is a statue somewhere in this house. Best Tongue."

I sigh. "Really a missed opportunity on her part. When I get you to nine, you'll give me an award, right? Not an Oscar statuette. It needs to be something tongue-themed."

"I'll try to remember if you beat your record."

"*When* I break my record."

"If."

"When."

"Sebastian!" she whines. "I think my clit would fall off."

"It won't," I tell her cheerfully. "My tongue will fall asleep and basically cramp like a bitch though."

"Seriously? It falls asleep?"

I nod. "Yup."

"Why do you continue to do it then? If it falls asleep? Surely women are fine with one, two, or three orgasms. I'd have been fine with just that first one," Isabella says, a hint of pink creeping onto her neck. Interesting that demanding I lick her pussy doesn't embarrass her, but talking about the number of orgasms does.

"Because I love getting a woman off. I get off on watching your reactions. What expressions you make, and how your body responds. I'd fucking live between your thighs if I could, baby." I press a closed-lips kiss against her, then jostle in surprise when her tongue tentatively slips between my lips. She swirls it around my tongue, then stops the kiss.

I open my eyes to see her looking thoughtfully at me. "It's not as bad as I expected, but I'm not a huge fan."

"What?" I ask.

"How I taste on you. It's okay," she says with a shrug, and I can't help the laughter that bubbles out of me. God I love this woman. I'm still laughing when she shimmies my pants and boxer briefs off my hips, then uses her feet to push them down the rest of the way. The laughter dies in my throat as my cock bounces against her core. "Um, I'm not on birth control. It really messed with my hormones, and I didn't like how it made me feel. But I am STD-free. I got tested after I found my ex cheating."

Still furious that she walked in her douchebag ex and her best friend, I try to stifle my anger as I nod. "I have condoms. And I'm clean too. I got checked when you moved in. I wanted to be safe, and I hoped we'd end up here. Not that it really matters, because it's been a while for me. In fact, this will probably be a lot shorter than you expect. Not only because it's been a while, but because it's *you*, and I'm struggling not to come right now just because I can feel the heat emanating from your pussy, and it's driving me insane."

Isabella smiles softly. "I think that's why I came so quickly. Because it's you."

Choking on emotion, I drag my gaze from hers as I lean toward my nightstand. Opening the brand-new box of condoms, I bashfully look at her through my lashes. "I just bought these. Again, I had hopes. But I didn't expect it. Not that I'm complaining, *mi Cielo*. Getting you in my bed was a hope, but not a goal."

"I think it's okay if you call it a goal," she teases, as I sit up and open the condom.

"It wasn't." Sliding the condom on, I meet her eyes again. "Getting your heart was always the goal. Sex is just a bonus."

"Sebastian," she whispers, holding her arms out to me. I fall into her embrace as she wraps her legs around me, and my cock notches at her opening perfectly. "Go slow to start, okay? You're bigger than I've had. Then you can go hard."

I'm struggling to respond as I slowly inch into her channel, the hot walls of her pussy clenching me tightly, and I rest my forehead against hers. Fucking hell. I'm about to blow. "Baby, I may not make it to going hard. You feel too fucking perfect."

"Would a distraction work to calm you down?" she asks.

"I don't know. Maybe?"

"Okay. I once heard my brothers talking —"

I groan. Wait. That worked. "Yeah. Keep talking about your brothers."

She laughs, but the sound is breathy and so fucking sexy. "They didn't know I was listening. They were talking about things they did to keep from coming too quickly. I can't remember which one does this, but one of them chants 'old man balls' over and over again in his head."

"Luca," I pant as I bottom out, my groin against hers. "It's Luca. I remember him telling me that once."

"Sebastian," Isabella moans. "You feel so good."

I groan as my head falls against her shoulder. "You have no fucking idea how perfect you feel."

I wait a moment as I focus on my breathing. I know with every beat of my heart that I just pushed into the only woman I'll be with for the rest of my life. This is it. This is my forever.

"Gonna be quick," I mutter as I pull out slightly, then slide back in. Isabella digs her fingernails into my back, and I hope she does it hard enough to break the skin. I want her nail marks tattooed there. She cries out as I quicken my pace, and my orgasm barrels toward me. Old man balls, old man — fuck, this isn't going to work.

"Sebastian," Isabella stammers, "I think I'm going to come again."

And that is my undoing. When my perfect girl holds her breath as she comes, her pussy clamps down on me so hard that I have no choice but to follow her over the cliff. I roar as rope after rope fills the condom, black spots dotting my vision, and I feel the condom fill completely. This is the hardest I've ever come, and I'm not remotely surprised. Of course it would be this way with Isabella.

I collapse on top of her, my softening dick still inside her, but I can't seem to make myself move. This connection is so perfect, so exquisitely unique because it's her, that I don't want to separate. Right now, there's nothing between us. No jobs, families, or crazy ex-boyfriends. It's just me and Isabella, in our own bubble, and I want to stay here as long as possible.

It's a few minutes before Isabella speaks. "I didn't know it could be like that."

"Neither did I," I confess. Lifting my head, I see her confused gaze. "I figured it would be the best I've ever had, but that wasn't even on the scale. That was spectacular, and I can't wait to do it again. I just need thirty to forty-five minutes. Maybe less."

Isabella giggles. "Twenty minutes?"

"Don't count on it. I'm an old man."

"Thirty-six is not old," she says with an exaggerated eye roll.

"I didn't know you knew how old I am."

"I've always known," she admits shyly. "I had a crush on you, Sebastian. No one knew, I think. I just couldn't wrap my head around you being interested in me. We seemed to be on opposite sides of the spectrum."

I cup her cheek, my thumb dragging lightly across her lip. "Opposite sides of the spectrum balance each other out, *mi Amor*. And there's no one more perfect for balancing me than you. I'm relieved you finally see the same thing I've always seen. That we're perfect together."

A BUZZING NOISE WAKES ME UP, AND IT TAKES ME A MINUTE TO RECOGNIZE the weight sprawled across me is Isabella. A sleepy smile covers my face as I breathe in her perfect sugared vanilla scent. I wasn't kidding when I said I planned to keep her up most of the night. I make a mental note to order more condoms, because I'd only ordered a box of six, and now only have two left. Isabella's pussy is my nirvana, and I plan to camp out there as often as she'll let me.

The buzzing happens again, and I root around the nightstand to grab my phone.

> Mom: We're driving down your driveway.
>
> Mom: We're parking the car.
>
> Mom: Sebastian! Is it safe to come inside?
>
> Mom: I better not see something inappropriate in there.
>
> Mom: We're getting Camila her breakfast.
>
> Mom: Two minutes, and I'm sending her up to wake you up. Then YOU can explain why Isabella is in your bed.

As much as I'd love to tell Camila that Isabella and I are together now, I don't exactly want to have the birds and the bees conversation with my five-year-old right now. And it should definitely be something Isabella is ready for.

Shit. We haven't really talked about what happens now. Moving forward. How should we act together? Can I be affectionate? Should we remain relatively professional in front of Camila? Dammit. I meant to bring this up last night, but clearly my dick began running all the blood in my body, and I could no longer form constructive thoughts.

I carefully extract myself from under Isabella, holding my breath as she sighs and rolls toward the other side of the bed. I respond to my mother as I'm tiptoeing into my closet.

Me: Keep her down there. I'll be down in a minute.

Mom: I assume things went well?

Me: How much information are you hoping to get here, Mamá?

Mom: Much less than you assume, mi bebé. Did you put your heart on the line? Does she know that you're in love with her?

Me: I've never shied away from telling Isabella how I feel. Now I know she actually believes me.

Mom: What will you be telling Camila?

Me: Mom, can we discuss this in a few minutes when I get downstairs?

Mom: As if your daughter will allow us to have an adult conversation.

I chuckle quietly as I throw on a pair of shorts and a loose tee-shirt. She's not wrong about that. It isn't that Camila expects to be the focus whenever she's around adults. She has too many questions about the world around her, so it makes carrying on a conversation a bit challenging. But I love watching her mind decipher information, and how she learns is pretty remarkable.

As I jog down the stairs, I follow the sound of my beautiful girl excitedly chirping about what she hopes to do today. "Hi Daddy! Did you miss me?"

I nuzzle against her head as I scoop her into my arms. "Of course, *mi Chiquita*. The house is quiet without you."

"You know what we need?" Camila asks, and I see the calculated look in her eyes. She's about to ask for an animal of some kind, I just know it.

"What, Camila?" I reply, sighing as I deposit her in her chair in the kitchen. I notice extra marshmallows in her cereal, and I raise an eyebrow at my dad. He stifles a smile as he buries his head in a magazine.

"Well," Camila begins, "I spend lots of nights with *Abuelito* and *Abuelita*. You must be so lonely here. And Butterscotch doesn't make nearly enough noise to keep you company."

"No, Butterscotch is a fairly quiet cat." He's also pretty dumb, but if he makes Isabella happy, he's fine with me. I squeeze my eyes closed because I know I'll give my daughter whatever she asks.

"He needs a little brother," Camila says innocently, beaming at me. Her eyes dart to the stairs as Isabella shuffles into the room holding Butterscotch. Camila squeals and Isabella immediately places the cat in her lap.

"Who needs a little brother?" Isabella asks, yawning. Her eyes have yet to catch mine, but my parents both stare in awe at her. In fact, I'm staring at her.

Even though she has most of her wardrobe hung in the guest room closet, she went into my closet and grabbed my things. I have a visceral reaction to seeing her in my plaid pajama pants and a worn tee-shirt from one of Luca's first games with the Denver Wolves. He signed it, and I proudly showed my parents afterward. They know it's mine.

I could play this cool. Wink and move on. But in this moment, knowing that only a few short hours ago, I was buried to the hilt inside her after wanting her for years, I'm through with being nonchalant.

She notices me striding toward her and her eyes widen dramatically. For a half-second, my steps falter as I worry I'll push her away, but then I see a grin tug at the corner of her mouth. With one hand on her hip and the other into her beautiful hair, I take her lips in a kiss that is definitely not PG, but not obscene either. I feel Isabella's hands clench at my shirt as she sighs into my mouth. Breaking off the kiss, I smile softly. "Good morning, *mi amor*."

"Hi," she whispers, biting her lip as her fingers absentmindedly trace across my chest. When my father clears his throat, I reluctantly step aside, but slide an arm around her waist.

"Alright. Ask your questions," I say.

"I don't have any questions, *bebé*. It was only a matter of time. Your story is written in the stars." My mother smiles widely at us before walking over to give Isabella a hug.

"I'm sorry it took me so long," Isabella says remorsefully, once my mom lets go.

Mom scoffs. "Nonsense. It isn't a race, and we weren't keeping a stopwatch as we waited. We know our son, and he'd do it all again if the same outcome was guaranteed."

I nod in agreement. I may have had a momentary setback last night, but I know I'd have come up with a plan by this morning, had Isabella not made the first move.

My eyes drift to where Camila sits quietly with Butterscotch in her lap. While she doesn't look mad, she doesn't look happy either. Going to her, I crouch next to her chair. "Talk to me, *Mija*."

Her eyes bounce between me and Isabella. "I know you love her, Daddy. Do you still love me?"

"Oh, Camila," I say quietly. "No one will ever displace my love for you."

"Are you sure?" she whispers.

I nod solemnly. "Absolutely."

"Do you promise not to be mad?" she asks.

"Why?" I ask, a sense of paranoia drifts down my spine. "Is there something that you think I may be upset about?"

She nods as she looks up at my mother. Mom smiles ruefully at me. "Butterscotch really does need a little brother."

I groan as I throw my head back, eyes closing. Fuck. Please be something normal, like a cat or dog. With Camila, anything is possible. She went through a complete fascination with tarantulas, excitedly accompanying me to southern Colorado for a tarantula migration. There was a brief interest in penguins, as well as marmots, courtesy of that stupid marmot that wreaks havoc on Eternity Springs. Camila even commented about a classmate having a corn snake a few weeks ago, and I literally might have a heart attack if my parents got her a snake.

"Daddy, it's okay. I want to call him Oreo, cuz then he'll match up with Butterscotch." I hear a very small mewl, and I open my eyes to find the cutest black and white kitten staring at me. There were rumblings of a kitten recently, but I made it clear to my mother that I had no interest in taking on an animal. I'm not sure if this is the same kitten, but the look of hope on my daughter's face is one I simply refuse to crush.

"Oreo, huh," I muse, taking him from my mom. Butterscotch sniffs the kitten once, hisses, then bolts from Camila's lap. "I think it may take some time for Butterscotch to learn to be friends with Oreo."

"It's okay. It takes time to make friends," Camila says matter-of-factly. Her eyes jerk toward Isabella again, and she lowers her voice to a whisper. "Is she my mom now?"

A pang of sadness overtakes me as I ghost a hand over Camila's hair. Her blue eyes look at me so hopefully, and I hate that she recognizes the absence of her mother. I also refuse to lie to my daughter. "No, *mi Chiquita*. That's not how it works."

"Oh," she says sadly, her eyes dropping to the floor. "All my friends have a mom. I thought that maybe ..."

I hear a sniff as my mom listens. I hand her the kitten while I pull Camila into my arms. I walk her into the great room and sit on the couch with her in my lap. "I know you want a mother, *Mija*. And while I can't say for certain that Isabella will or won't be in your life for a long time, we aren't ready to assign any role to her. But I know she cares for you a lot, and she likes spending time with you. Now the three of us can spend time together."

"My friend Amanda said she's always with a babysitter cuz her mom goes on dates. What's a date?" Camila asks.

"A date is when two people go out together somewhere because they like each other."

"So I'll be at *Abuelita's* a lot," she says sullenly.

"No. Absolutely not. You are my priority, Camila. You are the number one girl in my life. While I may want to take Isabella out occasionally just the two of us, I promise I won't leave you at *Abuelita's* any more than I do now. I can't come between the two of you and your special cookie afternoons, now can I?"

Camila giggles as she shakes her head. "*Abuelita* always lets me get a cookie with candy inside it."

I chuckle. "That doesn't surprise me at all."

Chapter 17

ISABELLA

I've never been a woman who likes to kiss and tell. Personally, I feel that what happens in the bedroom should stay between the couple. No one needs to know specifics about orgasms, positions, or moves.

It makes no sense to me why I immediately call my sister Arianna, as soon as I get a moment alone, to gab about how amazing the sex was with Sebastian.

"Is this normal?" I whisper, hiding in the guest room closet. Sebastian's parents left soon after bringing Camila home, and Sebastian took Camila into the backyard to play. Butterscotch has made himself a comfortable bed out of a pile of shirts I never hung up, and Oreo sits hesitantly in the doorway of the closet. He got too close to Butterscotch, which resulted in a hiss and a smack to the face. I know they'll make friends eventually, but with cats, it takes time.

"Normal? I don't know if I'd call it normal," Arianna answers. "But I know what you're talking about. It's different, and oh so good. I'd never experienced anything like it until Stone. Definitely never ... finished the way I do with Stone."

"Finished?" I ask.

Arianna lowers her voice to a whisper. "Little ears are listening, Aunt Isabella. Think about it. Finishing."

Oh. *Oh.*

"I understand. Yes, the finishing was something new, and I discovered that what I thought about the caliber of the finisher was not correct."

"You can say the words, Belly. You're not on speaker. I'm just watching what I say, because I don't want to have to explain anything," Arianna explains with a laugh.

"Oh. Well, before last night, I'd come with a man before, but it wasn't anything like this. This was …" I trail off. How do I explain the feeling?

"Life-altering. Mind-blowing. Toes curling so much they almost pop out of their sockets. Like you finally met your match, and you've been rewarded a million times over. Did I ever tell you about the time Stone hid under my desk and ate me out while Hannah was at the door, talking to me?"

"No!" I exclaim with a giggle. Honestly, that doesn't surprise me. Arianna and Stone have a very vivid and explosive sex life. I know this, because she tells me all about some of their more unusual experiences. Sometimes in graphic detail.

"Yup. Hannah told me I should eat breakfast after Stone finished his, and then left the room laughing. Mom and Dad caught us in the office a couple of months later. They asked us to keep the shenanigans at home."

"Which you didn't do," I pointed out.

"No, we just bought a better lock for my office door. It's a little harder to get away with things at the barbershop, considering the front of the shop is a wall of windows, but we make it work. Those spinning chairs bring a new level of excitement to finishing."

"How is it you could say that Stone ate you out, but you can't talk about an orgasm?"

"Because my mini-me left the room for a minute to go get another toy, and now she's back. So I'll continue using synonyms unless you want me to move to pig Latin."

"We could talk about something different," I offer.

Arianna is silent for a moment. "No. This is too good. You never call me and want to talk about this stuff. Who do you talk to about relations with a man?"

"Relations with a man," I repeat. "I haven't really talked to anyone about this. I used to talk a little to Amelia, but clearly that isn't going to happen anymore."

"You never talked to anyone about men and relationships?" Arianna whispers. "How is that possible? I think I'd actually explode if I didn't get all of my feelings out."

I shrug, reaching out to scratch Oreo's head. "It's not news that we have differing personalities, Ari. I've never been one who needs to verbalize every thought. I take a while to wrap my head around things before I feel the need to talk. But this ... this is different, and I needed to confirm that it's okay, what happened between me and Sebastian."

"It's absolutely okay, Belly. I think in your case, you're finally comfortable with a man because you know he accepts you for who you are. You get to be you, and he gets to love you. I bet that's a new feeling for you, which is why you're so nervous about it. And, even though I doubt you'll admit it, you're falling in love with him, and you're scared things might change, or that he'll regret being with you. Which is dumb, because that man is so far gone for you."

It's rare, but sometimes my family can read me so quickly. No one, it seems, reads me like Sebastian can. "I am falling for him. It's scary, especially because of Camila. There are so many factors I have to take into consideration."

Arianna is silent, before her voice lowers into a hiss. "Who the fuck is Camila?"

"Arianna! Your daughter is right there!" I shout.

"Don't you dare try to redirect this conversation. Who is Camila? I swear to God, Isabella, if that man has another girlfriend, or an estranged wife, I will march over to that Clubhouse and cut his balls off myself."

"Camila is his daughter, Ari. Calm down."

"Sebastian has a daughter?" she yells. "How? When?"

"I'm fairly certain you know the how portion, since you have been pregnant. And Camila is five, so I'm guessing six years ago. Her mom isn't in the picture."

"Stone!" Arianna screams, and I hear Stone run into the room. "Why didn't you tell me Sebastian is a dad?"

"What the fuck?" I hear Stone say. "With whom?"

"That's what I'd like to know. How long have you known, Belly?"

"Uh, since I moved in with them?" I answer daringly.

"Why didn't you tell me?" she screeches.

"I assumed you knew! Stone and Sebastian are friends, for fuck's sake. I thought I was the only one who didn't know!"

"Why would you be the only one who didn't know?" Arianna asks.

"I don't know. Seems like I'm not 'in the know' with everyone because I don't have a husband," I admit woefully.

"But five years ago, when Seb's daughter was born, most of us weren't married or in relationships. We wouldn't have consciously hidden something like that from you."

"I think a lot of people forget about me. I'm quiet and reserved, I keep to myself, and I don't really fit in with the Santo mold."

"What exactly does that mean?" Arianna asks quietly, her voice dangerously even-toned.

I sigh. "Everyone in the family is average-sized or smaller. I'm not saying I'm less-than because of that. I'm stating a fact. I weigh more than everyone in the family. Even my skin is lighter than everyone else's. Half the time, it looks like I'm adopted."

"You have Mom's nose and Dad's eyes, Isabella. And your hair is so damn pretty. You've got these natural highlights that I covet, and the only reason I don't pay up the wazoo for them is because Stone does them for free."

"For free?"

"Well," she says with a breathy giggle, "we have an agreement. Highlights for blow jobs. Honestly, we both really win."

I find myself smiling. "I'm sure there is an inspirational quote in here somewhere. 'Marriage is about bartering and blow jobs.'"

"'Blowing marriage out of the water,'" she jokes.

"'Marriage: where one blow job fixes everything,'" Sebastian says from the doorway, and I scream as I instinctively throw my phone at him. He catches it easily, then bends down to scratch behind Oreo's ears. Handing my phone back to me, he raises an eyebrow. "You good?"

His expression is concerned, but the love emanating from him is palpable. I smile goofily as I nod. He leans in, wrapping a palm around my neck as he pulls my lips to his. I let out a breathy sigh as his tongue traces my lips, and only vaguely hear Arianna cat-calling us as Sebastian ends the kiss.

"Damn girl! Get a fucking room!" she whoops, and I look down to find Arianna gleefully smiling at me.

"How — what —" I stammer. How did we go from a phone call to video?

"I don't know, but I'm not sad about it. The chemistry you two just showed me? Holy hotness. Do I need to pay for that show?"

Sebastian chuckles as he looks down at the phone. "Free of charge *this* time, Mrs. Dixon." One quick kiss to my forehead as he leaves, but he looks back at the last second. "We'll discuss how you think you don't fit in with your family, baby. And I swear I wasn't eavesdropping. I came up to tell you Camila is downstairs coloring, and she asked if you'd join her."

I inhale sharply as he smiles, taps the door frame, then leaves. His daughter wants to color with me. With me, the woman she witnessed kissing her father this morning. What does this mean?

"Belly, you're spiraling. Take a breath," Arianna whispers.

Grabbing the phone, I bring it shakily up to my face. I stare at my sister in shock. "He kissed me in front of her this morning. This has to be incredibly confusing for her. She doesn't have any relationship with her birth mother. How the hell should I act? Do I take on the motherly role, or act like a friend? What if she wants details about our relationship?"

"She's five, Isabella. They don't want details. Kids are naturally self-involved. She'll just want to know how your relationship impacts her, and whether you make her dad happy or not. Oh, and if you can get her treats. Bianca hits Luca and Hannah up for candy every time she goes to their house, because she knows they always have Skittles."

"So you're saying I should give her Skittles?" I ask, my tone bordering on crazed as I stand up. Exiting the closet, I begin pacing. "I don't have Skittles. I don't think I have any candy at all! Would gum work? I might have some gum. Shit, my bag is downstairs. I can't check. I could make her cookies! That's the next best thing, right? Or cupcakes? I'm already fucking this up and I haven't even done anything yet!"

"Jesus Christ," Arianna mutters. "Listen. If you go downstairs and start talking about making cupcakes or cookies, she might think it's odd. Just walk downstairs and start coloring. Ask her about her day. What her favorite animal is, or things she likes to play when she goes outside. It isn't rocket science, Bells. You're overwhelmed right now, and definitely blowing this out of proportion, but it's pretty amazing how you're worried about his daughter's opinion of you."

"Of course I am, you brat, I can't marry him if she doesn't love me too," I snap, then gasp. Holy shit.

"Woah," Arianna breathes. "Man. When you fall, you go down

with a blaze of glory, don't you? Crap. Bianca just dropped her glass of milk. I have to go. Good luck!"

I don't register Arianna ending the call as I fall onto the bed, my phone dropping onto the bedding undetected. Until this very moment, I've been able to stay in the present with Sebastian. Why focus on a future that may not happen? Besides, every other man has realized, for one reason or another, that they don't want to be with me. I guess I assumed Sebastian would end up doing the same thing.

Unbeknownst to my conscious mind, my heart has been busy making plans. I knew I was in danger of falling for him. But I've stayed well out of the part of my brain that thinks about long-term relationships and marriage. I wasn't even sure if I wanted to be married and have kids. But Sebastian is slowly changing my hopes and dreams.

I take a handful of minutes to calm myself down before I leave the guest room. Up until now, I would have referred to it as 'my' room, but now things are different, and I'm hoping Sebastian wants me to sleep in his room. I don't know the etiquette of that though, and the only person I can contact about it is Kate. She lived with my brother Dominic before they married, but her circumstances were quite different than mine.

"Isabella! Are you coming to color?" Camila asks excitedly as I walk into the kitchen. Sebastian sits at the table with a laptop, and — oh my fucking God — he's wearing black-framed glasses. With his hair in slight disarray, and a white tee-shirt covering his ample chest, he looks so distractingly virile and masculine. I may have just come.

"*Amor*? Are you okay?" he asks, a smirk on his face. He knows exactly why I've lost the ability to speak. He probably doesn't even need glasses. "Close your mouth, sweetheart."

God dammit. I'm really sitting here ogling the man in front of his daughter. Slamming my mouth shut, I clear my throat as I take a seat next to Camila. "I'm here to color. What are you working on?"

Camila launches into a long and winding tale about her favorite animal, which spirals into her dislike of a specific Disney movie about a dog and a fox, then ends with her telling me her favorite color is blue, but specifically the Elsa blue. "Not the other blues. Just the Elsa one."

I do appreciate specifics.

"Can I ask you a question, Isabella?" Camila asks.

"Sure."

"Why are you living with us?"

Way to be direct and blunt, kiddo. "Well, your dad is worried about my safety, so he asked if I would stay here."

"Your safety?"

Sebastian closes his laptop and pushes it to the side. "There are some men who went into Isabella's apartment when they shouldn't have, and we aren't sure why. So it's safer for her to stay here right now. Plus I like having my favorite girls under the same roof."

"Daddy," Camila huffs, rubbing at a lock of hair that sits on her forehead. Without thinking, I reach over and brush it out of the way, tucking it behind her ear. "Thank you. Daddy didn't braid my hair today. *Abuelito* did, and he's awful at it."

I laugh. I'm sure my dad would also be pretty bad at it, if forced to braid anyone's hair. "I'm always braiding my own hair. Would you like me to take a go at yours?"

Camila's eyes widen. "Yes! Do you think you can do one called a fishing rod braid?"

I swallow a laugh. "I think you mean fishtail braid, and yes. That's one of my favorites. I do that all the time for work because I can't have my hair down while I'm baking."

Sebastian watches, his elbows on the table and one hand under his chin, as I take Camila's long hair in my hands. Her hair is absolutely gorgeous, and an exact shade match of his. I make small talk as I go through the steps for a fishtail braid. It's slightly different when braiding on the hair in front of me, instead of behind my own head, but I quickly get the hang of it.

As soon as I announce that I'm done, Camila jumps from her chair and runs to the bathroom to see how it looks. I hear her excited squeal, and she skips back to the table before launching herself into my arms. "Thank you! It looks so much better than what Daddy and *Abuelito* can do. Only *Abuelita* does as good on it. I wonder why? Do boys not have long hair ever?"

I laugh. "Some do. But most boys keep their hair short. I think it's up to the owner of the hair how they'd prefer to keep the length."

"I want to have hair down to my butt," she says excitedly.

"My hair used to be that long. But it's a lot of upkeep, and it got to be too much. This is the longest it's been in a few years." I take my own braid out, and run my fingers through my hair. I don't miss the obvious darkening of Sebastian's eyes as he stares wolfishly at me.

"You are both beautiful, no matter the length of your hair," he says, his voice husky as he takes us in. "It's time for me to start dinner. Which one of my girls wishes to help me?"

Camila sighs, crossing her arms over her chest as her bottom lip protrudes out in a pout. "*Abuelita* made me help her last night, and I didn't get any time on my tablet."

Sebastian chuckles. "You've got thirty minutes, *Mija*. Looks like Isabella wins by default."

"Yay!" Camila skips out of the room, jumping up each stair on the way to her room. I hear her door slam shut as I stand up.

"I actually enjoy cooking, so it's not a problem for —" Sebastian interrupts me by grabbing my hand, yanking me toward him, then pushes me against the nearest wall. His lips are on mine immediately, and I moan into his mouth. I lift one leg, trying to get it around his waist, and he helps by lifting the other leg, settling my core against his in the most perfect way. He kneads my ass with both hands as he kisses down my neck.

"How quiet can you be?" he murmurs as he lets his tongue dance across my collarbone.

"Sebastian!" I hiss. "Your daughter is upstairs!"

His head pops up. "I wasn't exactly expecting us to fuck in my kitchen right this minute, *mi Cielo*, but I like how you think. I was more asking about how quiet you might be tonight. If my memory serves me correctly, you were pretty loud last night."

"I was not that loud."

"Yeah, baby, you were. In fact, when you did that thing where you just had to show me you could do a backbend off the bed while I was inside you, you screamed so loud I bet the guys at the Clubhouse heard you," he teases, making me roll my eyes. "I'm just saying I doubt I'll be able to keep my hands to myself once we're in bed."

"I wasn't sure if you'd want me in your bed," I whisper, closing my eyes as I wait for his response.

"Eyes open, Isabella," he commands, and I immediately open them to find him staring intently at me. "Of course I fucking want you in my bed. I want you with me everywhere. If I could figure out how to move your bakery next to my bar, I'd do it, but I don't think that would be close enough. We're finally on the same page, and I've got years of unrequited love built up that I'm dying to let out. I will never want you in another room, another house, your old apartment, or across town. I. Want. You."

A smile breaks across my face so fast it hurts. "I don't want to be away from you either."

"So you're saying I can move your bakery?" he jokes.

"No, but you could move your bar. There's a rumor that the guy who owns the distillery a few doors down from mine wants to retire," I offer. "You could move, or open up a second location."

"That's actually not a bad idea. I'd get to expand, and see you every day for lunch."

"I usually work through lunch. The bakery is only open from seven to two."

His brows raise. "I didn't say anything about *you* eating. But if you're willing to lock the door for ten minutes, I could certainly eat."

"Sebastian!" I pause. "Only ten minutes?"

He leans in to kiss the tip of my nose. "Maybe fifteen, if you're a good girl."

Chapter 18

SEBASTIAN

I doubt Isabella thought I'd seriously consider opening up a second location just to be close to her, but I'd fired off a text to a commercial realtor within a few minutes after our conversation. Seeing her more often? Yes. Eating her out at lunch? Fuck yes. Keeping an eye on her now that I know her main employee is a couple cards shy of a whole deck? Absolutely.

Shit. I really need to tell her I own the bakery.

Isabella also mentioned Arianna has started visiting her more often at work, which makes me realize I definitely need to be closer. Arianna is wonderful, and she makes Stone happier than he ever thought possible. But if anyone could convince Isabella to set fire to the town square, my money is on Arianna.

Then again, the whole lot of the women in that circle are two degrees away from a felony. Alex's woman is an elementary school teacher, and she's the scariest of them all.

So when Isabella casually mentioned she'd be having her book club in the basement of the bakery, I sighed. My mom and grandmother are invited this month, and I've heard rumblings of previous events being a little bonkers. How chaotic can a bunch of women be when they're sitting around discussing books? My mind goes to classics from Shakespeare or Jane Austen, or maybe a book of poems. When I asked Isabella, she nonchalantly said, "I doubt you'll know the book."

Needless to say, my interest is peaked, and I plan on staking out the bakery in case I'm needed. I don't have to eavesdrop, because I know *Abuela* will give me a play-by-play. But it's probably good to stay in the area. My dad is taking Camila out to eat and then to a playground, so I know she's taken care of.

Doing a little recon of my own, I peruse the distillery a few doors down. The bones of the space are good, with rustic wood beams crossing the high ceiling, and dark paint on the walls. Picture frames highlight Eternity Springs events, as well as the famous people who are from here. Closing my eyes, I can visualize a mahogany bar, warm and cozy booths along the back wall, and tables along a wall of windows. What is now being used for storage of extra bar stools would be the perfect location for a dart board. I'm getting more excited the longer I sit here.

"I bet you're just here because of that damn book club," Alex says as he pulls up a stool next to me. A baby strapped to his chest, he smiles widely at me, and I notice how the pain that was always evident in his eyes has disappeared.

"That's one of the reasons, yeah. Plus my mom and grandmother are attending for the first time," I tell him.

His eyes widen comically. "You're letting your *Abuela* go to that shitshow? Damn, Seb. I thought the only senior citizen crazy enough to go was my *Nonna*."

I frown. "A shitshow? It's just a book club. How wild can they get?"

"You'd be surprised. Five or six months ago they had the cops called on them."

"No fucking way."

He nods. "Yup. Wives of a couple of guys I work with attend, and they managed to sweet-talk their way out of tickets and fines. Excessive noise and disorderly conduct."

"What the hell do they do there?" I ask incredulously. My Isabella, leading a book club so out of control the police have to intervene? The beautiful soul who only recently began to smile directly at me? "Is this really a different group, and they call it a book club to cover up something else entirely?"

"No, there's a book. Not sure if they read anything other than the sex scenes though," Alex says as I take a sip of my rum and Coke, and I immediately inhale, choke, gag, then cough up everything in my lungs.

"What the fuck?"

"It's romance books, Seb. And they usually have lots of wine and make some sort of phallic-shaped treat. Explaining the box of cock cookies to my kids was interesting, but now Nat knows to bring the treats directly to our bedroom when she gets home." He pauses. "Kinda weird eating food shaped like a dick though."

"Are we talking about the same book club? At the bakery? Isabella's bakery. *My* Isabella?"

He rolls his eyes. "Yes, *your* Isabella. She's not as tender and quiet as you think once she's comfortable around you. Stubborn as a mule with a petty and vindictive side that is quite long. Clearly you know that, considering what she did to her ex-boyfriend's apartment."

I chuckle. "That was pretty creative. I'll give her that."

"I try to stay close because usually at least a couple of the ladies require a ride home. The local rideshare drivers have caught on to their shenanigans, and they camp out all night as well. With around fifteen women each month, and the amount of alcohol they imbibe, it's good to have safe options. Usually I wait until the book club has been going for an hour or two, but this little dude," Alex says, smiling peacefully down at his son, "was getting restless. Car rides always seem to calm him down."

"Dude, I asked her about the book club, and she blew it off like it was nothing. Told me I wouldn't know who the author is."

"In her defense, she's right. Natalie showed me the book, and it's some romance author I'd never heard of."

I raise one eyebrow at Alex. "And you've heard of a lot of romance authors?"

"Some. Natalie talks about them. Plus there are two that live in Mountain Springs, where my cousin lives, and they've both come up here to be special guests at the book club." Alex peers down at his son, who gives me a gummy grin. "Best part is when Natalie comes home, she almost always wants to reenact at least one of the spicy scenes. So I'm all for this off-the-rails book club."

Alex's phone chimes with a text, and his face falls. "Shit. We gotta go. Nat just texted me the code word."

"Code word?" I ask, draining the last sliver of whiskey before throwing a twenty on the bar for a tip.

"If she texts me 'sausage,' it means it's gotten too out of control, and we need to step in before the cops get called again. The new lieutenant isn't a fan of my family, and he's looking to set an example."

"Why your family?"

"Evidently his dad had a thing for my mom, but my dad stole her away from him. Then my damn *Nonna* got involved and said some less than stellar things about the lieutenant's family. It was a whole big thing, and now he makes my work day hell, but it is what it is."

"That's fucked up," I comment as I follow him out of the bar.

"It is. But I know it's temporary. He'll either be fired, or I'll quit. I've been talking to Leo about possibly starting a business together. But he's been pretty quiet about things since his injury, so I'm just playing it day by day."

The code word suddenly sinks in. "Sausage? Really?"

Alex grins. "My wife loves a double entendre."

I count the number of steps it takes me to get from the door of the bar to Isabella's door, and I'm pleased to find it's twenty-two steps. Should she ever need me, I could be here in less than a minute. Alex bypasses the front door, heading to a side door I've never even noticed. "This is the way to the basement."

Fucking hell. I've been trying to keep her safe and I never noticed a goddamned door here. Trace has told me about the door, but I rarely walk past the tight alleyway between buildings, and hadn't noticed the dilapidated entrance.

I hear the noise even with the door closed, then laugh when Alex yanks his bag from around his shoulders, opens it up, and pulls out a set of noise-canceling headphones. Placing them on his son's head, he then opens the door. Smart.

Heading down the rickety old stairs into a dingy basement, I'm surprised to find around twenty women in varying stages of undress. My grandmother is standing on a stool, swinging what appears to be a piece of black licorice above her head. My mother sits with Isabella's mom, and they're both crying.

Guarantee they're planning our wedding, which makes me smile.

Isabella's two sisters have their arms around one another as they belt out an off-key rendition of a Taylor Swift song, and her three sisters-in-law are throwing marshmallows at each other, attempting to catch them in their mouths. A woman I don't recognize has removed her shirt, and another seems to be missing pants. That's when I notice my grandmother is wearing two different shoes.

"My baby!" I hear shouted, and Natalie wobbles over to snatch her son out of Alex's arms. She leans toward both of us. "I figured you were close by. I'm sorry. Someone pulled out a bottle of Hooch and it went downhill fast." She hiccups, then giggles as she buries her head in Alex's chest. He smiles down at her, and I can see how utterly besotted he is with his wife.

"Sebastian? What are you doing here?" Isabella asks, coming out from underneath the stairs. Her hair is in disarray, and the near constant dusting of flour is evident on her cheek. I step around the other women quickly, needing to be next to *my* woman.

I want to kiss her. I feel like I have to kiss her.

Fuck it.

Sliding a hand into her hair and one around her waist, I tip her slightly as I capture her lips with my own. I love how she sighs into my mouth every time, like she's remembering once again how spectacular our kisses are and she's so thrilled to re-live them. The sugared vanilla scent is more potent tonight, mixed with a subtle hint of cherry. Forcing her lips apart with my tongue, the tanginess of cherry bursts onto my tastebuds, and I break the kiss to ask her what it is.

"Cherry for the candy we made," she whispers breathlessly, and I finally detect her hands wrapped around my neck, her fingers playing with my hair. Staring into her eyes, I feel like I'm finally experiencing the real Isabella.

Wanting to tease her a bit, I say, "Oh? Can I have some? I'd love to try it. I didn't know you made candy too."

The panic-stricken expression that covers her face is comical. "Oh, um, they aren't ready yet. They have to cool. And we only made enough for everyone to take home a portion."

"Oh. Then I'll wait until you bring home your portion." I raise my eyebrows as I smile innocently at her.

"I don't bring things home myself," she stammers. "I eat so many sweets here that I never bring them home."

I lean in and smile. "Liar."

Her eyes dart behind me to see Alex, and he throws me under the bus. "He knows you make dick shit for this disaster of a book club."

Isabella lets out a sound of indignation as she steps back from me and slaps my arm lightly. "You jerk! How long were you going to let me go before you told me the truth?"

"Probably about the same amount of time until you told me the truth about this book club. I thought it was some boring meeting where you discussed a classical fiction novel. Now I know you're actually discussing some good old fashioned cliterature. Tell me, baby, did you have a favorite scene from this month's book that you'd like to recreate at home? I'm all for promoting reading."

A slow smile spreads across her face as she bites her lower lip. "I may have a favorite scene, but it involves a knife, so I think maybe you won't be interested. Although I'm more aggravated about the possibility of ruining a mattress than the actual knife."

I stare at her as she watches me, her eyes sparkling. "I may need some clarification. There's a sex scene with a knife? Ruining a mattress, I understand. Is there actual stabbing with the knife? Will one of us bleed? I'm pretty partial to all of my limbs."

"The mattress gets ruined because of the knife, not because of the sex. Does that make sense?"

"No," I reply slowly. "Who is this author? Are we sure it's a romance book? This sounds like a thriller."

"Well, there are some deaths, and the mafia is involved, but yeah, it's a romance book."

"Author, Isabella."

She sighs. "Navessa Allen. The book is called *Lights Out*."

Pulling it up on Amazon, I say, "Oh, there's an audiobook? I like that even better."

"The audiobook is phenomenal. And there's a cat. But I really think you may want to read a different book. This one is ... dark." Isabella looks at me tentatively, and I can read the nerves on her face. I slide my hand around her waist, palming her ass as I pull her toward me.

"I want to read what *you* read, baby. And now I need to know how the mattress gets ruined by a sex knife."

She bursts out laughing, throwing her head back. I love this side of Isabella, the carefree woman who trusts me enough to show me her real self. "I don't think I can view that scene the same now, knowing it's a sex knife."

"I'll let you know what I think of it, once I get to the scene," I murmur, leaning in to peck her lips with a quick kiss. "So how does this shindig end? Do you have to kick everyone out? Anyone we need to drive home?"

"Oh, I assumed I'd get a ride with someone, or get an Uber," she answers.

I shake my head. "Why do you think I'm here? I'm perfectly capable of taking my woman home, and I can drive anyone else that needs a ride."

Her lips twitch with a cute smile. "You really are a sweet man underneath this bad boy exterior, aren't you?"

"Do you like the exterior, *mi Cielo*?" Leaning in, I whisper in her ear. "I can be a bad boy too, if that's what you'd like."

Before she can respond, a woman I've never seen before tentatively walks up to us. "Hi, Isabella, I wanted to thank you for allowing me to crash your book club this month. I heard you say you might need a ride. I'm heading out of town to my boyfriend's, so I can take you."

The hair stands on the back of my neck. I know this woman, but I can't remember how. A few inches shorter than Isabella, she has curly blond hair that ends at her shoulders, and hazel eyes that keep darting to me. Her posture is stiff and jerky, like she's ready to make a run for it if needed. Extending my hand, I say, "Hi, I'm Sebastian, Isabella's man. I'll be driving her home. What did you say your name is?"

"Oh, um," she stammers, before hesitantly placing her hand in mine, "I'm Jenna."

Her name is not Jenna, that I know. I dated a Jenna in high school, and I'd definitely remember her name. How do I know this woman?

"Thanks for coming, Jenna," Isabella says warmly. "As you can tell, we get a little rowdy for the Triple C Club."

"Triple C?" I ask, trying to think of what CCC might mean. I groan as I realize it. "The Cocks and Cookies Club."

"How'd you figure that out so quickly?" Isabella asks.

I tap her temple. "Because I know how your mind works."

"None of my brothers have guessed it," she muses, making me snort.

"I bet they know, and they've chosen not to bring it up. I've got sisters, and I'd never utter the word 'cock' in front of them."

A few ladies call out their goodbyes from the doorway, and Jenna hastily makes her exit. Pulling out my phone, I text Trace a description of her, then ask that he see if he can catch her at the outskirts of town. If she truly does live outside of Eternity Springs, I want to know where, and I want to know how she found out about this underground cock cookie club.

"What do you need help with?" I ask Isabella as she begins collecting empty plates.

"I don't leave anything down here. I'm scared even a crumb will attract rodents." She shivers. "I don't do mice."

"Good to know. Is there a way upstairs without going through that alley from here?"

"Yeah, but it's more like a pulley system. It's not a full staircase. It's big enough for me to get through, though, because one time a snow squall came through, and I needed to get a big bag of flour. I refused to go outside."

"And the exterior door has a good locking system?" I ask.

"A lock and a deadbolt. Should I add more?" Isabella inquires.

I try to keep my expression and voice calm. "I'm being overprotective. I have to have guarantees you're safe, sweetheart. Now that I finally have you, I have to make sure."

"Okay, weirdo," she mutters. "I think my dungeon is safe from criminals. If they feel the need to steal a fifty-pound bag of sugar, they can have at it."

That's not what I'm concerned about.

Chapter 19

ISABELLA

Sebastian is oddly quiet on the drive back to his house. I've begun referring to it as a compound, because the entrance to the Clubhouse is the same as his driveway, and there are always cars coming and going.

"Are you okay?" I ask quietly.

He looks over at me. "Yeah. I'm thinking about what you make for your book club. Does it get boring making cookies shaped like dicks over and over again?"

I giggle. "We don't make them all the time. We make other equally raunchy items, but most are dicks."

"What could you make ..." he mumbles, trailing off as he taps a finger to his chin. "What did you make today?"

"Cockers."

His mouth drops open. "Clearly not the dog breed. A cocker? Alright. Has to be a play on words. Cock plus something that ends in -er. Holy hell, Isabella. Did you make cock-shaped lollipops?"

I nod enthusiastically. "Yup. Cock plus sucker equals cockers."

He shakes his head as he chuckles. "How do you make those?"

"Well, I commissioned someone with a 3D printer to create molds so we could have cock-shaped candy. There was something lost in translation when they arrived, because the molds were much bigger than I'd anticipated —"

"If I had a nickel for every time I've heard that before," he interrupts, deadpan, making me laugh.

"Well, the guy reprinted them the size I expected, but he told me to keep the molds."

"Yeah, I doubt a guy would have much use for a dozen dick molds."

"It was twenty molds, but yes, I agree."

"Did you use the bigger molds or the smaller ones for the cockers?"

"The bigger ones. No one wants a one inch cocker, Sebastian. You should know that," I tease.

He chortles. "As you know by now, I don't hear about one inch cocks at all. I'm clearly blessed in the cock department."

That he is. I'm routinely doing measurement assessments as I bake, and I'd put Sebastian at a very healthy eight inches. "So far, I have no complaints."

"So far! Damn, woman. That's cold."

Feeling emboldened, I reach over and lay my hand in his lap. "Feels pretty warm to me."

"Jesus Christ," he mutters, but his hand covers mine as he presses down. I feel his length grow, and I try to run my fingers along the zipper of his jeans, but he stops me. "I have no problem pulling this truck over and fucking you against the door, so be careful how much you want to push me. All I know is I've dreamed about having your hands on me for so long, and now that it's happening, all the blood is rushing to my dick, and black spots are dancing in my vision. I'd really like to get us home in one piece."

I'm way too excited about the prospect of Sebastian needing me so badly that he takes me on the side of the road. I've never had a man want me like that. The thought makes me whimper. "What if I said yes? What if I need you so badly that I can't wait?"

He groans, the sound guttural and full of the same tension I'm feeling. It reverberates around the cab of his truck, and I feel it in my soul. "The only reason I won't is because I don't want another person on this entire planet to see you come. But as soon as Camila is asleep, I plan to improve my numbers on the orgasm count."

I inhale sharply. The three in a row he gave me last night made my legs shake, and every time after that, I wouldn't let him push me past one. Still, I came six times in twelve hours. Six. Times. Sebastian seems to think that number is low, whereas I know it's the most I've had in one night ever.

We're both quiet as we continue the drive, but I notice Sebastian increases the speed. My hand doesn't move until we turn into his driveway, and he gives me a look like he's pouting, making me laugh. "Relax, big boy. You need to calm down before you see your daughter. By the way, your grandmother is a hoot. I'm so glad she and your mom came tonight."

"Might have been a good idea to brief her beforehand so they knew what they were walking into," he mutters.

"Oh, they knew."

His eyes whip to mine. "The fuck? They knew?"

I nod. "My grandmother invited them, and told them all about it. That made them even more excited to come."

Sebastian sighs loudly as he swipes a hand over his face. "Do me a favor. Never again utter the words 'excited' and 'come' in a conversation about your cock cookie club and my grandmother."

On that note, he parks the car, turns it off, and jumps out. Jogging over to the passenger side, he opens the door with gusto before taking my hand and helping me down. I'm immediately pushed against the side as he covers my mouth with his. God, this man can *kiss*. He's able to weave a story with his mouth, like he's making love to me with his tongue. So much for him calming down before we go inside, since I'm trying to climb him like a tree and shamelessly dry humping him for anyone to see.

When we break apart, we're both breathless. He gives me a lopsided smile as his hooded eyes stare at my lips. "You can call me big boy anytime."

"Of course that's what you'd focus on. Such a typical man," I tell him, a teasing tone to my decidedly husky voice. Sebastian's grin grows bigger, and he closes his eyes as he takes two steps backward. I watch, intrigued, as he silently mutters something over and over again. "Are you trying the Luca thing of saying old man balls?"

"Yup."

"Is it working?"

"Nope."

"Maybe think about specific old man balls. Your dad's balls? Wait!" I whisper-shout. "*My* dad's balls. Nick Santo old man balls."

"Fucking hell," he mutters. "That worked like a goddamned charm."

"I'll have to remember that for the next time I tease you in public," I say cheerfully as I skip past him, but he wraps an arm around my waist, pulling me against his chest.

"You should know that I'm fine with the teasing, as long as I get to tease you right back."

Game fucking on.

CCC

When Isabella Santo began hosting her romance book club, many Eternity Springs residents were thrilled at another opportunity for an extracurricular activity. Now well into its second year, there is an ample waiting list to attend, as over half the membership consists of Santo family members. Recently, I became aware of the name of the book club, and suffice it to say, I was gobsmacked.

The second and third C's stand for Cookie and Club. I'll let you, dear reader, guess on the first C. At every event, Isabella excitedly shares a baked good or sugary treat. They all have a theme, and they're all shaped a certain way.

I immediately put my name on the waiting list.

Me: How does this damn website get information so fast?

Arianna: No clue. I'm beginning to think it's someone extremely close to our family.

Hannah: It really has to be. Who else would know the personal details about all of our relationships?

Kate: What if it's someone IN the family?

Me: No. Right? It couldn't be. Some of the things the articles have insinuated were pretty nasty. I can't imagine anyone in our family doing this.

Arianna: I don't know. My spidey senses are tingling.

Hannah: If that's happening, you aren't using the vibrator right. Jeez, Ari. Get it together.

MUCH TO SEBASTIAN'S DISMAY, CAMILA HAD A ROUGH EVENING, MEANING his hope of sex right away was dashed. Maybe it's a woman's intuition thing, but I quietly told Sebastian I thought she might be coming down with something. I remember Arianna when she was so sick as a child, and there was always a way her eyes would look when she came down with a virus. I suggested popping Camila in a bath, which he did. She requested cuddles while reading some books, and when I checked on them an hour later, they were both asleep in Camila's twin-size bed. I quietly took out my phone for a picture, then covered them both up. Tiptoeing out of the room, I decide to take a relaxing bath myself. I haven't yet used the rose bubble bath Sebastian got me, and it's calling my name.

As soon as he learned I love baths, tons of products arrived. Epsom salts in every scent imaginable, and gallons of bubble bath. Battery operated candles for 'mood lighting,' he explained, as well as a Bluetooth speaker so I can play calming music without having to keep my phone next to me. Is there a love language for taking care of a partner? Because Sebastian thrives when he's taking care of someone, and I'm all too thrilled it's currently me. I've never had a man devote this much time and energy in a relationship. He's learned my favorite kind of coffee, how I make it at home, and how I like my eggs. He knows I sing Taylor Swift when I'm happy, but switch to Sara Bareilles when I'm in a more subdued or depressed mood. I've learned that I shouldn't interrupt him on the rare visit from one of his MC guys, and that he can't stand eggs by themselves.

This relationship is new, but it also feels like I've been dating him for an incredibly long time. Maybe it's because I've known him for years, and we've always been destined to be together. Whatever the reason, I know I'm the happiest I've ever been.

I undress as the tub fills up, and the scent of roses overtakes the bathroom air. I slip beneath the bubbles and let out a sigh of contentment. Baking every day is hard on a body, and this bath was desperately needed. It's only a few minutes later before Sebastian shuffles into the bathroom, sleepy-eyed and adorable with his hair sticking up in every direction.

"I guess I'm more tired than I thought," he murmurs, then yawns. "I really want to join you, though."

"Baths are relaxing, but I know if you join me, you will not be relaxing," I tell him with a soft smile. His gaze rakes down my body, as if he can see through the bubbles, and the bulge in his plaid pajama pants grows.

"It would be worth it." He yawns again.

"Go get into bed, Seb. I'll be in later."

He nods absentmindedly as he turns back toward the bedroom, before he looks over his shoulder. "I know I've mentioned it before, but I like you calling me Seb."

I smile tenderly. "I know."

"You've always called me Sebastian, and it used to irritate me. It was like your way of letting me know you wanted nothing to do with me. But then I liked it because you're basically the only person who calls me by my full name all the time, so it became special to me."

Just when I think I have this man figured out, he throws a curveball at me. "Do you want me to stop calling you Seb? Since everyone else calls you that?"

He thinks for a moment, his eyes losing focus as he stares beyond me. "No, I like it too. But don't stop calling me Sebastian. I'd be okay if you call me baby, too. No one has ever called me that. Or *Papi*."

"Your mom calls you baby in Spanish," I remind him.

"That's different. I am literally her baby. Besides, it's you, so it's very different."

"How so?"

He looks directly at me with a look so intense it makes my breath catch in my chest, and my heart rate increases quickly. He studies me for a minute before finally speaking. "It's different because you're my forever."

I'm at a loss for words as he walks out of the bathroom, quietly closing the door behind him.

NOT TOO MUCH LATER, I EXIT THE EN SUITE FEELING RELAXED AND PRUNY. The only light Sebastian left on is the one by my side of the bed. I watch him as I cross the room, noting the slow way his chest rises and falls. He's already asleep, and I'm able to study him. Sebastian is without a doubt the most beautiful man I've ever seen. All put together, with his hair slicked back and his beard trimmed perfectly, he's gorgeous. But this Sebastian, with hair in disarray and one arm slung haphazardly over his head, he's breathtaking. He said he didn't want anyone else to ever see me come, which I understand, because I never want anyone to see that either. But this version of Sebastian is so perfect, so exquisite, that I believe I would cut someone if they experienced it. This view is just for me.

I carefully climb into bed, after turning out the light, and hope I don't wake Sebastian up. It's moot, because the moment I settle my head onto the pillow, an arm clamps around my midsection, and I'm yanked into the middle of the bed, where Sebastian is the big spoon to my little spoon. He buries his head in my hair and lets out a sigh of contentment. I relax into his embrace, falling asleep almost instantly. I only vaguely remember hearing him whisper, "God, how I love you."

UNFORTUNATELY, I WAS RIGHT ABOUT CAMILA. IN THE MIDDLE OF THE night, the pitter-patter of tiny feet woke me up. I opened my eyes to find her pitiful face. "I frew up."

"Oh, baby," I coo, chucking the comforter as I get to my feet.

The smell hits me once I'm standing beside her. "I think you need another bath."

She sniffles as she nods. "I didn't make it to the potty."

I follow Camila into her room, stopping on a dime when I realize Sebastian is still in bed. She came to me.

The aroma of fresh vomit permeates the air, and I quickly open her two windows. I motion for her to go into the attached Jack-and-Jill bathroom. "Go get undressed while I strip your bed." I don't usually do well with vomit, but this is Camila. She needs me.

Turning on the light, I survey the damage. Holy hell. It looks like an exorcism took place in here. How she got the puke on the wall six feet from her bed will be something she takes to the grave, because I'm not asking for a story. I gasp when I see her favorite unicorn plushy is soiled, knowing Camila cuddles with it every night. Poor girl. The vomiting probably woke her up from a dead sleep.

I quickly strip the bed, wad everything into a pile, and drop it into the hallway. I hear Camila calling me, and as I step into the bathroom, she vomits again. I softly stroke her back as she gets it all out, then usher her into the shower. "Why did I frew up?"

Could it be any cuter how she pronounces that? "It's throw up, honey. And it means there are germs in your tummy that your body wants to get out of there as quickly as it can. Your tummy will be back to normal soon."

Her disgruntled expression makes me hide a smile. "Well, I don't like frowing up. And I got it on my unicorn. How am I gonna sleep without her?"

Tears immediately start, and a horrifying wail leaves her mouth. A moment later, Sebastian runs into the bathroom. "What happened?"

"She threw up." I tilt a cup I found on the shelf, onto the back of her head. Camila quiets down as I begin to slowly shampoo her hair. "I've stripped the bed, but it needs new sheets. Also the wall across from the bed needs to be cleaned. We need to check the carpet between the wall and bed as well."

"Violent puking runs in my family." Sebastian says it so matter-of-factly that I let out a laugh. "I'm serious. I thought it was just a me thing, but she does it too. It's like that scene from *The Exorcist*."

"Daddy, I don't like frowing up, but Isabella shampoos my hair so much better than you," Camila says clearly, her eyes closed as my fingers massage her scalp. Sebastian lets out a laugh.

"I'll handle the bed. You get our girl all cleaned up," he says. When my head whips around to stare at him, he gives me a sly smirk and a wink before tapping on the door frame as he walks out.

Our girl.

Sebastian Garcia has a way of leaving me speechless.

Chapter 20

SEBASTIAN

"Her name is Berkley St. James. She's from a very wealthy family in Boulder, but she's gotten mixed up with a rough crowd. Probably due to boredom if I had to guess," Trace tells me the following morning about the girl who claimed her name was Jenna at the book club last night. Trace wouldn't even talk about it until he'd walked around the office at my bar with a weird contraption that looked like a walkie talkie, but with a swirled wire on the top. When I asked what it was, and how much it cost, his response was, "It's scanning the room for listening devices or cameras. Basically anything that emits a wireless signal. And since it's not technically on the market for regular consumers to purchase, you probably don't want to know the price."

I probably don't.

I stare bleakly at him as I yawn and rub a hand over my beard. Camila threw up three more times overnight, and only one of those times did she make it to the toilet. It was a pleasant surprise to see how Isabella jumped into action, never shying away from my daughter with her projectile abilities. What shocked me to my core was how Camila gravitated toward Isabella.

I thought maybe Camila had tried to wake me up, and that maybe I was in a deep sleep. When I asked her, she said, "Daddy, I don't have to wake you every time I frow up now, cuz Isabella is here."

I'm not complaining about her connecting with Isabella by any means, but I certainly didn't think it would happen so quickly.

And with puke.

Whatever the case, Isabella decided to stay home from work today, leaving the bakery in the hands of her psychotic employee, Ava. She's made comments to Trace about taking a ride on his Harley, but with the suggestive undertones and the nonstop winking, clearly she has a different ride in mind. Trace is legitimately scared of her, using the very evident age difference as the main reason he plans to stay away from Ava.

So, when I left this morning to meet my guys at the Clubhouse and then head to my bar, Isabella and Camila were cuddled up in our bed, sound asleep and holding hands. I snapped a picture and made it my phone background. It's everything I have ever wanted in one picture.

Knowing my girls are safe in our home, I'm finally able to fully focus on tracking down the douchebags who had the nerve to come after Isabella. "Does Berkley have a connection to Isabella's ex?"

Trace shakes his head. "Nothing that I can find so far, but she's got connections with a known drug trafficking ring that has ties to the Salazar Cartel in Mexico. These dumbass white kids who grew up wealthy want to experience life on the wild side, so they get involved with drug distribution. Berkley does have a connection to that jackass Devon, who broke into Isabella's apartment."

Blood boiling, I grab onto the edge of the bar, tightly squeezing it until my knuckles turn white. I shook that woman's hand. She infiltrated the book club and I had no idea. "So you're saying Isabella's ex-boyfriend was distributing drugs, although we don't know what kind —"

"Fentanyl, probably," Trace interrupts.

"And he told his drug buddies that she took the drugs, and they go after her. Then, when they still don't find anything, they send in a woman to scope things out at a book club, while none of us have a fucking clue. Jesus Christ. How the hell am I supposed to protect her if I don't even know what — or who — is coming?"

Trace smiles bitterly. "I think we've reached the end of our abilities here, Prez. We keep things by-the-book in Range Riders, and anything from this point on begins to fall in a gray area. If you want to move forward, we need to bring in authorities. If you want to continue without anyone else, we at least need to bring it to a vote at Church. Some of these guys have families, and they deserve the right to step aside."

I nod. "I don't want to do anything that jeopardizes our guys. The whole point of RMRRMC is to provide a place where veterans find consistency, healing, and comfort. I'm not fucking with that. Who do I need to call?"

"I'd start with the Colorado Bureau of Investigation and the DEA. They'll tell you what we need to do. Knowing how the Salazar Cartel operates, I'd definitely be careful who you talk to, and only make phone calls when you know no one is eavesdropping. I'll give you the scanner that detects any devices."

I let out an aggravated breath as Trace exits my office. It's not that I don't want to involve authorities, but I hate when I can't control the entire narrative. It's especially concerning because this impacts Isabella. And if something happens to her because some dipshit junior officer in the FBI decides to have a pissing contest with me, I will not be judged for how I choose to react. An eye for a fucking eye.

Before I can make any calls, I know I need to explain everything I've uncovered with Isabella and her family. I pick up my phone, and close my eyes as I wait for her to answer.

"Hey you," she says quietly.

"Hi, baby."

"You okay?"

"Why?" I ask with a chuckle.

"You don't normally call in the middle of the day. You've been known to text, but calling is unusual. And your voice is different. I have to assume it has to deal with me," she answers hesitantly.

"It does," I say simply. "I think it's time we have dinner with your family."

I'M NOT SURPRISED WHEN WE ARE PULLING ONTO THE STREET OF Isabella's childhood home to find virtually no parking, because every one of her siblings is already here. Our family dinner is the day after Trace and I realized the connection to drugs is worse than we feared.

Isabella's brother Leo waits at the top of the driveway, his posture stiff as he casts wary glances all around. He motions for us to park on the driveway, like they saved this spot for us. The guests of honor. Or maybe I'm the grim reaper, about to deliver some really bad news.

"Are you sure it's okay that we came?" My mom asks.

"Of course, *Abuelita*. Everyone loves you," Camila answers matter-of-factly. I glance in the rearview mirror of my parents' SUV, and find my daughter dancing in her booster seat. *Abuela* is next to her, with my parents in the third row. It's not ideal, but it got everyone here.

Isabella looks over at me nervously. Reaching over to her, I cup her face. "It's going to be fine, *Naranja*."

She smiles, but it's a strained pursing of the lips with no

sparkle in her eyes. She pulls on the hem of her shirt nervously as we unbuckle our seatbelts and exit the vehicle.

Leo walks up to me, his gait off, as he seems to only put his weight onto his right foot. I know his convoy hit an IED overseas, and he was injured, but he's never gone into detail about what happened. Knowing what I do about veterans, I can tell he has a significant leg injury, most likely to his left leg. Both arms appear to have scars scattered haphazardly across his flesh, most likely from shrapnel, but his face doesn't appear to have any lasting injuries. His eyes, however, tell me a different story. The pain I can see tells me he has trauma and guilt built up so much he probably can't see the top.

"You need to tell me right now what we're dealing with. Before we go in. I have to know what I need to do, and who I need to call," Leo says aggressively. It's possible this is triggering for him, as his posture is tightly wound, like he's expecting an attack at any moment.

"I would rather tell you all at the same time," I answer gently. He's like a spooked deer, and I'm trying to get him inside before he throws himself into oncoming traffic. "I have multiple sources I plan to contact, and I'm more than happy to go over them with you. But for now, let's go inside."

"But —" he starts, before Isabella interrupts him.

"I love that you're all riled up for me, Leo, but let's hear what Sebastian has to say before we jump to conclusions." She rubs her hand along his arm reassuringly.

"Excuse me," Camila says, coming to stand between the three of us. Leo looks down with surprise. "I need to use the bathroom."

"Uh, okay?"

"I'm Camila."

"I'm Leo."

"Oh. You're very tall, Uncle Leo."

Leo's eyes bounce between the three of us. "I didn't say — I mean, I — what the hell is happening right now?"

Isabella smothers a laugh. "Leo, this is Sebastian's daughter, Camila. She's five. She demanded that we also bring her grandparents and great grandmother, so it's a full house tonight."

Leo looks to me. "Anyone else in the car? Are you part of a clown circus, and siblings will start falling out of there?"

"No, my two sisters moved out of town. One is up in Loveland, and the other is in New Mexico. This is it. I can call my MC Club guys, if you want to have more people attend," I volunteer, pulling my phone from my pocket.

"No, we're good. Although I've been told I should talk to you about that club of yours," he says, scratching the back of his head.

"I'll give you my number before we leave. You call whenever you're ready to talk."

Leo nods, then motions for us to walk down the sidewalk to the front door. "Oh, Bells, in case you forgot —"

"Shit," Isabella grumbles.

"Daddy, we need a swear jar. I heard about it at school. Why is everyone waiting at the door?"

I look up and find thirteen adults and a handful of children staring expectantly at us. "I'm not sure, *Mija.*"

Isabella grabs my hand. "Has anyone ever told you about the stupid threshold thing that Alex made up?"

I struggle to keep my expression nonchalant. "That's real? I thought it was an urban legend."

"It sort of was, until everyone failed it. Then suddenly one by one, everyone sailed right through. So it's a big thing, and they're expecting us to do it now."

"I'm sure it'll be fine, *Naranja.* I can carry you perfectly well."

She looks toward the sky and sighs. "I have to carry you."

"Who is carrying someone?" *Abuela* asks loudly.

"Rosario? Is that you?" I hear shouted from the Santo family.

"Annamaria! We finally got them together!" A loud cackle sounds from both women as my grandmother shoves me aside to shuffle over to her octogenarian friend. They link arms and slowly walk into the house, obviously done with whatever embarrassment is going on here.

"Let's get this over with," Isabella mutters.

"What exactly is going on here?" My mom asks. Isabella turns to her and quickly explains.

"My brother Alex came up with this stupid tradition where we have to carry our partner across the threshold of our childhood home. It was funny, until everyone failed the task, even Alex with his first wife. Then suddenly, everyone started passing it, and the silly tradition became lore. If we've found the person we're supposed to be with, we'll be able to carry them across the threshold."

"And you've done this before?" I ask. I know the answer, but want to hear it from her perspective.

Isabella nods, and I hear my own teeth grinding. She explains, "I tried with my high school boyfriend, but I fell. Then the first time I brought my college boyfriend over, we attempted to explain it, and he freaked out. Bolted before I could even try. Since then, I haven't bothered."

"So you didn't try with Rick the Dick?" I blurt out, making Isabella laugh.

"No, I didn't try with him. There's been no one worthy of the task. That is, until ..." she trails off, looking up at me hopefully.

I take her head in my hands, cradling it gently, as I bend to give her a sweet kiss. Resting my forehead against hers, I breathe her in.

Isabella sighs softly. "Until you."

I hear a couple women whisper how cute we are, then one of her brothers grumble about 'getting this show on the road.' Probably Dominic. He's basically the most likely of the bunch to be an asshole.

"Alright," I say, clapping my hands together and looking at Isabella. "You ready?"

"Ready as I'll ever be. Camila, don't you need to go potty?" Isabella asks, and Camila gives her a smile.

"I don't anymore. Are there kids here? Do they have pets? When can I call you Mommy? I'm hungry. Can you do the fweshold thing so we can eat?" Camila chatters on, completely unaware of how she just rocked Isabella.

"Oh, yeah," Dominic says casually. "Sebastian has a daughter."

I see Isabella's mom kneel down, beckoning Camila to come to her. She whispers quietly to Camila, then takes her hand and walks her inside. Meanwhile, Isabella is silently crying.

"Baby, talk to me," I whisper. "Good or bad tears?"

"Happy tears, I promise," she stammers. "Is it okay that I think I fell for your daughter before I let myself fall for you?"

My heart bursts wide open as I pull her into my embrace. "I wouldn't have it any other way."

"Alright, let's go. The food is getting cold." That was definitely Nick Santo, the patriarch of the family. He has whatever the male version of resting bitch face is, and his current frown is rivaling that constant expression from the Jeff Dunham character, Walter.

"You ready?" I ask my girl, and she nods. "How do we do this?"

"So far, the girls have carried best in a piggyback stance."

God. I outweigh Isabella by at least fifty pounds, and I've got six or seven inches in height. "Are we allowed to be right next to the door so you really only have to take one step?"

"Yes, but if you fall back out of the doorway, it doesn't count. I'd prefer to get a few steps in before I drop you," she teases.

"Can you try to not drop me?" I murmur.

"I'll do my best."

Standing behind Isabella, I watch as she moves her hair over one shoulder, and I notice what appears to be the corner of a piece of Saniderm, the bandage that is used to cover new tattoos. I've studied every inch of this body, and there isn't one speck of ink anywhere. Touching the corner, I whisper, "You got something for me, didn't you?"

I see her gulp as she nods. "You and Camila."

I groan. "Goddamn, baby. I can't get hard right now."

"You didn't have to ask me about it!" she hisses, as I wrap my arms around her shoulders, linking them at the base of her throat. "Give me a knee. You have a tattoo for me, so I figured it was only fair that I do one for you. Other knee. Honestly, I kind of loved it, and now I want to get a lot more. Is that normal?"

"Yup, totally normal," I answer. "How do you think I got all of these? But when did this happen? Today, when you said you were at Arianna's?"

We're slowly moving into the house, but Isabella doesn't stop. "Yes. I'm sorry for lying, but I wanted to surprise you. And all of your tattoos have meaning. They're poetic. I want mine to be too."

The closer we get to the living room, the more I'm wondering what the tattoo is. Pulling at her shirt, I'm able to maneuver it to uncover the shoulder tattoo. It's an outlined circle, with half in script so small I can't read it. "Is that an orange?"

"Yes."

Holy fucking shit.

Forcing my legs out of her hands, I drop to the ground. Hands on her shoulders, I whirl her around. "Did you get an orange for me? Because I call you *Naranja*?"

She nods. "But the shape of the orange has dates along the edges."

"What dates?"

Isabella's eyes soften as she smiles up at me. "Your birthday.

Camila's birthday. The day I met Camila. The day you kissed me. And the day I realized that I'm in love with you."

Pulling her shirt down, I squint at the small writing, and time stops.

3.25 12.12 6.18 7.02 9.13

The world ceases to exist. The entire football team of Santos and Garcias roaming around Isabella's childhood home fade into the background as she slides her arms around my waist. "You love me?"

Her eyes appear glassy as she nods. "I really do. I'm sorry I didn't realize it earlier, and that I didn't give you a chance."

"We happened at the exact time we were supposed to happen, and you'll never be able to convince me otherwise. I wouldn't change a thing about how we got together," I tell her quietly. "Well, maybe the whole Rick the Dick thing. I could really have done without him being in our story."

She laughs lightly. "Honestly? Me too. But I'm glad he forced me to finally see the amazing man I've had standing in front of me for years. I had blinders on, thinking we could never work. But you see me for me, and you accept me anyway, bad traits and all."

I apply a quick kiss to her forehead. *"Mi vida estaría vacía sin ti."*

"What did you say?" she whispers, her gaze riveted to me.

"My life would be empty without you."

"It sounds so much better in Spanish," she jokes.

"Well, you know I call you *Naranja*, which means orange, but it also means 'my other half' or even my better half. *Eres mi media Naranja*. You're my better half, Isabella, and I swear on my soul that I'll spend the rest of my days showing you how beautifully loved you are."

"I love you too, Sebastian," she says solemnly, before pushing onto her tiptoes to give me a soft kiss.

A throat clears, and we break apart to find Leo standing next to us. "It's great that you love each other. Really. But go get some food, because I have to leave in an hour. Unless you want to explain why we're all here right now, on an empty stomach."

I'm not sure which is the better option: nausea because of an empty stomach, or puking because of nerves with a full stomach. At least I can mostly place the blame on my daughter for either option.

Leo looks back again, a tiny smile on his face. "I guess I'm the lone holdout now."

"For?" I ask.

He points toward the door. "The threshold. True love. All that bullshit."

Isabella gasps. "Oh! I didn't even realize we'd done it!"

I slide an arm around her waist, pulling her into my side. "If I'd have convinced you to try this ten years ago, do you think you'd have believed we were destined to be together?"

She shakes her head. "I'm glad it didn't happen that way."

"Why?"

Her gaze drifts to where Camila animatedly talks to *Abuela* and *Nonna*. "Because we wouldn't have her."

Chapter 21

I barely ate a thing from the smorgasbord my family managed to put out for us with only a day's notice. Sebastian's mother and grandmother brought a couple of dishes as well, and I realize the combining of a large Italian family with a Puerto Rican family will mean we will never go hungry.

"Belly," Arianna says quietly. "Are you doing okay?"

We're sitting on one of the couches in my parents' oversized family room. These couches have seen many family meetings, Christmases, and celebrations of birthdays and new babies. I never thought we'd be meeting to discuss my safety and an ex-boyfriend who may or may not be out to get me. Two large brown leather couches face each other, with a floor-to-ceiling stone fire-place covering the wall on one side. Two small chairs with a side table surround the couches, and my parents have pulled every dining chair into the space for our large congregation to sit. Alex's oldest daughter, Abbie, corrals all the children into the basement so they're out of hearing distance. I watch as Camila excitedly waves to me before she takes Abbie's hand and goes into the basement.

I sigh. "As good as I can, I guess. This is all incredibly surreal."

She takes my hand, squeezing it. "We're here for you, and we'll get you through this. Well, whatever *this* is."

I give her a small smile, but my insides are churning.

Mom sits on the other side of me, patting my knee reassuringly. Sebastian watches from the other side of the room, surrounded by my brothers, as they pester him with nonstop questions. His eyes warm as he gives me a small smile, and I notice his finger tapping along his hip bone, pointing to the spot where my tattoo is on his body. My entire being relaxes, melting into the back of the couch.

I love that we've both marked the other on our bodies. I love that, no matter what, I'm carrying him with me. Looking back, I can see how he slowly infiltrated my heart. While it may seem sneaky, I know it wasn't. He did it patiently, only when he knew I was open to it. He's always listened to me and respected my boundaries.

"Girl, you better quit looking at him like that, or you might end up pregnant right now," Arianna teases. "Although I'd sure love another niece or nephew."

"I basically just gave you a five-year-old niece. Can we maybe wait to breed me for a little bit? I'd like to enjoy Sebastian by myself right now."

Mom sighs. "He is one attractive man."

"Mom!" Arianna and I say simultaneously.

She shrugs. "What? I'm not allowed to look at the merchandise? It's window shopping, ladies. It's fine as long as I don't touch or purchase."

"For fuck's sake," Arianna mutters. "I think we got our ho tendencies from her."

"Speak for yourself. I have never been a ho," I tell her.

Arianna giggles. "Oh I definitely was for a hot minute, especially when Stone would piss me off, acting as if he wasn't attracted to me."

"You get your ho from *Nonna*," Mom offers. We both turn to

her, horrified. "You don't want to know the things I've heard about. You should be thanking me that I always made sure to lock the bedroom door."

Hannah comes up behind me. "It's worse for me. I married into it, and I've already experienced sexual situations with more than one of you hoodlums. So I appreciate a locked door."

"Alright, let's get started," Sebastian says, clearing his throat. He looks so handsome and controlled. His aura takes over a room, commanding it. Even Dom looks smaller than my man. "How many of you met Isabella's ex-boyfriend, Rick?"

Only a few people raise their hands. Looking back, I realize I didn't bring him around to family events much because I knew it wasn't a long-term relationship. I think I was more embarrassed about him cheating on me with Amelia, than actually hurt by the action. My decision to destroy his apartment was mostly due to it being the final straw. I was so sick and tired of being stepped on by men. Overlooked and discounted. Glitter bombing his space was me taking back my life, and vowing to never let a man become more important than me in my own fucking life.

Sebastian holds up a picture of Rick, then one of Rick and Amelia. He looks at me apologetically. "This was taken yesterday. One of my guys followed them. They were loudly arguing about some missing items. While they never clearly said specifics, it was insinuated that the group Rick was distributing for is getting more aggressive with scare tactics."

"It's definitely drugs?" Dad asks, and Sebastian nods.

"We were able to access the doorbell camera footage from the person across the hall from Rick. Only thirty minutes before Isabella and Arianna entered Rick's apartment, an unidentified person went in."

"How did you access the camera footage?" Dominic asks.

Sebastian's eyes meet mine, and I swear a slight hint of a

blush creeps onto his cheekbones. "I, uh, well, maybe I shouldn't say."

Leo raises a hand. "Let's just say it was liberated from the Internet, and we'll leave it at that."

Everyone turns to Leo, myself included. "Liberated it from the Internet? Have you done that before, Leo, or were you secretly involved in this project?"

His lips twitch. "It's classified."

I roll my eyes. "Uh-huh. Sure."

My parents turn to Arianna. "You were there too?"

Arianna has the decency to look relatively embarrassed. "Well, I wasn't going to let Belly go there by herself. Honestly it was so cool to see her stand up for herself. The girl has massive balls for someone who stays pretty quiet and introverted. No one piss her off, though. She's pretty creative when she's vindictive."

Looking around, I find all of my siblings staring at me with varying looks of amusement, but I can tell they're impressed. Beaming, I look at Sebastian, and find the biggest smile on his face. Even without their pride, I know Sebastian will always be proud of me, and that's all I want.

"The person who entered before my sisters. Male or female?" Leo asks. He stands uncomfortably by the staircase, using the banister to support his weight.

"We ran it through some software and found the person's height to be only around five-six, and due to the overall size being thin and lanky, we're safely saying it was a woman."

"Did she enter by breaking in, or with a key?" Leo asks.

"The apartment complex is fairly new, and the doors have keypads where residents input a code. Whoever it was knew the code, and entered quickly."

My mouth falls open. "Rick wouldn't give me the code. I looked over his shoulder once to see it. He'd never give it out to anyone, not even his family."

Sebastian watches me. "Do you think Amelia might have the code?"

I ponder that thought. "I don't know. Maybe. I don't even know how long they were sleeping together. Their interactions were few and far between. I don't know if they knew each other before we started dating, or if I actually introduced them."

Alex murmurs something quietly to Sebastian, and he nods. "Moving on. We've managed to connect Rick to a drug distribution ring within the Denver metropolitan area. It has connections to the Salazar Cartel in Mexico. The main drug they transport is fentanyl, which explains why both Rick, and the man who broke into Isabella's apartment, referenced tablets. But Rick also asked where the Molly was, which is a version of ecstasy."

"Damn," Luca mumbles. "When the quiet ones fall, they bring all the drama."

"Luca!" Hannah hisses. "Way to support your sister."

"What?" he says innocently. "I'm proud of Belle. She's finally taking ownership of her life and making things interesting. Yeah, it's a little more dramatic than we'd all like, but she's happy. Look at her. Everyone, look at Isabella. Has she ever looked this fucking happy before?"

I watch, enraptured by all the smiles of my family members, as they all shake their heads.

"Exactly. Seb, and his family, are Belle's perfect match. We could do without the drug thing, but it is what it is. I'm still just thrilled for my sister." Luca looks pleased as he slings an arm around Hannah.

"So what happens now?" Stone asks, casting a quick glance at Arianna. I can see the worry in his eyes, whereas Arianna has no idea she might be in danger. Just for her proximity to me, and the fact that she was also inside Rick's apartment, could mean these people come after her.

"We've contacted the Colorado Bureau of Investigations, as

well as the DEA and the FBI. And before you ask, I did a complete scan of my office before I made any calls, to ensure no one could potentially be listening," Sebastian says, his eyes darting toward me every few words.

It's as if a brick is dropped into my stomach. If he's worried about his office, could everything else also be susceptible? Is Camila in danger? A sheen of tears covers my vision, but I feel Sebastian crouch in front of me. If I brought danger into her innocent life, if I'm the reason why that sweet child experiences even a second of pain, the sheer torment I'll feel will be immeasurable. Sebastian's hand cups my cheek as his thumb strokes across my skin. "Baby, I've got it under control. Do you trust me?"

I nod, but the tears spill onto my cheeks. I whisper, "If something happens to her, I'll never forgive myself."

"Nothing is going to happen to either of you. I swear on my life," he says vehemently, taking my head in his hands, and swiping the tears from my cheeks. "It will be a cold day in hell before you and Camila are hurt in any way. My men and I guarantee it."

"If you've contacted authorities, why call this family meeting?" Gianna asks. "Are we in danger too?"

Sebastian swivels to sit on the ground in front of me, then grabs my hands to lay on his shoulders. I can feel the tension, and I wonder if my touch is helping to ground him. "I figure I had two options. One was to keep everyone in the dark, then only tell you afterward if needed. Since I assumed at least one of Isabella's brothers would take offense to that —"

Alex interrupts him. "We all would."

Sebastian chuckles. "My other option was to get everyone together and explain it all. I'd rather tell everyone at once, where I give the facts, instead of playing a messed up game of telephone where details get muddled in translation. Do I think you are all in danger? No. But I'd rather you all be prepared, be aware of your surroundings, and who you're with, so you can be ready."

"It's not like we don't know everyone in this town. A newbie comes in, we can basically smell them at the edge of town," Kate says with a laugh.

"That's where you're sort of wrong," I state, my voice trembling.

"What? Why?" Kate asks.

Sebastian speaks up. "The guy who broke into Isabella's apartment has a girlfriend. She came to book club, and I thought she looked familiar, so I had a friend tail her out of town. She said her name was Jenna, but it's actually Berkley. Berkley St. James. It's not about being untouchable in this town, thinking that your last name protects you, because it doesn't." I watch as every female's face pales dramatically. Sebastian's hand covers mine on his shoulder, and I grab it, squeezing it tightly. I need the grounding.

"They might have stayed at the hotel, or purchased pastries from me. Stone, they could have gotten a haircut from you, or done a tour of Travis's ambulance and the fire station. We have no idea how deep they've already dug into our family." My voice is quiet but resolute. Looking back in hindsight, I have no idea how often I'd possibly interacted with someone associated with Rick or the cartel. If I can't recognize a threat, how would my family?

The mood in the room noticeably shifts. I don't mean to put fear into my family, but just like with Camila, I have to protect them. If something happens to anyone because of me, I won't forgive myself.

But if something happens to Sebastian ... I won't be able to survive that.

We're all quiet on the way home, lost to our own thoughts. Camila chats about all her new friends, who she explains she knows will be family once I'm finally her mom, and asks when we can have more fun adventures with them.

Sebastian takes Camila up for a bath, and I take a moment on the covered patio. Nights are becoming cooler, and there's a crisp scent in the air that tells me autumn, and snow, aren't too much further away. The Colorado mountains can get snow virtually any month of the year, but ours usually happens at the beginning of October.

"Isabella." I jolt, looking over to find Sebastian's father. Julian Garcia is a striking man. He's an older version of Sebastian with salt-and-pepper hair, and deeper smile lines around his eyes and mouth. "Are you alright?"

I nod, but I know it lacks enthusiasm and believability. "I'll be fine."

He sits on a large swing, motioning for me to take a seat. "You don't have to lie. I can understand lying to your own family, but with us, I'd prefer the truth."

I let out a long exhale, trying to formulate my response. "I'm petrified. I feel like my life is finally getting started. I'm confident in my own skin, and I have a man I love that I know truly loves me, and now it's in jeopardy. There's a beautiful little girl in there that only sees the good in things, and I'm scared to death that something might happen, to change her outlook. Scarring her for life. But if something happens to her …"

"I know," Julian says quietly.

"And if something happens to *him*, I won't come back from that," I confess, the words whispered so lightly I'm not sure if Julian hears them. But I needed to say them out loud.

"There aren't many men in the world who I trust with my life, but my son and MC men are some of them. You are absolutely in the safest place you could be, and he will not let anything happen to you."

I don't respond. Julian and Sebastian can say those things, but they can't predict the future. If a girl could easily infiltrate my silly underground book club, what else could these people do?

A wave of nausea overtakes me as I realize they've probably already scoped out the Clubhouse. "There were two prospects that creeped me out. I've only been to the Clubhouse a couple of times, and was there once with these two guys. It's the first time Sebastian sort of 'claimed' me," I use air quotes, "and then explained why he wanted everyone to know I was spoken for. What if they've already gotten cameras or devices in there, listening to everything?"

"Then my son will handle it. Honestly, these degenerates are coming after the wrong group of guys. Every single man in RMRRMC has at least five years of military experience. Some of them finished their full twenty years. They've got SEALs, Army Rangers, Intel, and combat veterans. I have no doubt your four brothers will be involved in Sebastian's plan, and I'm not too proud to admit that your brother Leo scares me a little bit," Julian says with a wry chuckle, making me smile.

"I think he scares most of my family, actually," I answer.

"He's a bit intense. I know he was injured overseas, and those experiences change people. Coming back to civilian life, when you're physically and mentally not the same person as when you left, is undoubtedly incredibly challenging. Has he confided in anyone about what happened?"

I shake my head. "Certainly not me. I don't think he's told his twin, my sister Gianna, either. If anyone could get it out of him, it would be our oldest brother, Alex. Their shared military experience is probably why. But Leo has always kept his thoughts and feelings close to his chest. Him internalizing things isn't something new, but there's an air of anger and frustration I've never seen with him before."

"Sebastian is going to get him to join the Range Riders," Julian says nonchalantly.

"How? I thought you had to ride. Leo doesn't, or at least he didn't. Now I'm not sure if he *can*."

"It's not a requirement. Studies have shown that men establish bonds over shared likes or activities, but for Leo, it's more important for him to have an outlet with other veterans who know what he's been through, or men that can at least understand the risks of a deployment."

"That's true," I murmur. It could be so good for Leo to find a support group who empathize with him. Dom recommended a therapist when Leo first came home, and Dom was lucky to walk away unscathed. I'm not sure I've ever seen Leo so pissed off. We have a lot of big personalities in our family, but I always felt like Leo and I were cut from the same cloth. However, that last deployment really changed him. Now he's been medically retired, and I think he's quite lost. He's living in Natalie's old studio apartment while doing odd jobs around Everlasting to help out the family.

I hear the sliding door open, and I turn to find Sebastian and his mom. They're talking softly as they approach us, but Seb smiles at me when our eyes meet. Julian and I stand to greet them, and Seb slides an arm around my waist.

"Is *Abuela* still in the car?" Sebastian asks.

I nod. "She said she wasn't getting out until it was time to leave."

"Stubborn woman," Sebastian's mom, Gabriela, mutters. "We'll talk tomorrow. You have a lovely family, Isabella. I'm familiar with your mother and grandmother, but it was fun to meet your siblings and their families. I imagine we'll have many more Garcia-Santo events in the future."

Once they leave, Sebastian motions for me to sit back down on the swing, and he sits beside me, slinging an arm over my shoulders and pulling me into his side. "How are you feeling?"

"Overwhelmed," I say with a sigh. "I don't exactly regret messing up Rick's apartment, but if I knew then what I know now, I never would have gone anywhere close to his space."

"I know," he murmurs, placing a soft kiss against my temple. "Is there anything else you have questions about? How can I help ease some of your anxiety?"

Turning, I stare at him. "Promise me you won't do anything dumb."

"What?" he says with a chuckle.

"I'm serious. Promise me you won't be an idiot and sacrifice yourself to try and save me."

The smile dies on his face. "Isabella, I —"

I interrupt. "No. Don't try to justify anything you might do. I just told you I'm in love with you. But what I haven't said, and what I think is imperative for you to know, is that I know I won't survive if something happens to you. It isn't about me being heartbroken. It's that I will be completely broken and incapable of moving on. Maybe I've always known I'd fall so damn hard that it would destroy me, and that's why I haven't trusted my heart to anyone. Until you. But I also know you, I *feel* your heart, and I can see you sacrificing yourself to save me."

The tortured expression on Sebastian's face will haunt me. "What am I supposed to do, then, if it's you or me? How the fuck am I supposed to move on if I know you were hurt or died because of me? I can't live with that guilt. I can't fucking live without you, *mi Reina*. My queen. I call you my fucking queen, Isabella, because my entire kingdom will cease to exist if you're not in it."

"What about Camila?" I whisper, and he closes his eyes, torment evident in how he slumps against the back of the swing.

"She can't lose you, Sebastian. Sure, she has grandparents. But it isn't the same as having you in her life. You can't do that to her."

"How am I supposed to pick between you? How can I pick between the one who lives in my heart, and the woman who feeds my soul? My daughter is desperate for you to be her mother. What will I tell her if something happens to you?"

I throw a leg over Sebastian's thighs, straddling him, so I can grab his face. "Something might happen to me tomorrow, Seb."

"Don't you even suggest that. Don't put that shit out into the universe," he growls, his eyes suddenly heated and volatile.

"But it's true. Something could happen to you as well. We can't predict the future. All I'm asking is for you not to go out of your way to stack the deck for my benefit."

Pain slashes across his face as he reluctantly nods. "I don't like talking about this. I don't like the 'what if' game."

"Typically, I'm the one playing the 'what if' game, and you're the one being the glass-half-full guy, with never-ending optimism about the future. This is an interesting turn of events," I tease, and he manages to give me a half smile. "I can't spend however long it is before the guys are caught, thinking about you getting hurt. My anxiety is high enough as it is, but focusing on the negatives will make it skyrocket. I'm trusting that you and your men have things under control. And what you can't do, the authorities will cover just fine."

"Do you struggle with anxiety?" he asks.

"Occasionally. Arianna has it much more often, but since she married Stone, her anxiety has settled down as well." I'm not surprised that Arianna struggled with anxiety. Her health history would be hard for anyone. But Stone has given her such peace, and he's so accepting of her. I've seen a new level of contentment in Arianna I could have never imagined for her.

"Will you tell me if you get anxious? So I know?" Sebastian whispers, a raw and uncertain look on his beautiful face. I nod, unable to form words. Just when I think I know everything about this man, he reveals a new layer to me. He is my own orange, the other half of my soul, showing me the deepest parts of him that only I get to see.

"I'm anxious now," I tell him. I need him to make me see only him. Make me feel surrounded by him.

"You are? How can I help?"

"Make me forget everything but you."

Chapter 22

Make me forget everything but you.

"Done." Yanking her against me, I crash my lips to hers. I can make her forget the world. The only thing she'll remember tonight is that she completes my world.

Isabella slides her hands around my neck, up into my hair, clutching the strands tightly between her fingers. The brief twitch of pain is refreshing. It's keeping me grounded and focused on the gorgeous creature in my lap.

When she sighs against my lips, I take the opportunity to stroke my tongue on hers, circling it and reveling in the velvety softness as her taste overwhelms me. Isabella absentmindedly chewed a piece of gum on the way home from her parents' house, and a hint of mint still resides in her mouth. The overwhelming flavor of sweet vanilla is there, a flavor I've come to realize is how her entire body tastes. Vanilla is so inherently Isabella that I'll never be able to smell it and think of anyone but her.

As if I could ever think of anyone but my beautiful queen.

Grabbing Isabella's ass, I grind her down against my engorged cock, feeling her intake of breath as pleasure courses through both of us. The heat from her pussy soaks through every article of clothing, and I'm desperate to get my mouth on her so she can soak my face.

I break off the kiss to trail my mouth down her neck, finding the buttons on her shirt as I go. I get frustrated when I can't get the buttons undone with one hand, because I've slipped my other hand down her shorts to grab a handful of her luscious ass, so I rip the shirt off. I assume Isabella will be mad, but she surprises me once again.

"That was way hotter than it should be," she moans. "But you're replacing it."

"I'll buy you whatever you want as long as I get these tits in my mouth right fucking now," I murmur, yanking down the cup of her bra and sealing my lips around her rosy nipple. Isabella clutches my head against her as I suck hard, and she lets out the deepest moan I've ever heard. The sound reverberates through the trees, and it makes me wonder if I should move this indoors, but I'm too far gone to care. If any member comes up to me and admits seeing this, they're booted from the club. They know to steer clear of my home, so if they're watching, they've already broken a rule.

Lavishing the same attention on the other breast, I manage to slide my hand further between Isabella's thighs to reach her center. She's positively dripping, and after making my fingers wet, I retreat slightly to press against her untouched hole. Isabella gasps as her body stiffens, but as I swirl my finger gently, she relaxes into me.

"So good," she mumbles. She tilts her head back as I switch between her nipples, then apply a little more pressure against her ass, pushing the tip of my finger just past the ring of muscle. She's tight, so damn tight, that once I finally take her ass, I know I'll come immediately. Just the thought of anal makes pre-cum leak out of my cock, painfully aroused against my boxer briefs, but I'm not whipping him out until Isabella comes.

"You like this, baby?" I whisper, and she nods emphatically. "You like me fingering your ass?"

"I do. God, Sebastian, this makes me want you to fuck me there," she cries out, and bucks against my hand, making my finger slip in to the first knuckle. Another gorgeous moan as I nibble on her nipple, and she rests her forehead against mine.

"I've never seen you looking so gorgeous. The sounds you're making, how you can't stop grinding on me. It's fucking intoxicating, Isabella. You're going to come now, with my fingers in your ass, and then you're going to beg me to fuck you. Then I'll bury myself so fucking deep inside of you that we won't be able to tell where you end and I begin."

"God, yes, please," she moans. Sucking on her nipple again, tonguing it in torturously slow strokes, I carefully squeeze a second digit into her ass. She groans so deliciously as her body begins to tense, and I push my length up against her clit to hit three erogenous zones at once. "I'm about to come ..."

"Soak me, *Mami*. Let me see that orgasm."

Isabella's a vision as she comes, her entire body shuddering as her head thuds against my shoulder. Releasing her nipple with a satisfying pop, I stare down at my beautiful woman, a hint of a smile on her face as she pants.

"Does it make me sound ridiculous to say that I love when you call me *Mami*? It's incredibly sexy for some reason," she finally says, making me chuckle.

Carefully sliding my fingers out of her, I reach across the swing for a roll of paper towels. I'll go inside in a moment to more thoroughly wash my hands, but I want to ask her something first. "I like that you find it sexy. But what's your favorite name that I call you?"

Isabella ponders this for a minute as her breathing slows. "You asked me once before, and I think I said *amor*. But now I want to amend it to *mi amor*, because calling someone 'love' can be pretty basic. But saying 'my love' is better. It's concrete and resolute. It's about you and me. And I really like that."

"I do too, *mi amor*." I peck her lips quickly, then move her to stretch out on the swing. "I'll be right back."

I quickly jog inside to wash my hands, and debate on running upstairs to get a condom, but I don't want to presume what may happen next. We could sit outside and cuddle, and I'd still be fucking ecstatic. But I don't get an opportunity to meet her back on the swing, because she silently creeps in behind me, sliding her arms around my waist. "Missed me already?"

"I did. But I had ulterior motives for coming in here," she says, her voice decidedly husky as she squeezes between me and the counter. I place my hands on either side of her, bracketing her in, and she smiles like it's exactly what she wanted me to do.

"Oh?" I cock an eyebrow. "What motives do you have?"

Her smile is sweet, but her eyes are deceptively sparkling. There's a devilish glint, and as I'm trying to decipher the look, she drops to her knees and has my pants undone in seconds. Opening her mouth wide, Isabella takes me to the back of her throat, and my knees buckle.

"Goddamn, baby," I choke, but a hand grabs onto her hair, holding her against me. I want to fuck her face so badly. I want to see mascara running down her cheeks, and feel her choke around me. It's probably a little sick and twisted, but as I watch Isabella's pupils blow out with desire, I think she might just like a little pain with her pleasure too. "Do you want me to fuck your face?"

She nods, taking a hand and placing it on top of mine, pushing her head against me even harder. She swallows, and black spots dot my vision at how phenomenal it feels. "Tap my thighs twice if you need me to stop."

The vixen shakes her head, then winks at me, before sliding her mouth off my cock. "I want it to hurt, Sebastian. Make it fucking hurt."

Holy fucking Christ.

"You want it to hurt?" She nods. "You want me to make it

hurt, maybe treat you like my little slut?" Her eyes close in bliss, and she moans as she sucks me deep into her mouth again. Fucking hell. Her mouth should come with a warning label. Sweet and quiet Isabella Santo, the introverted baker, deep throats like a porn star.

Wrapping her hair around my fist, I begin thrusting into her mouth, every few strokes holding my cock as deep into her throat as possible. She moans happily, fondling my balls, then hollows out her cheeks to suck hard. I hiss as I fight off my impending orgasm, wanting to live in this moment for as long as possible. She's a vision on her knees before me, and she knows it. Grasping her hand in mine, I intertwine our fingers together as I continue to rut into her mouth.

"So fucking good," I grit out. "Gonna come down your throat so hard. Be a good girl and swallow every drop. Good girls get to come again. Good girls get to sit on my face and drown me. Are you a good fucking girl?"

Sucking as hard as she can, she doesn't answer. Instead, she slips a hand between my ass cheeks, and slips a fingertip right against a spot I've only touched myself. The orgasm shoots up my spine so fast I barely have time to ready myself, and I certainly don't have time to warn her. Rope after rope of cum shoots down her throat as I roar her name.

I'm shaking as I rest one forearm on the counter, my vision blurry as Isabella licks me slowly. She drags her tongue around the tip sensually, making my body shake, and one last drop appears. She sweetly licks it off, and that's when my knees can't hold me up.

"Oof!" Isabella groans as I fall half on her. "Are you okay?"

"I should be asking you that," I reply, my voice as hoarse as I've ever heard it. "What the actual fuck was that?"

She smiles at me as she stands to wash her hands. "What? A girl can't pick up some tricks here or there?"

I chuckle breathlessly. "I low-key want to murder whichever men taught you all of that, but I also want to thank them tremendously."

Isabella giggles as she dries her hands and joins me on the ground. We're laying on my kitchen floor after the best blow job of my fucking life, and I don't have the energy to move. "Some things I've learned along the way, but porn is pretty dang educational when you want to learn stuff. Granted, I'm lucky that I don't have a gag reflex, but how to give a good blow job is essential for any woman. It turns out I also really love giving them, so I put effort into the craft."

"I fucking love you," I mumble, and she cackles. "Now get up here and sit on my face."

"Sebastian!" she hisses, her eyes darting to the stairs. "Your daughter is right up there!"

I manage to rise to my elbows and stare at her incredulously. "Are you kidding me? You just sucked me off in the same space. How is it any different?"

"I don't know, it just is," she says, exasperatedly. "Camila coming downstairs and witnessing a blow job is more easily explained as I dropped something, your zipper broke, or I was fixing my shoe. Me naked from the waist down, sitting on your face? How do we explain that one, Mr. Smartypants?"

Good point.

"Just so I'm clear on the Isabella Santo sex rules, am I allowed to eat your pussy in our bedroom?"

"Yes, as long as the door is locked." Camila mastered unlocking the door well over a year ago, but I'm not telling Isabella that.

"And the shower?"

"Again, with the door locked." Isabella sits up so we're eye to eye.

"What about the couch? Dom said something about him and

Luca coming over tomorrow, and baby, I really want to fuck you there before then. I want to know you've come on my face, and then my cock, before your brothers have to sit right there." Yeah, it's weird. And no, I'll never blatantly tell them that they're sitting in a place where I fucked their sister. But just the thought of knowing that I've had her, right where they'll inevitably sit in the future, is oddly intoxicating.

Isabella stares at me, wide-eyed, and I wonder if I've gone too far. That is, until she says, "Get your ass in the other room before I change my mind."

Yes, ma'am. Scrambling to my feet, I pull my pants and underwear up, then grab Isabella around the waist and throw her over my shoulder. She shrieks, covering her mouth with her hands, as I jog into the living room. I lie on the couch, then motion for her to climb up. "I wasn't fucking kidding, *Mami*. Sit on my fucking face."

I expect her to be self-conscious, or tentative, but she surprises me once again by dropping her shorts and scrambling up my body. "You left your thong on."

"Rip it off then," she retorts, depositing her pussy directly on my mouth. I groan as her scent and taste fill my mouth, and I suck her clit into my mouth through the flimsy fabric. She gasps, groans, then covers her mouth with the corner of a throw pillow. Gyrating shamelessly on my face, I watch, mesmerized, as she positions herself exactly where she needs. "Suck my clit until I come."

"I fucking love when you tell me what you want, baby," I rasp, snapping the thin sides of her thong so I can get direct access. I slide two fingers inside her, and when I find that rough patch of nerves on the inner wall, I simultaneously suck on her clit. Her back arches as an orgasm overtakes her, robbing her of the ability to breathe. Head thrown back in bliss, I only wish I could see her face as she comes. Pussy fluttering around me, she shakes and moans as she rides the aftershocks. Isabella collapses against the back of the couch, and I frown as she moves away from my mouth. "I wasn't done."

"For now you are," she says breathlessly. "I want to get to the sex part. I've never had two orgasms during penetration, so I figure you can try for that."

"I do like a challenge," I muse. Looking around the room, my gaze latches onto something I forgot about this room, and I'm fearing how to explain it to Isabella. "If I tell you something, do you promise you'll believe me when I say I absolutely forgot about it, and this was not in any way intentional?"

Her head pops up. "That's only slightly concerning."

"Well, when everything happened with you, I wanted to be completely prepared in case anyone decided to pay me a visit at home. I figured your ex may have tattled that I was in the bakery that day, and I knew Devon would tell them all about me in your apartment. So I increased my security here."

"That makes sense. I mean, you have Camila to think of, and your parents are here pretty often —" she stops suddenly, and I see the dawning in her eyes. "How many cameras do you have in here?"

"Three," I respond simply. "One at the front door, one at the stairs, and one pointing toward the kitchen."

"And in the kitchen?"

"Two."

Isabella shifts backward, and I have a momentary sense of panic until she settles herself against my cock. "Do you have any outside?"

"Many," I grit out as she rocks against me.

"With a view of the swing?"

"Yes," I groan. Her breathing has quickened. Is she getting off on thinking about us essentially making a sex tape?

"And if I said I wanted to watch the footage, would you be

okay with that?" she asks breathlessly, rising slightly so she can move my pants and boxer briefs out of the way, then settles herself directly onto my dick. The heat from her pussy is euphoria-inducing. One inch to the right, and I'm slipping inside her tight pussy.

"Baby, condom," I growl. I'll force her off in a minute. Just one minute to feel this, as my eyes close in bliss. "This feels so fucking good."

"What if I said I didn't want a condom?" she whispers, and my eyes pop back open.

"I thought you said you weren't on anything."

"What if ... I'm not?"

Never thought I had a breeding kink until right this very fucking minute. The thought of fucking my seed into her? A very pregnant Isabella in my home, my bed, my life? Goddamn, I'm two seconds away from blowing. "You okay with that? Making a baby with me?"

"I wouldn't be against it, if it happened," she says breathlessly. "I do enjoy the trying part."

I surprise her by flipping us over. "Let's get something very clear here, sweetheart. If I get you pregnant, that's it. You're done. I'm never letting you go. Do you understand that? You'll be mine."

"I thought I already was yours."

"You are. But then you'll really be mine."

She rolls her eyes, a smirk covering her face. "Like you were going to let me go anyway."

I smile as I lean down to give her a harsh kiss. "I'd have at least let you think you had a choice, *Mami.*"

"Then fuck me like you mean it ... *Papi.*"

Fuuuuuuuck.

I groan as I grab her thighs, positioning them to wrap around my waist, and then I begin a vicious pace. I'm not going to last long, but Isabella's pussy is already fluttering around me, so I know she's right there with me. Sliding a hand between our sweaty bodies, I pinch her clit between my thumb and forefinger, and she detonates. Her walls clamp down tightly, so tightly I can barely move, and I unload inside her. It's the first time I've ever come bare inside a woman.

Collapsing on top of Isabella, I note that our hearts are beating against one another with the same beat, and I smile as I think of the symmetry there. She's had my heart for years, so it only makes sense they'd beat as one.

A Puerto Rican-Italian Mashup

While it may have started as fake, it's clear to anyone that the relationship between Isabella Santo and Sebastian Garcia will stand the test of time. What we didn't know, however, was the fact that our favorite biker boy also rocks the title of hot dad!

Other online news sources may give you his child's name, gender, age, and all the details I'm privy to, but I will not be doing that. I firmly believe children should stay off the Internet. Is the child gorgeous? Absolutely. But I will not feature them at all.

The child's biological mother chose not to be part of their life. And while Ms. Santo may never have viewed herself as maternal, I have no doubt she will be an excellent mother. This author hopes Mr. Garcia and Ms. Santo choose to procreate, as whatever offspring they produce will be absolutely breathtaking.

Isabella: WTF!

Me: What?

Isabella: That stupid website just posted an article about us, Camila, and any potential offspring!

Me: Did they print Camila's name? Because I have no problem going after them for that.

Isabella: No, they claim that they feel children shouldn't be on the Internet that way.

Me: Well. Shockingly, I agree with them.

Me: I also agree that you'll be an excellent mother.

Chapter 23

ISABELLA

Summer fades into fall, and I get comfortable in my new normal. Sebastian moved forward with purchasing the distillery a few doors down from my bakery, and spends most of his days working from my kitchen. At first, I was aggravated at having him invade my space. My kitchen has always been my sanity. It was where I could go to unwind, process things, and find my confidence. But slowly, Sebastian has become my saving grace. My person. The one who gives me peace and confidence to be exactly who I'm meant to be. There's something so incredibly tranquil about working in my kitchen while Sebastian sits beside me, quietly typing on a laptop. Every so often, he'll ask what I'm working on, or reach over to touch me in some way. A light caress of my cheek, a kiss on my temple, or a massage of my neck. Somehow he knows when I need it. I think it grounds us both.

From a baking perspective, autumn is my favorite season. I love making things with pumpkin, apple, cranberry, and cinnamon, as we get ready for the holidays. Apple dumplings, cranberry bars, maple blondies, and my favorite thing of all: pumpkin cheesecake bites. People can't seem to say no to an adorable little ball of orange bliss, shaped like a pumpkin, and rolled in sugar. Even when I make dozens at a time, they'll sell out before noon.

"What are you working on?" Sebastian asks quietly.

I'm rolling out dough for my second most popular item. "A sugar cookie with a maple glaze."

"Bet the kids love that one," he comments.

"They do, but my frosted Christmas ornament in November and December is much more popular."

"Ava is up front, right?"

"Yes. She's here until close." My lovely employee with the lead foot didn't even bat an eyelash when I explained the situation with my ex-boyfriend. In fact, she seemed even more excited. Sebastian is convinced she has some sociopathic tendencies.

"Good. I need to run down to the bar. I should be back in fifteen or twenty minutes. Will you be okay?"

Sebastian hates leaving me alone here, even for a few minutes. "I'll be fine. No one knows I'm back here. I'm hoping to go home early today anyway. Can we leave when you get back?"

He smiles. "Of course. Camila is having a sleepover with Hannah and Luca, so we'll have the house to ourselves."

Camila is pretty much obsessed with all of my nieces and nephews, but especially Luca's two kids, Melanie and Caleb. She's older than Melanie, but they love playing with all of Melanie's stuffed animals. Caleb is very much still a Momma's boy, but he's fascinated with watching his big sister and Camila play.

"Do you have plans for me, Mr. Garcia?" I ask coyly, and he wraps his arms around my waist, pulling me snugly against him.

"I always have plans for you," he whispers seductively against my ear, his hot breath sending a shiver down my spine. "I'll be back soon."

"Hurry. Now I have plans for you too," I call out as he strides from the room. I hear his loud laughter all the way out the bakery door.

Shaking my head, I get back to carefully icing the maple leaf-shaped cookies, when I hear Ava ask me to come out front. Her voice sounds different, and I'm immediately on edge. I take off my gloves, grab my phone, and pull up Sebastian's contact. I hit 'call' and stuff the phone in my jeans, between my skin and my panties. I figure it'll be too obvious if I put it in my pocket, even though I know any conversation will be really muted under the fabric. But I'd rather have Sebastian alerted about nothing than have no way to contact him if something is wrong. And something tells me I'm about to wish Sebastian had never left the bakery.

"What's up?" I ask, rounding the corner and stopping on a dime when I see three men, one of whom is holding a gun to Ava's temple. "Let her go, please. She doesn't know anything."

"Bitch, I'll decide who gets let go," one of them snarls. Looking to the right, I notice one of the guys looks very familiar. He smiles, a sinister grimace that sends fear shooting down my spine.

"I think our girl remembers me," he boasts, making the other two laugh. He strides toward me, his chest out in arrogance. "Time to meet the boss."

"No," I whisper.

"No?" he repeats, raising a brow. I barely see his backhand before it lashes across my face, but the metallic taste filling my mouth lets me know immediately that I've been hit. "You wanna try that again?"

I back up against the closest wall, holding my throbbing cheek, my eyes darting between this man and Ava. Her eyes are terror-filled, as I'm sure mine are now as well. "I swear I don't know what you're looking for. I didn't take anything from Rick's apartment."

"You think we actually believe you?" he asks.

"It's true. My boyfriend got the doorbell camera from across the hall. You can see someone else enter the apartment thirty minutes before me, then come out a minute later."

"Why the hell would I believe you?" he retorts.

"Because I have no reason to lie?" I try to keep my voice calm as I reason with him. "I'm just a baker. I wouldn't know any drugs other than what I can buy at the grocery store for a headache. I like my life, and I'm not made to survive in prison, so I wouldn't take a chance on stealing drugs, and then selling them. I just wouldn't. I've never even taken anything from Rick. I was only there because I was pissed he cheated on me with my best friend."

"Which is exactly why you're the only suspect, you stupid cunt. But since you seem so sure of yourself, I'll give you one option to walk away —"

"Yes, yes, please. I'll do anything," I blurt out quickly.

"You sure about that?" he asks. "Because it's either you or her."

Confused, I look at Ava, but the guy shakes his head. "No, not this bitch. Her."

He holds up a phone, and I see a video of my sister, Arianna, with her two children at a playground near her house. Then I notice it's a video call. "Is that ..."

"Oh, it's live. You think I've only been tailing you? Took me a bit to find your sister. She was only on screen for a second at your boyfriend's apartment."

Confused, I reply, "She hasn't been to Sebastian's."

The guy sighs dramatically. "Rick's."

"Wait. Rick has cameras now?" I ask.

"Only one. In the bedroom. You're boring as fuck in bed, babe."

Blood drains from my face as his words hit. Rick had a camera? He was recording me — us — in bed? Without my consent or knowledge? I feel sick.

Sebastian seemed genuinely remorseful for his cameras. Is it the same thing, though? Did Rick just innocently forget to tell me he'd added cameras?. At least Sebastian told me as soon as he remembered. But I know if I'd said I didn't like it, he'd have deleted the footage and probably move the cameras somewhere else. Knowing the difference between Sebastian and Rick, however, tells me Rick would record me without telling me, and he'd never feel an ounce of remorse over that fact.

"Aw. You're upset." He gives me a fake frown. "Poor Isabella. She thought Rick was the one, and he'd never do her wrong."

I laugh bitterly. "No, I absolutely do know he'd be like that."

He looks surprised. "But he cheated, and you destroyed his apartment."

"So?"

He shrugs. "Doesn't matter. Let's go. You're gonna have to sit with the boss to see if he believes you or not."

I try to keep my voice even as I plead with him. "I'll go with you. But please leave Ava here. She really doesn't have anything to do with this."

He ponders this for a moment, tilting his head as he studies me, with one finger against his chin. "Nah. I think she'll come with us as collateral."

Using his gun, he motions for me to step toward the door, but then he slaps my ass twice. I jump, squeaking in shock, making him laugh. "Just checking to see if you're trying to be sneaky and bring a phone. Won't end well for you if you cross me, Isabella."

Ava grabs my hand when I get close to her, and I squeeze it reassuringly. She's completely terrified, and I feel awful for bringing her into this chaos. Still a teenager, Ava has her whole life ahead of her.

We're directed to the east, away from Sebastian's new bar, and I feel hysteria rising in my throat. He'd have seen us if we walked past. But now he'll walk back to an empty bakery and have no clue what happened.

I can only hope he's silently listening on my hidden phone, and he'll be able to follow us, or track my location somehow. Here I am, hoping a man loaded tracking software onto my phone like he said he would.

We pile into an unmarked white van that doesn't appear

suspicious, and I'm thankful for the noise of driving because my phone is vibrating nonstop. Maybe the call to Sebastian didn't go through, or maybe he's texting responses instead of speaking. My phone is always on silent with vibration, and I'm now acutely aware of how loud vibrations are when the rest of the world is quiet. To add some volume to the air, I begin asking the man questions, as he rides with me and Ava in the back of the van. The other two men sit silently in the front seat.

"I recognize you," I comment.

"And?" he retorts.

"How did you infiltrate Sebastian's MC so quickly?"

He laughs sardonically. "That dumbass prospect we were with. He couldn't stop talking about the MC and how amazing the president was. He slipped and said the guy's name once, and all it took was an Internet search to put the pieces together as the man who beat up Devon. He never should have let Devon go, not that it matters. He was dying either way."

"Devon?" I ask, my voice incredibly quiet.

"Yeah. He failed a mission. Can't have that. Your man should have killed him. Dev knew he was on borrowed time, which is why we only caught him at the Mexico border. Dumbass was going toward the Cartel instead of away from it. They're even worse at torture than anyone up here."

Bile rises in my throat. The guy watches me, smirking, knowing he's affecting me. Ava and I are sitting together on a small wooden bench, while the man sits across from us, knees wide apart, with the gun pointed at us. He's short. Shorter than I remember, and my gaze falls to his feet. His shoes look odd, like the heel of his foot is nowhere near the bottom of the shoe. Are they lifted? I choke on a hysterical giggle as I imagine this guy waltzing into a shoe store and asking for something to give him height.

"May I ask who we are meeting today?" I finally ask, once I know my voice can stay even.

"I guess there's no harm in telling you. We're meeting Fernando Montoya. He runs the distribution ring for all of Colorado, Wyoming, Idaho, and Utah. He is a second cousin to the Salazar family, of the Salazar Cartel in Mexico. Or maybe he's not a cousin. Honestly, the whole family is incestual, and it's hard to keep track of who is related to who."

Ava whimpers next to me. Still holding her hand, I squeeze it, but keep it away from my stomach. I don't want her to give away the fact that I have a phone. "Why does the head of a drug ring want to meet with me?"

"Two reasons." The man dangerously spins the gun between his two hands, his eyes glittering at me. He wants to scare me, that I know. Unfortunately for him, I have two brothers who were in the military, and one of them is a police officer. I know guns, and I know his gun still has the safety on. "He doesn't believe that you're innocent."

"And the other reason?" I ask evenly.

"He wants a little background on your boyfriend."

"Ex-boyfriend," I growl, my teeth clenched.

The man smiles, a leering grin that makes my stomach sink. "Oh, no. Your current one, if you can even call him that. I guess maybe he is now? He certainly wasn't at the beginning, but after the way you sucked him off in his kitchen a while ago, I'd say you're at least friends-with-benefits."

I'm about to vomit.

I've only gone down on Sebastian once in the kitchen. I've done it a lot since then in other places, but never in the kitchen. Did this guy hack into the cameras to watch old content, or was he watching live? I feel sick that he's now tainted an amazing memory. A time when I've never felt more sexy or sensual.

The more I think about it, the angrier I get. This asshole has watched me sleep with two men now, without my consent. I'm more angry with Rick over that footage, but for this guy to watch me with Sebastian has crossed a major line.

"May I ask your name?" I ask.

"The name I gave you, or my actual name?"

"Does it really matter which one?" I snap, and his posture straightens. The cocky grin is no longer in place. His gaze is locked in on me, and I know I'm dangerously close to him getting violent again.

But this time, I'm expecting it. He will not take me by surprise.

"You know what? It really doesn't matter. I told them my name was Rico. It's really Diego. Well, my legal name is Rico Diego Delgado."

"Well, Diego," I tell him sweetly, "I think Sebastian is going to enjoy hurting you once he finds out you watched us without our consent. Well, more me. He won't care that you saw his dick, since he'll know his is much bigger than yours."

I see the moment the words strike, and his arm moves. The look in his eyes is pure hostility as he lunges toward me, but both Ava and I lash out. Ava swiftly punches him in the groin, and as he's groaning and doubling over in pain, I quickly poke both fingers into his eye sockets. The feeling is horrific, and I know I've done damage, but I don't have a moment to feel bad. Diego stupidly drops the gun, which Ava and I scramble to pick up. I hear one of the guys in the front seat stutter, "What the fuck?" right as I get my hands around the grip of the gun. Diego reaches up blindly, grabbing the gun, and as we both wrestle for ownership, my fingers hit the safety just as his hit the trigger. The loud boom ricochets around the van, and I watch as blood spurts out of Diego's throat.

"Bitch, what did you do!" The driver turns to shout at me, making the van swerve.

"I didn't! He shot himself, I swear! His thumb hit the trigger!"

Struggling to calm my nerves, I swivel and point the gun at him. "But the safety is off now, and I have no qualms about having you go with him. Pull the fucking van over."

"Montoya will kill us if we don't bring her in," the guy in the passenger seat says.

"You heard Diego. We're dead either way." He slams on the brakes, and I tumble into Ava. I hear a screech of tires, and the driver mutters a string of curse words. "We've got company."

"Shit. We've got a lot of company."

I hear the most beautiful sound I've ever heard. A sound I'll never forget.

It's the sound of many, many motorcycles.

Sebastian came for me.

"You should probably let us out," I announce cheerfully.

"The door ain't locked, bitch. Just get out," the driver says tiredly.

Ava lunges for the sliding door, swinging it open with gusto. As soon as her feet hit the pavement, she screams as she runs toward the motorcycles. Crouching by the door, I turn to the guys. "Is Fernando Montoya going to keep coming after me?"

The driver shrugs. "Probably. He won't believe us until he sees it with his own eyes."

"That's what I'm afraid of," I murmur. Stepping out of the van, I find Sebastian straddling his wheels in front of motorcycles as far as I can see. It's as if he brought every single RMRRMC member with him. "Sebastian isn't going to let me go with you now. He'll kill you both before he lets me go."

The driver sighs again. "I'm really sick of being threatened with death."

"No fucking kidding," the other guy mutters. "We need to get the hell out of Colorado."

The driver turns to look at me. "You won't all be allowed in the compound. But if you bring only him, I think Montoya will allow it."

I hesitate. "Do you think he'll kill us both? It's just … Sebastian has a daughter. Her mom isn't in the picture, so he's all she has. I can't put him in a situation where she might lose him."

"We know all about his daughter. Montoya is a sick fuck, but the one thing he doesn't fuck with is children. He's pretty adamant about it, actually. Diego wanted to abduct Camila, and Montoya threatened to hang him by the balls in a wolf enclosure."

Peering down at Diego's body, I shudder. "That's oddly specific."

"Isabella," I hear whispered, and I turn my head to find Sebastian at the edge of the van.

The driver sighs again. "Tell him to approach. You're the only one with a gun. Well, I assume he has one too. But we don't. Diego wouldn't let us carry. It was too emasculating for him."

Sebastian immediately steps alongside, an arm gripping me tightly. "Is there a problem?"

"Is Ava okay?" I ask quietly, and he nods. Turning toward the men, I ask, "Can I ride with Sebastian to follow you, or do we need to be in the van? I don't want to be near … that."

"Jesus Christ," Sebastian breathes.

"Your girl did that," one of the guys says.

"I did not!" I exclaim with indignation. "I swear, my hand hit the safety, and his hit the trigger! I did poke his eyes out, though."

Sebastian muffles a chuckle. "Where do they think you're going?"

"I need to go speak to this guy Fernando Montoya —"

"Absolutely the fuck not!" Sebastian shouts. "No fucking way. They were taking you to him? Seriously? Baby, do you know who he is?"

I nod. "They told me. But he thinks I stole all these drugs, and I told them that you got video from a doorbell camera that shows someone entered the apartment thirty minutes before me. If we tell Fernando that, I'm hoping he'll let us go. But I said if they think Fernando might kill us, that you shouldn't be involved, because I refuse to leave Camila without any parents."

Sebastian's eyes soften slightly. "*Mi Cielo*, I'm not letting you go in there alone. And you may not have given birth to Camila, but there's no one she'd rather have as her mother than you."

"I know, but I can't let you go if something might happen. She's too important to me," I sniffle.

The driver speaks up. "If it's any consolation, I told her that Montoya is violent, but he doesn't fuck with children. He would never harm your daughter, and knowing you're a single parent like he is, he's more likely to let you go."

"Dude!" the passenger hisses. "No one fucking knows that!"

"Oh. Whoops. You should probably follow us. We gotta get back because Montoya knows you're coming, and he gets mean if he sends out the troops to intercept people."

"We'll follow," Sebastian says curtly, before grabbing my hand, pulling me quickly toward his bike. "Isabella, I swear to God, I'm gonna light your ass red when we get home."

As soon as we get to his bike, he rips a spare helmet off the back. "I love you too, baby."

Sebastian glances at me before grabbing the back of my head and crashing our lips together. It's a quick, borderline punishing kiss, but it's full of love, pent up desire, and promise. "You didn't have to call me. I've got software on your phone, and there's a GPS tracker in the sole of your shoe."

"In my shoe?" I ask incredulously, my mouth open in shock.

"Yup. You wear the same shoes to work every day. I figured there was a chance you might not get to grab your phone, but you'd always have your shoes on. Turns out I had two ways to track you today. And I snuck back in through the basement, so I was in the kitchen listening for most of the conversation with Diego. He never knew I was there, though."

"Of course not. You're much smarter than him," I announce proudly, as he positions the helmet on my head. "And much more handsome."

"I did hear the part about having a bigger dick, though. I appreciated that," he says with a chuckle. "Hop on, but avoid these parts here. They'll burn you."

"I wasn't sure if the call dropped," I comment as I throw my leg over the bike.

"It didn't. I had myself muted in case they could hear me. I was texting you that I was on my way. Ava would probably love to know how many laws I broke getting to you as quickly as I did," he jokes as he climbs on.

A few months ago, I'd had a dream about riding on the back of Sebastian's motorcycle, my arms wound tightly around him, with one of his hands running up and down my thigh. While that part of my fantasy is coming true, I certainly never thought it would be so I could go speak to a someone in a cartel.

Chapter 24

SEBASTIAN

The only thing keeping me held together right now is Isabella behind me on my Harley. I've never considered myself to be a murderous person, or a man that would commit any crimes necessary to protect the woman he loved.

That changed with Isabella.

I would have no hesitation striking the match to light the whole motherfucking world on fire if it meant she would be safe.

As I follow the unmarked white van through Boulder, then into Fort Collins, I'm growing angrier. Why? Because I fucking *know* Fernando Montoya.

I know him. Several years ago, I'd have considered him an acquaintance, maybe even a friend. He came into my bar a couple of times a month, and we'd always end up chatting. Never once did he give off a drug lord vibe, or that he was high up in the Salazar Cartel. Maybe he wasn't at that time. He was just a cool dude who I felt a commonality with because of our Hispanic upbringings.

Montoya, obviously, is from Mexico. We were both raised closely with our grandparents, both brought up in the Catholic faith. We disagreed on sports, with me liking baseball, while Montoya stayed loyal to his first love, soccer. We bonded over our mutual distaste for springtime tourism in Colorado, because out-of-state tourists, especially from the south, have no idea how to drive treacherous mountain roads during an unexpected snow squall. I told him about my interest in owning a bar, and how RMRRMC came to be. But I don't think we ever talked about what he did for a living.

I wrack my brain, trying to remember where the connection is to Salazar, and how he got here. Have I been under surveillance all this time? Was the connection to Isabella completely coincidental, or did Montoya plan to use me once Tweedle Dee and Tweedle Dum got past the prospect stage in the club?

Isabella snuggles in closer to me, sliding her hands under my shirt. Intrigued to see what she has planned, I let her hand wander. She settles it over my heart, and I feel a long exhale against my back. I can't even begin to imagine how scared she must have been. I take one hand off the handlebars, placing it tightly over hers. It's too loud to talk, and I'm not sure if I have the words to express my thoughts.

I want to put her over my knee for getting herself in danger.

If I thought she'd actually do it, I'd make her promise never to go anywhere without me.

While I get why Isabella essentially offered herself up to ensure my safety, that shit isn't gonna fly again. Camila needs her just as much.

And mostly, I need her to promise — *promise* — to love, cherish, and honor me for the rest of her life. Legally. With a massive diamond on her finger, and maybe a tattoo on her forehead that says, "I love Sebastian Garcia." If I thought she'd do it, I'd make her carry around a sign, too.

I'm surprised when we drive north of Fort Collins, around the Colorado State campus, and head west into the foothills. As we slow into a residential area, I discreetly tap a tiny button underneath the visor that alerts Trace to my location. I figure we're gonna be checked for trackers immediately, and I wouldn't be surprised if they completely destroy our phones as a precaution. There's no way Montoya is going to be fine with us waltzing in there.

When we exit the residential area, and continue on a gravel road, Isabella's arms tighten around me.

"I know, baby," I tell her. "It's gonna be okay."

"I'm scared," she confesses.

Me too.

My phone vibrates in my pocket, and I assume it's Trace responding to my location. Hell, I'm surprised I even have service here. Only a couple houses dot the horizon. We'd worked out a code phrase for us to say whenever we had to share a location. The person at the Clubhouse would say, "Guys want to know if it's tacos or enchiladas tonight." Then the one out responds with tacos, if everything seems to be on the up-and-up, or enchiladas if the Range Riders need to get to us. The majority of the guys were with me when the van pulled over, and I assume they continued in the direction we headed. If needed, I hope they can get to us within an hour.

What seems like an eternity passes before we reach a large, motorized gate with a guard on duty. The guard approaches the van, then rounds the vehicle to open the sliding door. He rears back when he sees the body, and Isabella stiffens. "There's blood dripping out of the van."

So there is.

Well, if all else fails, my guys can follow the trail of blood like some fucked up Scooby Doo case.

The guard quickly closes the door, then motions for me to follow the van. He stares me down, and Isabella tilts her head down so he can't see her face. "Baby, you didn't even flinch when that guy was bleeding out in the van, but now you're scared to look a guard in the eyes?"

"Adrenaline. I don't know how I handled that," she says quietly.

We continue for another mile before turning a corner to see a beautiful home built into the side of a mountain. Floor to ceiling windows across the length of the home for all three stories look out onto the city of Fort Collins. We can see all the way to Greeley from here, and I bet on a clear night, downtown Denver might be visible.

Turning off my bike, I quickly dismount, then take my time removing Isabella's helmet. "No matter what you're asked, act dumb. Put it all on me. I know how to handle a guy like this, and I've met him before."

"Okay," she whispers, and the sadness of her tone makes me stop.

"You know I don't actually think you're dumb, right? Or that you can't handle yourself? I know you can, sweetheart. I'm honestly hoping my previous history with this guy can work to our advantage. I love you. We're gonna be okay."

"I trust you," she says, a tiny bit of oomph back in her voice.

I hear someone approach about the same time metal hits the back of my neck. "This is an interesting turn of events."

I slowly place Isabella's helmet on my bike, then remove my own. Turning slowly, but keeping Isabella behind me, I take a good look at Fernando Montoya. It's been eight or ten years since I've seen him, and the time has aged him tremendously. In his early forties, he'd once been lively and youthful. Now there are deep lines across his forehead, and what looks like a permanent scowl on his face.

But what gets me is that the fucker is wearing red silk pajamas while pointing a diamond studded pistol at me. "What? No comment about my outfit? You always had opinions before now."

I shake my head, chuckling. Eccentric motherfucker always wore something odd. I used to tease him about shopping at a consignment store straight out of the eighties. Knit sweaters in odd geometric patterns, bright colored trousers, and almost always with boat shoes. Who the hell wears boat shoes to a bar in Colorado?

"You weren't supposed to come with Miss Santo, Sebastian Garcia. What am I to do with you now?"

"Listen to an old friend, I hope," I tell him. "I always wondered what happened to you, Fernando. I never knew you were related to the Salazar family."

Fernando sighs as he lowers his gun. "I'm not technically family. My mother's brother's illegitimate son married a Salazar girl. They wanted to build up the distribution in Colorado, and here I am."

I feel like there is a lot more to the story, but I doubt he's going to offer up any information. "I'd really like to explain how Isabella got mixed up in this. For old times' sake, I hope you'll give us a chance. I know my word doesn't mean much to you these days, but there was a time when I thought you trusted me. I'm still that same man."

"And your *amor*? Will she be participating in this chat, or have you decided you're the only one who can talk?" Fernando asks, a glint in his eye as he waits for my reply.

"She can talk just fine," comes a muted voice behind me. Isabella peeks out nervously. "Sebastian is worried. I was coming here with or without him. I knew I had to speak with you and plead my case."

Fernando sighs again as his gaze strays to the side. "I own all of this land. Did you know that? Over ten thousand acres."

I'm impressed, but even I know the Cartel can buy anything. "I had no idea. I always wondered what your profession was."

He continues as if I haven't spoken. "A Salazar son is trying to force me out. He whispers into the ears of the kingpin, spreading lies about my leadership. It's only a matter of time before I'm sent to the gates of Hell with everyone else."

I hear Isabella's sharp intake of breath, and I know her heart is torn. She wants to feel hurt for the lost man in front of us, but also hates his part in wrecking our lives over the past handful of months.

"I can't remember the last time a guest came to see me," Fernando murmurs. I'm tempted to remind him that we are not, in fact, guests, but that information is irrelevant. He whips his gaze to mine with a look of determination. "Let's go inside. The house is beautiful. You'll meet my wife, Maria."

Fernando turns, walking quickly up a cement pathway, motioning back at us with his gun. Isabella gasps, hiding behind me. "I don't like the gun."

"I'm more concerned with the fact that he's got a wife hidden up here," I mumble, trying not to move my lips. "Who the fuck would choose to live as a hermit with a drug lord?"

"I get wanting to be alone. I'm an introvert. But this is overkill. How do they get groceries? Drone delivery?" she asks quietly.

I snicker. "Somehow I think even the drones get shot down."

"A Fort Collins grocery delivers at the gate," Fernando calls out, a good one hundred feet in front of us. "My hearing is excellent, and sound reverberates off the mountain. Keep that in mind, please. I do not like nasty backtalk."

Jesus fucking Christ.

Isabella's hand flails against mine as she grips it tightly. I hear a shuddered breath, and I know she's trying to control her emotions. Isabella has never been highly emotional. Out of all the Santo siblings, that honor goes to Arianna. But everyone has their breaking point, and I think we passed Isabella's quite some time ago. "I've got you, *mi Reina*. Trust me."

"I know," she whispers.

Fernando waits for us at the front entrance, two thick glass doors that lead into a stunning two-story foyer. A winding staircase creeps up the side, matching the white marble on the floors and walls. Everything is white.

"Wow," Isabella breathes, and Fernando beams. He motions for us to continue through a regal dining room, featuring a glass table and twelve chairs — who the hell is he expecting to eat here — and into a gourmet kitchen that has Isabella's mouth dropping open. "This is spectacular. Every chef's dream kitchen."

Fernando makes a show of pointing out every part of the space. An induction oven, restaurant quality espresso machine, and two massive refrigerators. The stove has eight burners, and a microwave only appears when a hidden button is pushed, making the appliance descend from a cabinet. He waxes poetic about a hot water tap near the stove, points out the three sinks spread throughout the space, and shows us the "mood lighting" that is color-coded and controlled by an app. Isabella is in awe.

We continue into a living room space, where Fernando encourages us to sit on a large sofa facing the windows, while he sits in a large chair to the side, which looks too much like a throne to call it anything else. Once we're all seated, a woman seems to materialize out of thin air. She approaches us, sitting on the arm of the throne chair. Her gaze is narrowed on Isabella, and the animosity comes off her in waves.

"Settle," Fernando says, tapping the woman's knee. Like a switch is flipped, she blinks and smiles sweetly at us.

"Hello. I'm Maria. Welcome to our home."

What the actual fuck.

I'm too shell-shocked to answer, so Isabella does. "Hello, Maria. I'm Isabella, and this is Sebastian."

"I know who you are. You killed Diego." The switch is flipped again.

"Forgive my wife," Fernando says calmly. "You killed her lover."

"I didn't kill him," Isabella says, her teeth clenched. "Why doesn't anyone believe me? His finger was on the trigger, mine was on the safety. But did you just say lover?"

"Yes. We have an open marriage. In fact, I'd love to discuss —"

"Absolutely the fuck not," I growl. Fernando's grin is immediate. "We are *not* in an open relationship."

"A shame, really. Ten years ago you would have had no problem sharing a woman." I growl again. He's baiting both of us, because I've never shared a woman with anyone. That is not my idea of fun, and I certainly won't share Isabella.

"I don't believe Sebastian ever shared anyone with you," Isabella replies quietly. "If you are attempting to get a rise out of me, it won't work."

"Oh? And how do you know this?" Fernando asks.

Isabella's brown eyes find mine. "Because I know him, and he's the most trustworthy man I've ever met. I know his heart. He wouldn't treat a woman like that."

Fernando grins like he won something. "It seems like Sebastian Garcia may still be the kind of man I remember. Now let's get down to discussing why you've traveled all the way here from Eternity Springs."

Isabella launches into a monologue about her relationship with Rick, finding him with her friend, and then destroying his apartment. She vehemently denies even seeing a bag of drugs on the counter, as well as denying knowledge about Rick's side gig of distribution.

Fernando looks at me when Isabella has finished. "I understand you've come across video that shows another person entering the apartment before Isabella?"

"I have. We've guesstimated the height of the person to be only around five-five or five-six, leading me to believe it's a woman." I pull out my phone, surprised no one took it from me when we got here, and show Fernando the video. "The person enters through the front door using the keypad code. They somehow snuck out without being recorded."

"Do you have any leads on the whereabouts of the young woman? Her name is Amelia, yes?" Fernando asks, smiling smugly as we both stare incredulously at him.

"Amelia? My best friend? The one I caught Rick with?" Isabella asks, and Fernando nods. "Wow. I — I had no idea. How long has Rick been distributing for you? When did Amelia get involved? How long were they sleeping together? How did you know it was her? They must have been doing this right under my nose. I guess I need to work on my situational awareness."

"Amelia and Rick are currently on their way to Mexico, I'm afraid. A reunion won't be possible, and I suspect your questions will go unanswered about their relationship. I will not be divulging any details about distribution, but I will say we'd suspected Rick of skimming off the top of deliveries for quite some time, so I had a hidden camera installed in one of the light fixtures of the kitchen. Someone was having a temper tantrum —" he says irritably, glaring at his wife, "— and changed the password to the server where the videos were downloaded. It took some time to find the footage, and I'd just been given a screen grab only an hour or two ago. Amelia took off her jacket, and I recognized her as the woman Rick had worked with."

"Then why are we here?" I ask, suddenly angry at Fernando. Two hours ago, we were driving through Fort Collins. We could have been notified and gone home. This is complete bullshit.

Fernando shrugs. "You were already on your way. And once I learned you were accompanying Isabella, I decided I wanted to see you again, and determine if you're still the stand-up man I remember."

"Am I?" I snap. "I'm sure you'll remember I'm not very fond of mind games."

Fernando smiles easily, leaning back into the chair. Maria still pouts next to him, her eyes shooting daggers at Isabella. "Ah, Sebastian. You're so easy to rile up."

"I don't appreciate Isabella being part of this. If I start aggravating your wife, don't you think it would make you fly off the handle a little faster?"

Fernando frowns, but shrugs with his hands up in a defensive stance. "Maria can fight for herself. I didn't marry a pussy."

"I'm not a pussy," Isabella murmurs quietly.

"No, you aren't," I respond. I can see the worry on her face. The confusion over why Fernando brought us here if he already knew she was innocent. The fear that we may not get out of here unscathed. Turning back to Fernando, I decide to nip this in the bud. "Now you know Isabella is innocent. I'm the same man I've always been. We would like to leave."

"Now, now, why rush out so quickly?" Fernando purrs, his eyes on Isabella. "Surely we can have a drink. Stay for dinner. Let's get to know each other better."

This motherfucker. "Fernando."

"Hmm?" he replies, his eyes dragging slowly down Isabella's body, and she folds herself closer to me.

"I don't fucking share."

"What?"

"Stop looking at my wife!" I shout, making Fernando smile wickedly.

"She isn't your wife yet."

I scoff. "It's a fucking technicality and you know it. So any plans you have of potentially seducing Isabella are out of the question."

Fernando looks at her, his brows raised in question. "Shouldn't the woman be allowed to speak for herself?"

Maria glowers at us, her bottom lip sticking out in a pout. I'd think it was adorable if Isabella did it, but on Maria, it makes her look immature, haughty, and a downright bitch. But I'm proud of my girl, who doesn't shrink back from Maria's intense gaze. "I have no interest in swapping."

Fernando sighs. "Worth a shot. We never have women to the compound. I've run out of options for myself."

"Then stop fucking the help, because they inevitably fall in love with you, and then I have to kill them!" Maria snaps. Fernando smiles sheepishly as he drags Maria into his lap. She swivels to straddle him, and we're suddenly getting our own live porno. Their kisses are completely disgusting, with way too much tongue and spittle. Isabella looks appalled.

"Fix your face," I murmur as quietly as possible. She immediately schools her expression. This is undoubtedly just another test we have to pass.

"Make them leave, Nando," Maria says as she peppers kisses across his jaw. "If I can't fuck him, then either shoot them or let them go."

"Jesus Christ," I mutter, rubbing a hand across my forehead. "I vote for the latter."

Fernando only has eyes for Maria. "Of course, my darling. And then you'll do the thing?"

She bats her eyes at him. "Does Daddy want me to eat his ass?"

Isabella makes a small choking sound, and Maria glares over her shoulder. Looking back at Fernando, she waits for his reply.

"Yes, my love. As soon as they leave."

We all stand, zeroing in on the impressive erection Fernando sports under his silk pajamas. He makes no effort to adjust himself or hide the erection, choosing instead to proudly stride through the house. He is the quintessential definition of a man who peacocks.

As we arrive at the door, Fernando surprises all of us when he yanks Isabella into his arms and plants a desperate kiss on her lips. I'm so shocked it takes me a few seconds to get my body to cooperate, and as I watch him force his tongue into Isabella's mouth, I step forward to push him away. At the same time, Fernando makes a muffled sound, stepping away from Isabella while holding his mouth, and I see blood on his lip.

God, I love this woman. She bit a fucking drug lord.

"You should know better than to kiss a woman without asking for her consent first," Isabella says hotly. She's absolutely fuming, and she has every right to be. If I didn't think I'd be shot on the spot, I'd deck Fernando right now.

Fernando chuckles. "Can't blame a guy for trying. Although now that I know you're a biter, I'm glad we won't be sharing a bed tonight."

I step closer to Fernando, lowering my voice. "Up until this point, I've played your games. I've respected our history, as well as your family. But you've crossed one hell of a line, Fernando. I will not allow you to assault Isabella again. If you do, there will be consequences."

"That won't end well for you," he muses, rubbing his chin.

I shrug. "It is what it is. I'll take great pleasure in ending your life, old friend. Remember that as you make your decisions moving forward."

As we walk out the open door, Fernando grabs my arm. "Your daughter is lovely, Sebastian. You are a good father."

"I know I am," I answer. "But don't talk about my daughter again. Evidently, you're also a father?"

Fernando chuckles. "Touché. I wish you well, old friend. It's unlikely we'll see each other again."

I note the sadness in his gaze, the way he seems resigned to his fate. "I wish you well, Fernando. Thanks for not killing us, I guess?"

He barks out a loud laugh. "It was touch-and-go, since I know you still think baseball is better than soccer."

"You're damn straight."

ISABELLA

I'm scared to death and also turned on at the same time. I want out of here, away from this despicable man, but watching Sebastian threaten a drug lord's life is actually really hot. Looking back at every relationship I've had, I've never been with a man who I thought would literally fight for me. There's a storyline in an old *Grey's Anatomy* episode where a guy kept hiding behind his girlfriend during an active shooter situation, and that's how most, if not all, of the guys I've dated would act.

Not Sebastian.

I fight the smile that twitches on my lips. Undoubtedly, if Maria and Fernando catch on to any of my thoughts, they'll start up some other ridiculous mind game. And if that man attempts to kiss me again, I will bite straight through his tongue. Gross.

Sebastian taps rapidly on his phone, and I assume he's texting Trace to update him. He shoves his phone in his pocket before grabbing my thigh, squeezing it tightly. Neither of us look back at the house, and I'm glad to be putting distance between us and Fernando.

Once we leave, and I'm safely tucked against Sebastian's back on his motorcycle, I let out a loud sigh of relief. The sun is setting behind the mountains, and the men who led us to Fernando's compound are nowhere to be found. We're on remote dirt roads, in the middle of nowhere, and it's getting cold. I tuck my hands under the hem of Sebastian's shirt, stealing some of his body warmth, and lay my head against his back. Closing my eyes, I let the vibrations of the road lull me into relaxation.

Just a short time later, the motorcycle comes to a stop. Yawning, I lift my head and open my eyes to find we're in the parking lot of a hotel. "What's going on?"

"I'm getting us a room. We're both exhausted, and we need to talk," he says curtly, extending a hand to help me off the bike. I'm quiet as he unstraps my helmet, and I wordlessly follow him into the hotel. We're alone in a room moments later.

I feel my heart beat increase, assuming the worst. He's mad, rightfully so. But mad enough to do what? End things? Demand I be grounded from going anywhere? Tell my entire family that I willingly went to a drug lord's home in an attempt to clear my name?

I watch as Sebastian removes his jacket, then toes off his shoes. When I make no move to get comfortable, Sebastian forces me to sit on the edge of the king-size bed. Kneeling before me, he removes my supportive but ugly white shoes, then hesitates before laying his head in my lap. I'm too surprised to react, until his arms slide around my body, hugging me tightly. Only when I hear a sob do I move.

"Talk to me," I whisper, gliding my hands through his hair. I can count on one hand how many times I've seen each of my brothers cry, and I'm incredibly ill-equipped to handle this. Sebastian is the strongest man I know. But today's course of events have clearly drained him entirely. His body shakes as he lets his emotions release.

"I am so fucking mad at you," he whispers, each word staccato as he tries to gain strength and calming, "but I'm also so fucking impressed by you. So in love with you. If something happened to you, *Naranja*, it would destroy me. I'm so wrapped up in you that I don't know how I'd be able to move forward without you."

"I love you too," I say softly, continuing to drag my fingers through his hair, gently scratching his scalp. "I know why you're mad, but why are you impressed?"

He leans his head up, resting his chin on my thigh. Eyes red with tears soaking his thick black lashes, I'm so overcome with his beauty that I forget how to breathe. How on earth did I end up with this man? A beautiful soul who wears his heart on his sleeve, loves fiercely, and waited years for me to finally get my head out of my own ass.

"You would have sacrificed yourself to save me, and I know you would have done it for Camila too."

"Of course I would have. She deserves to have a parent raise her. I won't apologize for that," I state. Every decision I made today was for Camila. Her mother abandoned her, and I won't be responsible for taking her father away from her.

"You know the kind of person that does that? Who is willing to die for a child?" he asks. I don't answer, not sure where he's going with this. He gives me a smile. "A mother is willing to sacrifice herself for the safety of her child. You get that, right? You were treating Camila like she's yours. You have given more to her in the last five months than anything her birth mother gave her. There aren't many women who would be so willing to do that, Isabella. That's why I'm impressed by you."

"Oh," I whisper bashfully. I close my eyes, thinking about the course of events from the day. I was ready to go to a drug lord's home, by myself, trying to save the day. By myself. What the fuck was I thinking? Fernando may have manipulated the situation to corner me, where maybe I didn't have a way out, an escape ...

what if I didn't get out? What if he didn't end my life, but kept me there? Emotion clogs my throat as my eyes fill with tears. "Oh my God. What was I thinking?"

I start sobbing, and Sebastian mutters, "There it is." He rises, scooping me into his arms, and turns so he's sitting on the edge of the bed and I'm crying into his shoulder.

"I didn't think, I just reacted," I cry. "I didn't want anyone else to get hurt. They said they were watching Arianna too, and I just reacted. I couldn't be responsible for a child losing a parent!"

"I know," Sebastian says quietly, slowly stroking a hand up and down my spine. "You did what you thought was the best option."

"What would you have done?" I stammer, sniffing hard.

Sebastian sighs. "The same thing you did. I'd have sacrificed myself."

My head pops up, and I absentmindedly swipe at my face, moving rogue locks of hair that are stuck in streaks of tears. "Then why are you mad at me?"

"I'm mad because I could have lost you. I'm mad because I had no control over anything that happened today. And I'm furious because that fucker stuck his tongue in your mouth even after you said you had no interest in what he was offering. In front of me. In front of his wife. I wanted to strangle him right then, and I knew I'd be killed, and who knows what he'd have done to you. And I'm more upset with myself because I thought about killing him anyway," he fumes.

"That's — that's not a normal reaction from you," I murmur.

"No, it's not. I'm not violent. I kick people out of the MC if they start fights for no reason. I always feel like disagreements can be solved verbally instead of physically. But the moment — the fucking *moment* that asshole looked at you with interest in his eyes, I wanted to launch across the room and rip his head off."

I ponder that for a moment. "Maria wanted you too, you

know. She'd have slit my throat if she thought you'd agree to be her next lover."

The look of disgust he gives me is comical. "Gross. First of all, not my type. Secondly, I'm not a fucking home wrecker, regardless of whether they claim their marriage is open or not. And lastly, she's not *you*."

I smile tenderly at him. His voice is evening out, and he no longer looks like he might collapse at any moment. "I'm sorry, Sebastian."

"You have nothing to be sorry for, *mi Cielo*. None of this was your fault."

"I started the ball rolling by glitter-bombing Rick's apartment. Did I understand that correctly? That Rick and Amelia are probably going to get murdered in Mexico?"

He nods, his lips pursed in a straight line. "That isn't your fault, Isabella. Fernando insinuated Rick had been stealing from him. If he's taking Amelia out too, then he must have evidence she's also stealing. The Cartel don't take too kindly to that. An eye-for-an-eye."

"And are you disgusted by me now? Because he kissed me?" I blurt out, blushing furiously as I ask the question I can't stop thinking about. Am I tainted now?

"What the fuck? No, baby. I'm not disgusted by you in any way. You didn't ask for any of this," he says.

"I feel a little dirty," I confess. "It's been a long day, and then being on the motorcycle, plus him touching me ... I feel like I want to scrub my skin off."

"Do you want to shower?" he asks.

I nod. "But will you shower with me?"

"Of course."

Sliding off his lap, I grab Sebastian's hand and pull him into the large bathroom. I think momentarily about taking a bath, as there is a large soaking tub in the corner of the space, but continue to the shower. Sebastian turns on the water while I remove my clothes. I frown when I think about having to put these clothes back on whenever we leave to go home, knowing it'll feel awful to slide into dirty clothing that is caked in flour.

I sigh in relief as I step under the hot water, letting it soak my hair. Sebastian steps in behind me, and I hear the pump of the attached shampoo bottle as he fills his hand. I moan much louder than I should when he begins washing my hair, his strong fingers massaging my scalp at the perfect pressure. He turns me to face him, and I lay my head on his chest. I feel his lips ghost over my forehead, and I smile.

When Sebastian speaks, his voice is husky and tender. "The first moment I saw you, I fell for you. It was like my heart began beating at the rhythm it was supposed to for the first time. Each time I saw you since, I became even more convinced you were meant to be mine. While these last few months haven't been ideal, I'll never regret getting to know you so deeply. Learning everything you like, watching you fall for my daughter, and seeing you trust me more and more each day. I've been half in love with you for years, Isabella, but there's nothing compared to how my heart beats for you now."

I look up at him, and he bends to apply the sweetest of kisses to my lips. The memory of Fernando is erased immediately. I'm exactly where I'm supposed to be, with the man that I love, and I wouldn't have it any other way.

Sebastian rests his forehead against mine as he pushes us under the water to rinse out the shampoo. His fingers dance across my hair and back perfectly. He continues with the conditioner, expertly applying the product where it should go, and he catches my smile. "This is where having a daughter with long hair has its perks."

"I guess so," I laugh. We take turns washing each other's bodies, then step back into the spray to clean off the soap and conditioner. Standing there, with Sebastian's arms tightly around me, I've never felt so cherished. It's intimate, comforting, and sexy all at the same time. I gaze up at him, starstruck at his beauty. His hair, so dark it's almost black, and how I love it even more when we're at home, because the unruly locks give him a boyish look. The perfect brows that arch when he teases me, but cover those deep brown eyes that only sparkle for his daughter and me. Flawless lips that look best when tipped up in a smirk, but also fit against mine so sublimely.

I stand on my tiptoes, pressing my lips against his. Sebastian sighs into my mouth as one hand tracks up my spine to grab the back of my head. He deepens the kiss as he turns me, pressing me into the tile wall. I shriek against the cold material, but then moan softly as he drops to his knees, taking a nipple deep into his mouth.

"You can do better than that," he murmurs, circling my nipple with his tongue, before lightly biting the tip.

"Do what better?" I ask, confusion evident in my tone.

"Moan. We aren't at home, baby. You can get loud." He sucks harder while pinching the other nipple, and I gasp. He kisses down my stomach. "Nah. I want you to knock the roof off this joint."

Throwing one of my legs over his shoulder, he attacks my pussy with gusto. Quickly sliding two fingers inside, he sucks on my clit with the same tempo that he scissors his fingers in and out. In. Suck. Out. Suck. It's exhilarating and maddening and oh God, so fucking good. I clutch his hair with one hand, desperately trying to control his angle, but Sebastian maintains his pattern, never quite giving me enough to fall over the edge.

I growl at him when he stops completely, making him laugh. "I'll get you off, Isabella. You don't have to worry."

"I was right there," I whine, close to stomping my foot like a toddler.

"And I'll get you back to that point in a second. Just wanted to look at you. You're so fucking beautiful. I honestly can't believe you're finally mine," he says quietly, and I look down at him. It's him who's gorgeous, with his tousled hair and my essence covering his lips.

"I feel the same way about you," I reply shyly.

"I love watching you orgasm, because your entire body goes pink. It's like nothing I've ever seen before. So I might be dragging this out a little bit, because I know it'll make you come even harder."

"Wow," I mumble, my vision going cross-eyed as a wave of pleasure courses through my veins. He's not even touching me, but his words alone are striking a chord so intense I have to steady myself.

Sebastian switches hands, sliding his left up to tweak my nipple, then onto my chin. I grab my leg behind my knee, holding it up to give him better access. He pushes two fingers into my mouth, then demands, "Suck them as hard as you want me to suck this needy little clit."

I let out a loud moan. The mouth on this man! If anyone else spoke to me like this, it would be an immediate dealbreaker. But with Sebastian, it works. Swirling my tongue around his fingers, I hollow my cheeks and suck, tasting myself on his skin. Sebastian immediately latches onto my clit as he shoves two fingers inside me, tapping my G-spot again and again. When his pinkie finger pushes against my back hole, I feel the orgasm barreling toward me like a freight train. I barely have time to breathe before white-hot pleasure starts at my feet, whipping up my legs and torso, before sliding across my chest and head. I ride the wave for a minute, forgetting to breathe, and as I crash down with aftershocks, Sebastian catches me, sliding us both down the wall and onto the shower floor. I shake as I catch my breath, straddling Sebastian with my head on his shoulder. One hell of an orgasm.

"You good, baby?"

"Mmm-hmm," I mutter, focusing on my heart rate as I come down from the high. Opening my eyes, I find Sebastian's expression slightly pained. "Are you okay?"

"I really want to come inside you, sweetheart, so you need to stop stroking me," he rasps through clenched teeth. I look down and find I'm gripping his dick tightly, the bulbous head red and angry looking.

"Oh my God! I swear I didn't realize I was doing that," I tell him, scrambling to get out of his lap.

"Any time you want to hold my cock, you're more than welcome to," he teases as he grabs me by the waist. "But right now, I need you."

"Don't you want to go to the bed?" I ask, pointing out of the bathroom. Although who knows what that bedding has seen. The shower may actually be less germy.

"No. I need you right fucking now," he says huskily, pulling me to straddle him. I hiss when the tip of his cock hits my incredibly sensitive clit, and I know a second orgasm will be easily acquired tonight. I slowly slide down his length, watching as Sebastian's eyes roll back into his head and he grits his teeth. Circling my hips, I find I can hit his pubic bone each time, giving me the friction I crave, and Sebastian silently lets me control the tempo as I chase another orgasm. It's nowhere near as intense as the first one, but still better than anything I could give myself. Sebastian waits until my eyes open before he speaks. "Can I take over now?"

I nod, and he wastes no time. His hands clamp on my hips, lifting me up, before slamming me down roughly. I let out a guttural moan as he does it again and again, the growls and snarls coming out of him like a damn aphrodisiac to my pussy.

"I want to try a different position," he mumbles, pushing me off to the side. He manhandles me so his front is to my back, then positions himself at my core again. "Gonna be intense, baby. Three, four, and five."

"I'm happy with two," I murmur, but he doesn't respond as he pushes into my channel. The new position means his cock slides along my G-spot, and within a few seconds, I'm coming again. The fourth orgasm isn't too far behind, and when I can tell Sebastian is close to coming, he reaches around to pinch my clit between his thumb and forefinger, making me come a fifth time.

"So. Fucking Good," he growls as he pours himself into my pussy. So good. I almost tell him that I hope I get pregnant, but manage to shut my mouth at the last second. While I think it wouldn't necessarily make Sebastian run for the hills, I'd rather not scare the crap out of him either.

Five orgasms in a short period of time means my legs are complete mush, and my vagina has a heartbeat. Sebastian moves me aside, cleans both of us off in the now cool water of the shower, then towels me off. He deposits me under the covers, turns off all the lights, climbs into bed, and yanks me against him. I nuzzle into his shoulder and sigh happily. I'm almost asleep when he speaks.

"Marry me," he whispers, and my eyes pop open.

Chapter 26

SEBASTIAN

"Marry me," I whisper, and her eyes pop open.

"What?" she screeches.

I chuckle, peeking out of one eye. "You heard me."

"I was just naked in the shower!"

"Are you aggravated I'm not on one knee? Because —" I stop talking, jump out of bed, and begin to lower myself onto a knee, but Isabella grabs onto me.

"No, I don't care about that. I always thought that was a weird tradition anyway."

"Well, historically, it's a sign of respect and submission."

She snorts. "Submission? You? That's not a word I'd use to describe your personality, Sebastian."

"Being submissive isn't a bad trait, Isabella. It also means that I fully trust you, and I know you have my best interests at heart. Submissive in the bedroom, now, that's a different story. Are you going to answer my question?"

"You didn't ask a question. That was a statement. You basically stated a fact."

I shrug. "I mean, you're not totally wrong. We're getting married. I figured you'd like to be in on the planning of it, though."

"This is so surreal. We were just in a long shower. I'm shriveled up like a prune."

I pull her into my embrace, my mouth millimeters from hers. "I didn't ask a question because it's not a question. It's a fact. We are in love. We don't want to spend a moment away from each other. We want to parent our daughter, and maybe have some more rugrats down the road. I didn't ask because I know your heart, *Naranja*. I know that when we're together, our heartbeats sync up. Half the time I know what you're going to say before you say it, and you respond to me before I've even spoken a word. I can't imagine a day when I don't get to fall asleep with you in my arms, or a time where you don't bring me peace just by being in the same room with me. You're mine, and I'm yours. I want your last name to be the same as mine and Camila's, and a giant ring on your finger so that no man thinks for a second that he can shoot his shot. Please, baby. Put me out of my misery and say yes."

"You didn't ask me a question," she whispers, a sheen of tears making her eyes glassy.

I laugh quietly as I kneel on the bedroom floor. "My love, my sky, my queen. You're my other half, and I will spend all of eternity cherishing you. Will you marry me?"

"Yes," Isabella breathes, dropping to the floor beside me and throwing her arms over my shoulders. I grunt as the movement jars my balance, and we topple over. I make no effort to move, so I take the opportunity to memorize every detail of her face. The tiny gold nose ring she got around her twenty-fifth birthday that her parents absolutely hate. The chocolate brown eyes that sparkle more now than they ever have, like she's finally living the life she never thought was possible. Her pert nose that scrunches up, usually in disgust, when she tastes a sweet treat that isn't up to her standards. And her beautiful smile that is a balm to my soul, especially when it's directed at me.

"I'm sorry I don't have a ring yet," I confess, swiping at the hair dangling in front of her face.

She waves a hand indifferently. "I don't care about that. I rarely wear jewelry, and I'm not going to proudly show off a ring."

"What?" I say, and I know I have a dejected look on my face. "Why?"

Isabella giggles. "I mean that it won't be the first thing I tell people about our engagement. I'll tell people about what you said. How you made me feel. A ring is wonderful, and I have no doubt you'll pick out something beautiful and way too big, but what you think is so much more important than that."

A smile breaks across my face. "So you're saying I can still buy you a massive ring?"

She snorts as she shakes her head. "Can we settle on something adequate?"

I scoff. "No wife of mine will wear an adequate ring, Isabella."

"How many wives are you planning to have?" She asks, teasingly.

I look at her adoringly as I slide a hand to the back of her neck. "Only you, *mi amor.*"

She pulls my head down to hers, and I take her lips in a searing kiss, hopefully pouring my love and devotion into her soul.

Isabella breaks off the kiss with a gasp. "But I can't wear a diamond while at work!"

I frown. I never thought about that.

Shit. Her work. I guess now is as good of a time as any. "There's something we need to discuss about your work, *mi Reina.*"

Her eyes darken almost imperceptibly. "If you're about to say that I don't need to work anymore because I'm marrying you —"

I interrupt her. "Oh, no. Not that. If you want to work, I wholeheartedly support that. But there is something about your bakery you need to know, and I really hope you don't get too mad about it."

"I already forgave you about the MC order, Sebastian. I know you were just trying to support me." She pauses, then her eyes widen. "SGI. You own my bakery?"

"I do. Well, I did."

She's silent for a long moment, and I can almost see the wheels turning in her mind. "But you've owned it for as long as I've worked there! Even before I took over the lease!"

I nod. "I bought it around the time you started your apprenticeship. I intended to sell it to you, but it never seemed right. It wasn't a way to get an 'in' with you," I use air quotes, "but a way for me to support your dreams."

"You've raised the rent every year," she comments. "I'm paying a similar amount to all the other tenants on the block. Do you own all of them too?"

"No, just yours. I've kept the amount on par with everyone else. The week after I had you move in with me, I added your name to the deed. It's yours, Isabella. Ours."

Her eyes fill with tears. "What?"

I nod solemnly. "If you want my name off the deed, say the word. It can be yours outright."

She shakes her head. "No. I want us both on there. Except for one minor thing ..."

"What?"

She gives me a beautiful smile. "I'd like it to reflect my new last name."

 with my woman wrapped around me. My fiancée. The love of my life.

Isabella tucks her hands under my jacket, her hands sliding up and down my abs. It's not sexual in nature. It's a comfort. A natural connection between us. Each day, Isabella becomes more comfortable in how she expresses herself with me. It's about intimacy and familiarity.

It boggles my mind how any man in Isabella's past fumbled her so badly. She's a diamond in the rough, and she's been waiting for someone to come along who sees her exactly as she is. Those men were dumb to leave her, but I'm not mad that they did.

As we slowly head down the driveway for both my house and the Clubhouse, I see Trace wave from the doorway with a quick nod of his head. He was incredibly worried about Isabella, and admitted in a text last night that he views her like a little sister. He also knows how much she means to me, and if anything happened to her, he'd be the one who would be tasked with helping me function.

"Do you think she'll be okay with this?" Isabella asks from behind me. I can hear the worry in her voice, and almost see her chewing on the inside of her cheek as she waits for my response.

"I know she will, sweetheart. She loves you. My parents do too. They will welcome you with open arms." I smile as I think about my grandmother, and assume she'll undoubtedly shower Isabella with all kinds of "gifts," that will all be tied to fertility in one way or another.

As we turn the final corner, our house comes into view. As expected, my grandmother, parents, and Camila all stand at the front door with wide grins. I may have let slip in another text that I'd asked Isabella to marry me.

As soon as I turn off the engine, Camila runs to us. I turn to catch her, then look on in surprise as she dances around me to get to Isabella. She squeals in delight as Isabella scoops her up while still sitting on my Harley. Quickly pulling out my phone, I snap a picture.

My world, all wrapped up in one perfect image.

Wrapping my arms around both of my girls, I kiss each on the temple. "*Naranja,* is it okay if we tell her now?"

"Tell me what?" Camila asks.

Isabella's eyes meet mine as she nods. "Can I tell her?"

"Of course," I answer, my smile so big my cheeks hurt.

Camila looks between the two of us as Isabella says, "Your dad asked me to marry him."

"Daddy," Camila whisper-shouts, looking at me with a grin, "I get a Mommy now! Is it okay for me to call you that now, Isabella? I think you'll make a good Mommy. Don't you, Daddy?"

I set one hand on Camila's back, as I wipe the tears clinging to Isabella's lashes with the other. "I agree, *Mija.* She'll make an excellent Mommy."

"Can I have another present?" Camila asks.

"The last time you asked, I got suckered into a kitten," I respond, deadpan.

Camila giggles. "I love Oreo. And Butterscotch. But I want something else."

"What do you want, baby?" Isabella asks softly.

Camila turns her beautiful blue eyes toward Isabella, and the love emanating from them steals my breath. "I want a baby brother."

Isabella inhales sharply before stammering, "Oh. Well, we don't get to pick boy or girl for a baby."

Camila harrumphs. "I guess I'll be fine with a baby sister."

"*Mija,* babies take some time, so you'll need to be patient," I tell her. "It may be a few years."

"Years!" she yells. "Why that long? Even the pet store doesn't make us wait that long to pet the puppies."

Isabella looks at me in confusion, and it takes me a moment to understand what Camila thinks. "*Mija,* babies don't come from a store. A baby sister or brother will grow in Isabella's tummy."

"Mommy's." Camila looks plainly at me. "It's Mommy's tummy."

I chuckle. "My mistake."

"Well, how long does he have to grow?"

"Nine months," I tell her solemnly.

"That's almost a whole year! I can't wait that long!" she screeches.

"That's not up to us to decide, sweetheart," Isabella coos. Already an excellent mom, and it makes me want to impregnate her tonight.

"Ugh. Fine," Camila says with an exaggerated eye roll. She jumps down from Isabella's lap, then skips over to where my parents and grandmother stand.

"She's going to make the teenage years very interesting," Isabella comments. Don't I fucking know it.

A COUPLE OF MONTHS INTO THE NEW YEAR, AND I'M A MARRIED MAN.

Isabella, not surprisingly, was a nonchalant bride. Other than wanting it to be small and winter-themed, she didn't care about much. We decided to let our mothers surprise us, and both matriarchs were up to the challenge.

Breaking from tradition, Isabella chose not to have her father walk her down the aisle. Instead, she and Camila walked hand-in-hand, in matching white dresses. They each held a bouquet, although Camila's was much smaller. Their dresses were simple silk, with sheer sleeves, and they each wore a jeweled headband instead of a veil. Camila was positively giddy to be included, and stood happily between us as we said our vows. From that moment we returned after I proposed, she began calling Isabella her mother, and she hasn't stopped.

Contrary to Isabella's hopes for something small, I got her a sizable diamond ring. Actually, a handful of diamonds. I intended to go with what she wanted, but as soon as I saw the ring with diamonds in the shape of a flower, I knew it had to be hers. It's unique, just like her. Her wedding band matches the white gold of the engagement ring, but I also got her a silicone ring that matches mine for while she's at work.

Only two months after our visit with Fernando Montoya, the Feds raided his compound. He'd mysteriously disappeared, and the trail ran cold soon thereafter.

Last week I received an envelope full of blank paper, post-marked in Montenegro. A subtle way to tell me he's not dead yet. The following day, one hundred thousand dollars showed up in Camila's bank account. I immediately donated it anonymously to fifteen different charities across the state of Colorado. I don't want, or need, drug money to raise my daughter.

"Wow, it's really coming down," Isabella comments from the passenger seat of my truck. It's snowing heavily in a typical Colorado spring snowstorm. Camila is staying at Luca and Hannah's tonight, and I'm happy to have my wife to myself.

I hope it never gets old to call her my wife.

"Can we stop at the grocery store before we leave town?" Isabella asks. While I live about fifteen minutes outside of Eternity Springs, the closest stores all reside in town. In this weather, once we get home, we won't leave again until the weather breaks.

"Sure. Do you want me to run in and get something?" I ask, turning into the parking lot for a small grocery at the edge of town.

"No, I know what I'm looking for. You'll just buy every option of the item because you'll second-guess what I actually want," she teases.

"I'm being a good husband, Isabella. Giving you options," I say defensively, but my lips tip up as I fight a grin. "I'll come in with you."

"No, it's okay —" she breaks off when my phone rings.

"Shit. It's the elementary school. It's after school, so this can't be good." Isabella smiles softly at me as she opens the door. Hiking the hood of her winter coat over her head, she gingerly walks to the store entrance before stomping snow off her boots. Turning, she waves gaily at me, knowing I'm watching. I chuckle as I answer the phone.

"Mr. Garcia, this is Principal Patterson calling," a female voice announces.

"Yes, hello." Every interaction I've had with the principal so far has been no-nonsense. While she doesn't come off as incredibly warm, I can tell she loves the children and wants them to succeed.

"Camila had some difficulty in school today, and I hope we can schedule a time to meet in person within the next week."

"Okay? What exactly happened?" I ask.

"There was a disagreement with another student over a preferred item during indoor recess. Camila was witnessed striking the other child. While we typically operate a no-tolerance view on violence in school, we also understand there are two sides to every story. Camila has never shown any aggression in class before, but when we spoke with her, she clammed up. I'm hoping if you and your new wife attend a meeting with us, Camila will be more comfortable in telling us her side."

"Wow. Hitting a child is incredibly out of character for her, Mrs. Patterson. I'm more than happy to sit down with you and get to the bottom of things. I'll ask Camila about it tomorrow as well, as she is staying with her aunt and uncle tonight."

"If you're able to come in Monday after school, we will set aside time."

"I'll make it work, as will my wife." Looking up, I see Isabella walking back to the car with a small bag. When she gets in the car, I try to see what she needed. "What's that?"

"Nothing," she replies quickly. "What was the principal calling for?"

"We have to meet with her Monday afternoon. Apparently Camila hit a kid today at school."

Isabella gasps. "What? No! What happened? That's not like her. She had to have been provoked. Is she in trouble? Do you want me to go too? I can't guarantee I'll keep my mouth shut, so tell me now what version of me you want. Shy and quiet, new stepmom navigating the waves, or feral mom who will cut a bitch for offending her daughter."

I let out a loud bark of laughter as I back out of the parking spot. "We should probably play it by ear, but I will likely pick the feral mom, just because I really want to see her in action."

Isabella beams at me. "It's a new position. I'm still learning the ropes."

"Learning the ropes of how to be feral, how to be a mom, or how to cut a bitch?"

"All of the above, I guess," she says with a snicker. "Watching Arianna and Alex's wife Natalie have given me a crash course in all three, but starring as the main character is still new to me. Digging the role, though."

I grab her hand, bringing it to my lips. "Good to hear, *Mami*."

Isabella coughs, dragging her hand away to hit her chest. "Swallowed wrong."

My eyes narrow as I watch her in my periphery. She's off. I can't quite put my finger on it, but something is definitely weird about her behavior.

I make idle chitchat as I carefully drive home, but when I pull into the garage, I quickly snatch the bag out of her hands before she can react. I know it's something about whatever is in here.

"Sebastian, wait!" Isabella shouts, causing me to pause. Her gaze is intense, her eyes imploring me to stop. "I'm not sure if you're ready for what's in there."

"The only thing I can think of that I might not be ready for would be a butt plug for me, and I highly doubt our grocery store has that ..." I trail off as I see a look in her eyes. Holy shit. I rip open the bag, staring at the two-pack of pregnancy tests. My eyes whip to hers. "Are you sure?"

"I don't know," she frets, wringing her hands in her lap. Tears fill her eyes as she chews on her bottom lip. "I'm late, but my period isn't always like clockwork. Then again, we've been pretty lax about birth control."

I chuckle as I lean across the center console, sliding my hand around to bracket the back of her neck. "We haven't been lax. We've been consciously going without. I've been trying to get you pregnant for months, baby. Now that I think of it, your tits are bigger than normal. I chalked it up to your period starting, but hopefully it means Camila will stop bugging us about giving her a sibling."

She gives me a watery smile and light chuckle. "How can you be so nonchalant? If I am pregnant, this changes everything."

I shake my head. "It doesn't change a damn thing about how I feel about you. How you feel about me. How happy we are. I've got all the love to give, sweetheart. And if you aren't pregnant, I'm still the happiest I've ever been, and I'll continue trying to knock you up every chance I get."

"I do enjoy the trying part," she whispers, leaning in to peck my lips.

"Let's go see if we're still in the trying portion of conception, or if we've moved into the production part."

I whisk Isabella inside our house, directly to the bathroom, only remembering to leave when she shouts at me that she'd like to pee in private.

Five minutes later, a tiny screen flashes the best word I've ever seen.

Pregnant.

Epilogue

ISABELLA

FOUR YEARS LATER

"Mom!" A loud screech is immediately followed by the slamming of a bedroom door. "Keep Nico outta my room!"

I sigh as Camila stomps down the stairs. I hear her huffing as she rounds the corner into the kitchen, where I'm quietly preparing dinner. Looking over my shoulder, I see my furious daughter, holding her favorite white sweater. Well, a sweater that used to be white.

"Oh dear," I murmur, logging the lovely colored lines that have been drawn all over one side of the fabric. Without looking, I can already assume my permanent markers, locked in an upper cabinet, will be gone. "I'll see what I can do."

"Mom," Camila whines, tears cresting her eyelids. "I wanted to wear this Monday for picture day at school. Why does he always go for my stuff?"

What I'd like to say is that Camila's room is a disaster, and it's easy to destroy things when they're left on the floor. Or that Camila leaves her door open, instead of shutting it and using the child lock we installed for this very reason.

"Your brother loves you so much, baby girl," I tell her quietly instead. It's not a lie. From the moment he was born, Nico Sebastian Garcia only had eyes for his big sister. For the weeks that we suffered through horrendous colic, and the nights where cutting molars was excruciating, only Camila could settle Nico down.

A loud scoff. "I know he loves me, Mom. But I don't want him in my room."

"Then lock the door," I say, aggravation evident in my tone as I clench my teeth.

My sweet and affectionate son crawled at five months, walked at eight months, and scaled the kitchen counters before his first birthday. He mastered riding a two-wheel bicycle on his third birthday, and has absolutely no fear about heights, speeds, or anything that normal children worry about.

My mother-in-law tells me Nico is exactly like Sebastian, which is only mildly infuriating.

"*Naranja?* Nico is on the roof again."

As I'm kneading dough to make dinner rolls, I shout back. "That's your DNA, Sebastian. You deal with it!"

I smile when I hear Sebastian's loud laughter, but he doesn't disagree with me. My brothers were wild, but even my parents say Nico takes it up a notch.

While Nico was a pleasant surprise, my pregnancy definitely threw a minor kink in our overall plans. With Sebastian owning two bars, he made the tough decision to hand over the reins of his original location, choosing instead to work from the Eternity Springs bar. Pregnancy did a number on my body, and I was forced to hire a store manager to oversee much of the bakery's day-to-day operations. Ava helped out when she could, but I was clear that I wanted her to focus her time on her college classes.

I've never been one to complain about the early morning wake-up that comes with owning a bakery, but pregnancy was a level of exhaustion I could not fight. I was either at work or asleep, and sometimes both simultaneously.

The hormones were ridiculous. Why did I need to have cystic acne cover my back? Hair on my chest? My nose grew like some fucked up version of Pinocchio. And the mood swings? Astronomically bad. It's a wonder Sebastian put up with me, patiently rubbing my back and giving me foot massages.

But worst of all was the fact that the concept of "morning" sickness was lost on me, as I had nonstop nausea. It also stayed the entire pregnancy. Needless to say, I was relieved when we found out Nico was a boy, because it meant we had a daughter and a son. Pregnancy just isn't for me.

"Momma." Looking over my right shoulder, I find my little boy, held tightly in his father's arms. His normally dark skin is even darker with what appears to be a layer of mud. Nico's beautiful face, normally a carbon copy of Sebastian's, is in an adorable pout as he stares at me defiantly. "I mad at Daddy."

"You're mad at Daddy? Why?" I ask.

He harrumphs. "Cuz he said no more roof time."

Sebastian's lips twitch as he stifles a smile. "Why did I say you aren't allowed on the roof anymore, Nico?"

Another harrumph as Nico crosses his arms. "Cuz it's not safe."

"Those weren't the exact words I used, *Mijo*."

Nico sighs. "Cuz I can't fly."

"That's right," Sebastian says with a nod. "Your feet need to be on solid ground. Or in a building with flooring beneath you. Not on a roof, where you might fall and hurt yourself."

We have learned to be specific with Nico, who, even at the tender age of three, has figured out how to circle around our words. We now have to specifically state he needs to go to his room, get into his bed, and go to sleep. Otherwise, he'll say we only said to go to his room, which means he can play in there. Technically, he isn't breaking the rules that way.

Nico's lip trembles as his eyes dart between me and Sebastian. "I like da roof."

"I know you do," Sebastian coos. "But it isn't safe, especially now that I know there are raccoons getting up there."

"Raccoons?" I shriek in excitement. "Did you see them? Where? Can we put a camera up there? I want to see!"

"See? Mommy like dem too," Nico snaps in frustration.

Sebastian gives me an exasperated look. "Could we cool it on how much we encourage the pipsqueak, please?"

Whoops.

I hear a commotion and see Nico slide down Sebastian's body so he can run to me. Turning, I squat down next to him, and I'm hit with a horrendous smell. "What have you gotten into, sweetheart?"

Nico shrugs. "Dirt on da roof."

I look up to Sebastian, and he nods. "Not dirt. I definitely need to clean the gutters, but the raccoons also appear to be using the roof as their bathroom. I believe he managed to get into both before I got to him."

My head swivels back to my child, horror filling my blood as I realize Nico is literally covered in shit and God knows what else. "You need to take a bath right now."

"No."

"Yes."

"Momma, no."

I sigh exasperatedly. "If you take a bath right now, you can have a lollipop before dinner."

He smiles sweetly, but I see the victorious look in his eyes. Nico hates taking a bath, but a barter was necessary. "Go take a bath."

"I want a cherry sucker," he replies, gleefully skipping past Sebastian to the staircase. "Come, Daddy!"

"Demanding little bugger," Sebastian mutters, leaning down to absentmindedly kiss the top of my head. "When does the window guy come out to put the child locks on all the windows and doors?"

I sigh. "In three days."

The amount of child-proofing we've had to do in our house is absurd. Multiple locks on every door, upper cabinet locks, all chemicals in a spot Nico can't access, and medications in a box with a keypad. Nico understands the concept of the word "no," but his curiosity takes over his impulse control way too often. He wants to know how everything works. Natalie has encouraged me to talk to our pediatrician about ADHD, but I haven't done it yet. He's only three. Even if he is diagnosed, the only thing we can really do at this point in his development is add occupational therapy. I want to wait a little longer, and let Nico be a kid, before we start the stress of doctors, potential specialists, and therapists. I don't like the idea of medicating my preschooler, and I've been researching more natural ways to help his activity and focus.

Not surprisingly, Nico hasn't taken too kindly to the changes.

"Thank fuck," Sebastian breathes. "This kid is running me ragged."

Don't I know it.

There were many nights when Nico was an infant that Sebastian and I were still able to enjoy our time together. Sure, we were tired. But a quick orgasm or two was a nice culmination to a busy family day. Now, however, we're both so damn exhausted by bedtime. We *want* to have sex, but neither of us has the energy.

Fortunately, Sebastian's parents take both Nico and Camila every Saturday night, with the expectation that we have a date night.

I'm sure they'd rather not know that we rarely leave the house, and a lot of times, Sebastian basically attacks me before the kids are even buckled into their car seats.

Tonight is a Saturday night, but the kids are with us later than normal. Sebastian's grandmother had some kind of event she wanted to attend in Denver, and she dragged my grandmother with her. Because no one in either family trusts two octogenarians to drive down the mountain to Denver, Sebastian's parents took them.

"When will *Abuelito* and *Abuelita* be here to get us?" Camila asks as I finish rolling out my dough balls, covering them with a dish towel so they can rise, and begin focusing on the sauce for my pasta dish.

"In an hour or so. *Abuela* wanted to stay at her craft thing a little longer."

"What craft thing?" Camila asks.

"Cross-stitch, I believe."

She scoffs. "*Abuela* doesn't cross-stitch. Does *Nonna*?"

I laugh as I shake my head. "*Nonna* only gets crafty if someone forces her to. She has never been interested in sewing or stitching of any kind."

"Why'd she go?" Camila asks.

I shrug. "Because your great-grandmother asked her to. I'm sure that they both had a great time, regardless of the topic. I have no doubt they enjoyed antagonizing *Abuelito* the entire time."

Camila giggles. "*Abuelita* probably encouraged it."

Now ten, Camila is growing up to be a beautiful young lady. She's already showing interest in following in Natalie's footsteps into elementary education. She loves the opportunity to watch her younger cousins whenever possible, and she asks a lot of questions about what life is like for a teacher. As she's getting ready to head into middle school, I'm so damn proud of how empathetic, intelligent, and loving she is. She may get irritated by her brother from time to time, but I have no doubt she'd be ready to throw down for him if needed.

"Sebastian!" I shriek, giggling as he throws me over his shoulder and takes the stairs two at a time. I slap his ass exuberantly, and he returns the gesture with a smack of his own. We may have accidentally figured out a couple of years ago that I find it incredibly arousing to be spanked.

Running into our bedroom, I'm tossed onto our bed with flourish. I laugh as I bounce, but when Sebastian manages to remove my shorts and underwear while mid-bounce, the laugh turns immediately into a moan as he covers my pussy with his mouth. I grab fistfuls of his hair, holding him in place, and I feel him chuckle against me, the hot breath against my clit sending a wave of endorphins throughout my body. It's a wonderful dance we play in bed: I attempt to move his head where I want his tongue, and he laughs as he refuses to give me control. I know he'll get me where I want to be, but I still fight him about it. Our odd version of foreplay.

"Loosen up, or I won't let you come, baby," he mutters against me, resting his head against my thigh, and I automatically let go of his hair. "That's my girl."

We may have also realized I have a praise kink.

Sebastian gives me a quick, harsh flick-flick of his tongue on my clit, then backs off, choosing to circle it slowly. I growl in frustration, making him chuckle again. "Enjoy every sensation, *mi Reina*. Relax. I'll get you there. You know I will."

From experience, I expect he'll get me there five or six times before he finally comes himself. Forcing myself to relax, I let out a long sigh as I close my eyes. Focusing just on the sensations, I moan as I feel him lick down to my ass, circling the tight bud over and over again. Our sex life has expanded since our marriage, and we've found that we both enjoy ass play. The hardest I've ever come was with Sebastian buried deep in my ass, and a dual action vibrator inside my pussy simultaneously stimulating my clit. The orgasm seemed to go on for minutes, and I've chased that high ever since.

When Sebastian slowly inserts two fingers into my pussy, I feel myself instinctively tighten around his digits as he taps my G-spot. An orgasm starts slowly at the tips of my toes, sweeping up my legs and onto my abdomen as it steals my breath. Fireworks explode behind my eyelids as I let out a loud and guttural moan. Sebastian patiently licks me through it, extending the pleasure.

Panting, I focus on my heart rate and only vaguely recognize movement as Sebastian rises from his position at the edge of the bed. When my breathing returns to normal, I open my eyes to find my husband staring at me, his eyes dark with lust. I scramble to my knees, expecting to repay the experience of sucking him off, but he shakes his head. "Foot of the bed."

Oh.

Directly across from our bed is a dresser with an oversized mirror. At the foot of the bed is a cushioned bench. As I crawl to the bench, I note Sebastian ripping his shirt over his head, then unbuttoning his jeans. He pushes them down, stepping out of them when they hit the floor, then meets me at the bench.

I stare up at him expectantly. "What now?"

He reaches up to drag a thumb across my lips, dipping the tip into my mouth. "I want to fuck your mouth, but —"

"No buts," I interrupt. "Let's do that."

He chuckles. "Oh, there will be butts, which is why I don't want to fuck your mouth. I have something better in mind."

I internally squeal. Is he going to recreate the best orgasm of my life? I reach out to grab the waistband of his boxer briefs, and only then do I notice a nondescript shipping box on the edge of the bench. "How long has this been here?"

"Since yesterday," he replies simply.

"But I've walked past it at least a dozen times without noticing it," I comment.

"Pretty sure we've talked about your shitty situational awareness, baby." His voice is light, with a teasing tone, and I can't help but laugh at myself. Sometimes I can't see my own hand in front of my face.

"Well, what's in it?" I ask, curiosity evident as I lean toward it, but Sebastian stops me with a hand to my décolletage as I reach out to touch the box.

"Not for you to know just yet. We're wearing too many clothes." His other hand lands on top of mine, pushing it down playfully. I roll my eyes with a smile as I drag his boxer briefs down his legs, quickly darting in to suck the tip of his cock into my mouth. He gasps, but lets me take his length deep into my throat before pushing me back. "You're too fucking good at that."

I preen at his praise, but don't try to push any further. I know I could. I know he'd let me, because while he might be considered the dominant in our relationship, I know I'm the one with all the power. In this moment, however, I can see the excitement in his eyes bubbling just under the surface, and I want to know what he has planned.

Sebastian sits on the bench, facing the dresser and mirror, then motions for me to stand in front of him. I awkwardly slide off the bed, removing my shirt as I do. I reach around to unclasp my bra, but he stops me. "No. Leave it on and turn around."

His hands find my hips as I slowly turn, then he pulls me down into his lap, kicking my legs out to be on the outside of his. His cock slides between my ass cheeks perfectly, and I inhale quickly. One hand stays gripped on my hip, while the other slides up my arm and across my collarbone. Sebastian brackets my throat with his hand as he watches me in the mirror. "I want to watch you. I want to see your face when you come, knowing that I'm fucking you so good you can't wait another second for me to come with you. And I want to know what it feels like with you so stuffed, so stimulated, that you cover me with your cream."

"I love when you talk like this," I moan, my eyes closing and my head dropping back to loll against his shoulder.

"I know you do," he whispers huskily. The hand around my neck drops down to cover my breast, and he pinches my nipple through my bra. At the same time, I hear a lid popping open, and I smile in delight. "I love how much you love me taking your ass."

"I know you do," I repeat, feeling him lean back slightly so he can reach between our bodies. His knuckles drag up and down my spine, and I know he's lubing his cock. The same hand dips between us to circle my hole.

"Stand for me, baby," he murmurs. As soon as I feel the blunt tip of his cock against my backside, I tremble in anticipation. "Touch yourself."

As Sebastian slowly swivels my hips around, I circle my clit. I can already feel an orgasm waiting, like I've been sitting at the cusp of an explosion all day. I hear a rustle as Sebastian reaches into the package, and I see him grab a long, pink device. "What is that?"

"A new vibrator for your G-spot," he answers. Another swivel of my hips, and another inch buried in my ass. I bite back a loud moan as tingles shoot down my spine, and I slow my finger on my clit. I'm not ready to come yet. "You aren't coming until I say you can. I can tell when you're getting close, Isabella, and I'll stop everything if you don't."

"I won't come, I promise."

Another inch, and this time, Sebastian groans. "Goddamn I love fucking you here. So tight. So perfect."

I mumble gibberish in response, so overwhelmed with white-hot pleasure I can barely see straight. I feel him notch the new toy at my opening, sliding it inside. It rubs against my upper wall right as he bottoms out in my ass.

"Don't come," he mutters as he turns on the vibrator, and I'm hit with such an intense wave of sensation that I scream. Sebastian wraps an arm around my waist, holding me up a few inches, then pumps into me from below. I'm assaulted with so many different feelings that I can't process which to focus on. "Eyes open, baby. Watch me fuck you. I wish you could see how perfect you look from my vantage point. Watching my cock bury itself into your ass is about to make me come."

I moan in delight. Knowing I can unravel this man makes me heady. "Sebastian, I'm going to come ..."

Everything stops.

"Noooo!" I wail.

He chuckles, but the sound is pained. "I'm not done yet."

My body shakes as I feel him lean toward the box of toys again. "I don't think I can take anything else inside me."

"This isn't for inside." I force my eyes to focus, watching as Sebastian brings a small object to my clit.

"What is tha — holy shit!" I scream, as he turns on the new device. It suctions hard on my clit, harder than I've ever experienced before, and my back bows as I attempt to breathe. Everything stops again, and a sheen of sweat forms across every inch of my skin. "Seb, please!"

"Please, what?" he grunts.

"Please let me come," I whisper. He drags what I'll refer to as the clit sucker three thousand back and forth across my sensitive nub, making me tremble in need and anticipation.

"One more minute," he says. "You'll come when I'm ready. Fuck yourself on my cock, baby. Get me there."

Barely even able to feel my feet at this point, I lean forward slightly, bracing my hands on Sebastian's knees. His head remains on my shoulder, his eyes locked with mine, as I find the strength to move. He groans loudly, teeth latching onto my neck, and I feel his cock start to twitch. He turns on the G-spot wand and the clit sucker together, and I immediately explode into an orgasm so intense, so mind-blowing, that I struggle to stay alert. Insane tremors wrack my body and never seem to end, but Sebastian also doesn't remove either toy, sending me into another orgasm of equal intensity. I close my eyes when they begin to cross, attempting to push his hands away, but he doesn't let up. When the third orgasm hits, Sebastian whips the G-spot massager out of me, and I feel my body gush. It feels like it's coming from everywhere, but I'm too exhausted to think about it.

Sebastian drops the toys, grabbing me from underneath my thighs, and stands, still buried inside me. He quickly walks us to the bathroom, turning on the shower and stepping inside. He slowly drops my thighs, allowing my feet to hit the ground, then carefully slides out of me. I hiss as he does, knowing I'll be incredibly sore for the next couple of days, but not caring one bit. I love everything Sebastian does to my body.

I settle against my husband as he quietly washes my body, shampoos my hair, and whispers how much he adores me.

Our love story isn't commonplace. It isn't perfect by any means. And sometimes I wonder what might have been had I let him take me out one of the first times he asked. But then I think about how Camila might not exist. And how much I grew those years by myself, knowing the exact person I am, and what kind of partner I needed. Knowing I'd get here, to my perfect little family in our big Italian-Puerto Rican world, I wouldn't change a damn thing.

BREAKING NEWS!

Is Leo Santo off the market?

Multiple reports suggest our favorite veteran has been seen escorting a single mother around town. Did he finally manage to lock down the one who got away?

Pre-order Leo's book today!

Want to start at the very beginning and read how Sebastian first asked Isabella's brother about her? Check out Luca and Hannah's story!

Ready for more? Start my new Mile High Sports Series, featuring Luca's teammate Gabe Dawson, in Blue Lines and Lullabies!

To keep up-to-date in all JJW news, please join my newsletter!

Want to join my Facebook group? Go here!

Want to grab the first Santo sibling story for free? Go get Gianna's story of how she met her paramedic hubby, Travis!

Acknowledgments

Wow! Book number thirteen is out in the world! This one was difficult to write, but not because of the characters. It was because of MY children, the muses for almost all the child characters I write. Summer vacation + mom working from home? Not a good combo. Nevertheless, I persisted, and courtesy of some very long nights, got this sucker done.

I'd like to thank my author friends, who have nicknamed themselves the Hot Flashes and the Emotional Support Bitches. Catie, Tamara, Becky, BJ, Breanna, Alina, and Nikki: I could not do this without you, ladies. You talk me off the ledge, you help me pick out model pictures, and you send amazing memes and reels that always give me a giggle. It's truly wonderful being in your orbit, and I'm so thankful I can call each of you a friend.

To my PA, Morgan, the rock star graphic designer who whips my shit together and (attempts) to keep me in line, you're amazing and I love you.

To Lemmy at Luna Literary Management: I don't know how you do it, but you're doing a phenomenal job at it! It's been a joy to work with you for the last four releases, and (hopefully) many more to come.

To the wonderful influencers who make each and every release so phenomenal: Taylor, Colby, Tiffany, Sierra, Isabella, and Abby. You are all absolute rock stars, and I'm so thankful I've met each of you.

To my editor, Brenda: I love how you fight for me when I tell you anything negative, and your incredible usage of the phrase "twat waffle". Our eighth book together ... I think. Can you believe it? Thank you for always making sure I use the Oxford comma correctly.

To my husband, who is so supportive of this venture, and routinely pimps me out to co-workers and friends, thank you. I know it took a while for me to find what gave me purpose, and I appreciate you never saying anything bad for the multiple forays into the MLM world.

Lastly, to the real Rick and Amelia. Rick, you're a mother-fucking douchebag, and I hope your life is paved with tiny LEGOS on the floor, plastic wrap on the toilet, opened milk behind the couch, and every damn battery stolen out of your house. Cheating on your wife while YOU were deployed is so basic. Karma is a bitch, jackass.

Finally, for the real dedication: this one is for my children. This book is proof that you can do hard things when everything is stacked against you. You can find the time in chaos to achieve goals. I love you both, and please never grow out of the need to give me hugs, because sometimes they're the absolute highlight of my day.

Also By

Forever Series

Forever Sunshine

Forever Yours

Forever Ours

Forever Mine

Forever Us

Forever Together

Eternity Series

Worth the Risk

Worth the Trouble

Worth the Vow

Worth the Test

Worth the Heat

Mile High Sports Series

Blue Lines and Lullabies (prequel novella)

Forecasting the Forward

Paws on the Playbook (coming winter 25/26)

About the Author

Jennifer J. Williams writes steamy romance full of sassy characters, epic banter, and delivers amazing HEAs in her sports and small town books. She was born and raised in Ohio, but currently calls Colorado home. A lifelong lover of romance books, Jen enjoys writing older characters because love stories don't end at twenty-five. Jen prides herself on delivering realistic characters that struggle with normal problems. She spends most of her free time within her zoo: two kids, two dogs, and two cats! When not containing the chaos, Jen can be found lounging on her covered porch, devouring books on her Kindle.